SECRETS OF THE SURVIVORS

Secrets of the Survivors

Mark L. Eastburn

Copyright © 2008 by Mark L. Eastburn.

Library of Congress Control Number:		2008901514
ISBN:	Hardcover	978-1-4363-2345-1
	Softcover	978-1-4363-2344-4

All rights reserved. No part of this book may be reproduced or transmitted in any form or by any means, electronic or mechanical, including photocopying, recording, or by any information storage and retrieval system, without permission in writing from the copyright owner.

This is a work of fiction. Names, characters, places and incidents either are the product of the author's imagination or are used fictitiously, and any resemblance to any actual persons, living or dead, events, or locales is entirely coincidental.

This book was printed in the United States of America.

To order additional copies of this book, contact:
Xlibris Corporation
1-888-795-4274
www.Xlibris.com
Orders@Xlibris.com
47813

CONTENTS

Chapter 1: To Save the World 9
Chapter 2: A Survivor Speaks 14
Chapter 3: The Conquerors 18
Chapter 4: Microbots and Neuro-links 22
Chapter 5: Ghet O'Malley 25
Chapter 6: Ten Thousand Miles 32
Chapter 7: Underground 40
Chapter 8: The Challenge 46
Chapter 9: atarkya.com 51
Chapter 10: Ready for Action 57
Chapter 11: Jean Diop 60
Chapter 12: Battle Dome 64
Chapter 13: PravaPort Game System 71
Chapter 14: New Recruit 78
Chapter 15: The Resistance Grows 85
Chapter 16: Invasion 93
Chapter 17: Ranid Surprise 99
Chapter 18: Counterstrike 108
Chapter 19: Retrieval 113
Chapter 20: The Hatching 117
Chapter 21: Hospital Room 121
Chapter 22: Moving Day 127
Chapter 23: Roda Capoeira 131
Chapter 24: Chinatown Mischief 138

Chapter 25: Swim Lesson 144
Chapter 26: The Big Test 149
Chapter 27: Freedom? 158
Chapter 28: Space Combat 165
Chapter 29: Hero 173
Chapter 30: Aftermath 175

DEDICATION

I dedicate this book to:
my children, for their inspiration,
my wife, for her patience and support,
and to a whole bunch of reptiles,
who gave this story new life.

CHAPTER 1

To Save the World

A shout of "Kill it!" first caught Alex's attention. Thumps from branches striking the forest floor drew him closer. Bullies often terrorized smaller kids in Sweetbriar Park, but Alex thought this commotion sounded different. *What the heck are those guys doing?* he wondered.

Alex tiptoed over November's dry leaves without making a sound. As he crept up a dirt pile to see the action, tree trunks cast shadows which helped hide his movements. Down below, inside a circle of older boys, a grayish-brown lizard was running back and forth in a desperate attempt to escape. When Alex realized how badly the reptile was injured, he searched for the courage to act.

One of the bullies shouted, "Watch this!" and hurled a rock straight at the lizard's head. He struck his target with a *pop* and cheered when the foot-long creature slumped to the ground.

Two girls named Katherine and Marie were hiding in the bushes nearby. Alex motioned for them to stay out of sight and calculated his next move.

Katherine, who could never keep quiet for more than twenty seconds at a time, leaned forward and whispered, "Billy's gonna kill you."

Alex didn't respond, but instead sprinted through a gap between Billy's friends and snatched the lizard. Turning to flee, he tumbled to the ground when something hard slammed into his forehead. Blood dripped down the left side of his face.

"It's that long-haired Mexican punk!" Billy yelled.

"He thinks he's a hero," another added.

Billy plucked a rock from the ground and said, "Let's show this stupid illegal what we do to heroes around here!"

Panicked by the pain he was about to endure, Alex felt an asthma attack start within his lungs. The noisy gasps which followed caused the bullies to pause for a moment.

"I'm calling 911!" a voice screamed from the dirt pile. It was Katherine, holding Marie's cell phone.

Billy and his gang ran for their bikes. In less than fifteen seconds, they were gone.

Katherine rushed over and brought Alex to a sitting position while Marie fished through his pockets for an inhaler. Two puffs of medication later, Alex felt relief when oxygen flowed back through his body.

"Thanks," he said quietly, embarrassed that a pair of girls had come to his rescue. "What happened to my head?"

"Billy hit you with a stick."

Alex felt pressure from Marie's sweatshirt on his forehead and asked, "How bad is it?"

Lifting her hand to check the damage, Marie said, "I don't think it's too bad."

"But what about all that blood?" Katherine blurted.

"Cuts on the head *always* bleed a lot, even when they're not serious." Since her parents were emergency room nurses, Marie was an expert on all sorts of injuries.

Katherine and Marie helped Alex onto his feet while he struggled to maintain a grip on the unconscious lizard. Alex was short for a fifth grader and not much taller than the girls—both of whom were two years younger than he. His smooth skin, like that of his sister Katherine, was a shade of tan halfway between their mother's pale complexion and father's brown skin. Though they looked alike in many ways, eye color was different—Alex had brown eyes and Katherine's were green. Their friend Marie's complexion was quite a bit darker, reflecting her roots in the African nation of Senegal.

All three left Sweetbriar Park as a mass of intertwined bodies, with Marie pressing on Alex's forehead and Katherine trying to keep his pants from falling down. Clasped between Alex's hands was the blood-spattered lizard, which was still breathing despite its injuries.

Twenty minutes later, everyone arrived at the place where Alex and Katherine had been living for the past few months. It wasn't much to look at—just a two-story brick house with an iron fence in front. Smells of fried food and cigarette smoke were thick in the air when they stumbled through the back door.

Mom was sitting at the kitchen table with a newspaper in her hands. Her blonde hair was tied back and her blue eyes were hidden behind thick glasses. Sweatpants and a tee shirt covered her round body. Glancing towards the doorway when Katherine asked for help, Mom let out a gasp of shock and shrieked, "What happened?"

While Alex explained the afternoon's events at Sweetbriar Park, Katherine snatched the lizard and hustled to their bedroom. She laid its limp body inside an empty aquarium they'd plucked from the neighbor's garbage and rushed back to the kitchen.

Moments later, Uncle Roy trudged in. The house belonged to him—a fact no one could ever forget. "Those kids aren't supposed to be back yet!" he scolded. "I can't hear the TV!"

"Leave 'em alone," Mom replied, dousing her son's forehead with iodine and dabbing at orange drops with a wad of paper towels.

"He get hurt or something?"

"Don't worry about it."

Uncle Roy shrugged his shoulders and made a move for the refrigerator. As soon as he spotted Marie in the kitchen, he pointed a finger towards the door and snapped, "Go home, you!"

Marie wasted no time in darting outside.

Mom huffed, "Roy, you're a jerk! She was just trying to help."

"Two kids in this house are enough."

"Oh, shut up and get out of here!"

Uncle Roy farted while leaving the kitchen with a bottle of beer in his hand.

"Go apologize to your friend," Mom said to Katherine.

An instant later, the screen door slammed shut and Katherine's footsteps raced along the side of the house.

"Stop slammin' that door!" Uncle Roy's voice thundered from the living room.

Mom turned back to Alex. "Don't listen to Uncle Roy. He's an idiot."

Eyes shut from the pain of antiseptic in his wound, Alex grunted, "Huh?"

"He's probably gonna whine about you two comin' inside before dinner, so just ignore everything he says."

Sadness weighing on his heart over Uncle Roy's stupid rules—not to mention memories of the life he'd left behind in Texas—Alex grumbled, "Maybe you should've let me and Katherine stay in El Paso with *Tío* Ramiro."

"Oh Alex, don't start that again! Philly will grow on you . . . trust me."

More of the same old crap. Mom says Philadelphia's a great city, but it's sucked so far. Alex didn't see the point in responding.

Mom's voice became more cheerful when she said, "Maybe you can call your *tío* sometime."

"Like prison, huh? Don't they give you one phone call?"

Katherine barged through the back door before Mom could respond. "Is he alright?" she wheezed between deep breaths.

Cobbling together a bandage from paper towels and tape, Mom winked and said, "I think he's gonna live."

With that, Alex rose on shaky legs and walked out of the kitchen with Mom by his side. They moved towards the "bedroom" he and Katherine were forced to share, which was really nothing more than a run-down family room with two beds, a desk, and a couple of posters taped to the walls. The cracked aquarium where Alex kept animals from Sweetbriar Park was sitting on the floor. Box turtles, toads, and even a garter snake had lived there at other times, but now it held something entirely different.

Stepping through the doorway, Mom caught sight of the new creature. "Oh Alex, what'd you bring home *this* time?"

"It's some kind of lizard. Those guys who hurt me were trying to kill it."

"That's my boy," Mom sighed. "Always trying to save the world."

Immediately after those words escaped from Mom's mouth, the lizard flipped over onto its stomach and stared at them with yellowish-brown eyes. Every injury on its body had disappeared. A full recovery in less than one hour was something Alex couldn't explain, but what surprised him even more was how the lizard reacted to his mother's comment. *It seemed to understand her.*

A blue tongue flicked from between the reptile's jaws.

"Ick," was Mom's reaction. "You sure that thing's not a snake?"

Alex shook his head and adjusted his bandage. "It has four legs. I think it's a blue-tongue skink."

"A skunk?"

"No, a skink. S-K-I-N-K."

"Well, I don't like the looks of it... Can't you just put it back in the woods?"

Desperate to keep his latest discovery, Alex decided to play on Mom's sympathies. "You know those guys who were gonna kill that skink *also* called me an illegal Mexican."

Clenching her fists as if she could punch all her son's tormentors at once, Mom said, "They have no right to say that, Alex. My pedigree's as all-American as George Washington."

"But Dad's wasn't." Since Mom never liked talking about why Dad wasn't around anymore, Alex often mentioned him as a way to get what he wanted.

"What do those blue whatcha-ma-hoozits eat?" Mom asked in an obvious attempt to avoid discussion of Alex's father.

"I think they eat fruit, leaves, eggs, and cat food. It doesn't get cold where they usually live, so he'll probably die if I put him back in Sweetbriar Park. I can take care of him, though—I've seen books about blue-tongue skinks at the library." The library reference was another attempt to trick his mother into allowing the lizard to stay. *Maybe I can change her mind if she thinks I'll read more.*

Mom took another look at the lizard and sighed.

"I can keep it, right?"

"It can stay for a *little* while, but only as long as you don't feed it mice or bugs or anything gross."

On the inside, Alex was smiling. His scheme had worked beautifully.

Before she stepped out of the room, Mom turned to say, "Just make sure I don't find that *thing* creeping around the house!"

Alex lay down on his bed and stared at his newfound pet. It looked straight back, flicking its blue tongue every few seconds. The reptile's face suggested some sort of ancient wisdom, but Alex didn't think lizards could be smart. He was wrong, though . . . *very wrong*.

CHAPTER 2

A Survivor Speaks

Late that evening, strange noises startled Alex from his slumber. The first thing he noticed upon opening his eyes was that the lizard wasn't inside of its aquarium. *Oh crap, I'm in trouble.* Alex lifted his head to scan the entire room, but he soon spotted the reptile near an old telephone on his desk. That phone had been strictly "off limits" ever since Alex and Katherine moved in, however this lizard looked as if he were about to make a call.

Moonlight caught the creature's face when it glanced at Alex and stammered, "Uh . . . you're just . . . you're just having a dream. Now lay back down and rest."

Unsure if he was really awake or not, Alex decided that the talking lizard must be telling the truth. *It's all a strange dream.* Returning to the pillow with his eyes closed, Alex heard the skink fiddle with the telephone for a moment. Then it spoke again.

"Hey mates, I think I've found a candidate for our mission here . . ."

While the lizard talked, Alex noticed it had an accent. *Must be Australian*, he concluded. *After all, that's where blue-tongue skinks come from.*

Several minutes later, the lizard finished his telephone conversation by chuckling, "I reckon these Yanks fancy me to be their pet, but I'll be at the meeting . . . no worries."

As soon as the receiver clicked, Alex realized his forehead was throbbing under the bandages. Since people had always told him you can't feel pain in a dream, he began to doubt he was sleeping. After a pinch to his arm which hurt like crazy, Alex sat up with eyes full of surprise. *I'm not dreaming.*

Standing on two short legs, the reptile turned from the telephone and said with a sheepish smile, "Can't say you're dreaming again, I reckon."

"Huh?" While the sight of a talking lizard wasn't exactly frightening, Alex was too stunned to say anything else.

"I won't trick you a second time, mate. I owe you something for saving my life, don't I?"

"I-I-I guess so."

Hearty laughter sounded from the creature's wide mouth. "Don't worry, friend. I come in peace."

"What?"

The lizard's blue tongue flicked from between his scaly lips and retracted again. "I should probably tell you something about us, eh?"

"Huh?"

Peering at a wall near Alex's desk, the blue-tongue skink remained silent for several seconds. A faded poster hanging there showed a menacing *Tyrannosaurus rex* locked in a deadly battle with a three-horned *Triceratops*. Ferns and pine trees dotted the prehistoric landscape behind them. The *T. rex*, jaws wide open, stood on one foot with claws digging into the earth. The other foot tore at the face of the *Triceratops*. In a move to defend itself, the three-horned dinosaur was about to stab the tyrannosaur in its ribs. Above this scene appeared the words, "Age of the Great Reptiles."

"I wouldn't say *all* of them were great," the lizard mumbled.

"Huh?"

"*Some* were great, but many were a real pain in the arse."

Alex struggled to make sense of the lizard's words. "W-w-what do you mean?"

"We had a civilization."

"Who did?"

"Reptiles."

"All reptiles?" Alex was starting to wonder about other creatures he'd found in Sweetbriar Park. *Were they smart, too?*

The lizard shook his head. "Only the *civilized* could walk and talk."

"Civilized reptiles?" In Alex's mind, the two words didn't seem to fit together.

Checking his surroundings, the skink leaned forward and asked, "Do we have to worry about *her*?" One of his tiny fingers pointed towards Katherine, who was under a pile of blankets on the other side of their "bedroom." A hand stuck out near the foot of the bed, but little else was visible.

"Nah, she sleeps through just about everything."

The skink flicked his tongue again and took a breath. "Even though you humans don't think much of us, reptilian civilization was more advanced than yours."

"But it's not around anymore?"

"It was destroyed."

"By who?"

"An army of aliens."

"Aliens?"

"You know, creatures from other planets."

"They came to Earth?"

The lizard nodded. "It all happened sixty-five million years ago."

"That's when dinosaurs died out!" It was a fact Alex knew well. Among the only books he ever enjoyed reading were those about dinosaurs.

"Dinosaurs didn't die out," the skink corrected. "Most of them were killed."

"Killed?"

"Murdered by the Scipion Legions—an alliance of conquerors from space."

Alex shuddered at the thought of alien invasion. For some reason, the idea had always haunted him.

"The Scipions wanted to make Earth part of their empire, so they sent warriors in giant spaceships against us."

"Didn't you fight back?"

"We tried, but it wasn't easy. If Ketoo hadn't been on our side, we'd all be dead."

"Ketoo . . ." Alex whispered, trying to commit the name to memory.

"Ketoo's the smartest reptile I've ever met, but you wouldn't guess it by looking at him. On the outside, he's just a yellow gecko with brown spots. I reckon you'd call him a—"

"Leopard gecko?" Alex blurted. He'd always wanted to get one as a pet, but Mom said they were too expensive.

The lizard smiled. "We owe a lot to that leopard gecko. He's the reason I'm still alive . . ." Pausing for a moment, he pressed his stumpy hands together and muttered, "But I'm off the subject. What I meant to tell you was that Ketoo developed a plan for resistance after violence broke out between dinosaurs and the alien soldiers."

"Dinosaurs attacked them?"

"Most dinosaurs got angry when Scipion invasion discs began landing, so Ketoo turned seven species into the greatest fighters this planet's ever seen. By changing their DNA and body structures, he made an army that couldn't be stopped. Not by *anyone*."

"Did you win?"

"Well, not exactly. We had problems with those warriors . . . *terrible* problems."

"What do you mean?"

His voice indicating he'd rather not dwell on the subject, the skink waved a hand and sighed, "It's a bloody awful story, mate. Millions of reptiles were killed. I'm sure you don't want to hear about it, so ask me another question."

Deep down, Alex wanted to hear the lizard's stories of death and destruction more than anything else in the world. Since this was their first conversation, however, he decided not to press for more information. After sitting in silence for several seconds, Alex slicked back his long hair and asked, "Um . . . do you have a name?"

The skink's face turned cheerful once again. "Sure do, mate. They call me Bluey. And yours is Alex, right?"

"Yeah . . . and my last name's Hidalgo."

"Alex Hidalgo, eh? You've got a Spanish last name?"

"My dad came from Mexico."

"That's a beautiful country. I've been there many times."

"Really?"

Bluey nodded. "Hidalgo's a common surname in those parts. Do you know what it means?"

Alex shrugged his shoulders.

"It comes from '*hijo de algo.*' That means 'son of something.'"

Running a hand over his cheek, Alex muttered, "I guess that makes sense. Sometimes my Uncle Roy calls me a son of a you-know-what."

"What's a 'son of a you-know-what'?" An instant later, Bluey seemed to understand and said, "Don't answer. I get it now."

The two continued their conversation until the first rays of the morning sun began peeking over the horizon. When Alex warned that his sister would soon be awake, Bluey shuffled back to his cage and hopped in. There were many issues the two still needed to discuss—most important among them being the return of the Scipion Legions . . . and their plans to destroy *human* civilization.

CHAPTER 3

The Conquerors

Far from where Alex and Bluey had been speaking, inside a warship orbiting the planet Jupiter, ominous events were unfolding in front of Commander Trod's eyes. Images of giant worms digging into the soil flickered across a video screen. Though the picture was fuzzy, the message was clear. *Another team of Sleerans has landed on Earth.*

"Landing number eighteen is a success," Commander Trod smirked to himself, thumping his muscular hand on a table and scraping three claws across its metal surface. "Humans don't stand a chance."

Commander Trod was a member of the most elite fighting force in the Scipion Legions—the Diapsids. Two clans of these monstrous warriors had been waging war across the cosmos ever since they crushed their mortal enemies—the so-called "five fingers"—in a bloody uprising many generations ago. Diapsids in the Wounding Tooth Clan stood nearly nine feet tall, with brownish stripes crossing tan scales on their necks, arms, legs, and jaws. Commander Trod was a Wounding Tooth.

Members of Trod's rival clan, known as Swift Runners, were similar in appearance. Every Diapsid had two legs, two arms, three fingers per hand, and flexible tails that touched the ground. Their bodies rippled with muscles that would put any human bodybuilder to shame. Differences between the clans came down to color, feet, and power. Swift Runners—the traditional leaders of Diapsid forces—had greenish scales, yellow eyes, and an enlarged "killing claw" on their second toe. Wounding Teeth, who were forbidden from serving in positions of authority, had orange eyes and three equally powerful claws on each foot. Needless to say, the sight of either type of Diapsid struck fear into all conquered species of the Scipion Legions.

Rising from his chair and straightening to his full height of eight feet and eleven inches, Commander Trod stretched his massive arms and thick neck, placed a four-horned helmet on his head, and marched down a dim hallway to the Throne Room of Admiral Dromeus.

The spacecraft where Trod walked was known throughout the Scipion Legions as Destroyer 3176. It was spherical in shape and gigantic in size, capable of housing one million Diapsid warriors when filled to capacity. At the present time, however, the ship's crew numbered little more than one thousand. Shock troops were scheduled to arrive and fill the ship once the conquest of Earth was set to begin.

Commander Trod passed through a doorway lined with yellow crystal, then lowered himself on one knee in front of a marble stairway that led to the throne of Admiral Dromeus. Since the admiral was one of the most important Swift Runners in the known universe, it was customary for a low-ranking warrior like Trod to wait on his knee until granted permission to speak. Despite the long history of this tradition, Commander Trod *hated* bowing before Swift Runners. His only comfort was the thought that Admiral Dromeus would soon be dead.

Dromeus sat upon his iron throne in the armor of a warrior. Having risen to his high rank through never-ending bloodshed, the outfit was appropriate. Jointed metal plates ran down his chest and stomach while lighter shields covered his thighs. A helmet with a row of sharp spikes sat atop his head and metallic spine covers protected his backbone. Except for a brown loincloth hanging from his waist, the remainder of his body was exposed.

Massive muscles flexed under the admiral's green skin when he leaned forward and growled, "Rise and give your report."

"*Hracha Kedru Husak Sek,*" Commander Trod replied. His words were a traditional greeting in the Diapsid language.

Admiral Dromeus slammed a fist into the armrest of his throne and roared, "Listen, Wounding Tooth! If we are to conquer the humans, you *must* speak their languages!"

"Understood, Lord Conqueror," Trod hissed, *Lord Conqueror* being a title reserved to address high-ranking Swift Runners. Clearing his throat, he continued, "I'm here to report the successful landing of another Sleeran team on Earth."

"No humans witnessed the landing?"

The commander shook his head. "They landed in a forest several miles from the nearest settlement."

"You're *sure* no one noticed?"

"I've been monitoring their television and radio programs," Commander Trod assured. "There's been no mention of killer worms from outer space."

"Are the Savages ready for the invasion?"

"No."

"You're taking too long! We must get our forces down there!"

"I need more warriors, sir."

"Nonsense. Push your lieutenants to work harder."

"Two of my lieutenants were eaten last week!" Trod raged. "Savages are more dangerous than you could possibly imagine!"

Dromeus clutched one fist over the other. "I've led Savages in *thousands* of battles, commander. Are you saying I'm blind to their power?"

With the knowledge that any answer to the admiral's question could be dangerous, Commander Trod chose his words carefully before saying, "Replacements for my dead lieutenants would allow us to prepare Savages at a faster pace."

Leaning back on his throne, Admiral Dromeus hissed, "I will consider your request, commander . . . but if you continue to delay our mission, you'll be killed."

Trod didn't respond, though he was confident that Dromeus was really the one who should be worrying for his life. *Soon I will sit in the admiral's place*, Trod smirked while kneeling in front of the stairway a second time and stepping back through the doorway.

In the hall outside of the Throne Room, Commander Trod spotted Vice Admiral Hati standing at attention. The commander thumped his chest armor with a closed fist—a traditional salute among Diapsids. Unable to return the gesture, Hati bowed his head and limped into the Throne Room to speak with the admiral.

Taller than most Swift Runners, Vice Admiral Hati had been injured years ago in a duel against another Diapsid. As a result, his body was mangled and lame. A hideous scar of light green twisted its way down his face, covering the few remaining pieces of his left eye. His left arm was also missing, with only a small stump of flesh and bone sticking from his shoulder. Despite such wounds, the vice admiral managed to kill his rival. A claw from the fallen enemy hung around Hati's neck.

Inside the Throne Room, Admiral Dromeus greeted his friend with a hard thump to the chest. After descending the twelve steps which led from his throne to the floor, he grabbed the vice admiral by his chest armor and pulled him close.

"How are our spy operations going?" Dromeus snarled.

"Commander Trod is planning something *big*, Lord Conqueror," Hati replied.

"You think he'll challenge me to a duel?"

"Could be."

"Keep him busy. That's the best way to keep these plans from coming to fruition."

Vice Admiral Hati nodded. "I will inform Captain Ripu."

"Imagine Trod's vanity," the admiral scoffed, "to think that a Wounding Tooth like *him* could take my place . . ."

"Ripu and I would never let that happen."

"Make sure it doesn't."

The vice admiral bowed his head and left the Throne Room without another word. Life on Legion Destroyer 3176 was growing more dangerous by the second.

CHAPTER 4

Microbots and Neuro-links

Alex was relieved the next morning when he woke up and saw the clock read 10:24. *Mom didn't force me to go to school today.* All she did was leave a note on top of his covers to say she'd be continuing her search for a job until late. If he got hungry, chicken nuggets and French fries were in the freezer. Without another thought, Alex crumpled the paper and tossed it towards an overflowing trashcan. As usual, he missed the shot. Stepping out of bed to retrieve the paper ball, Alex jumped when he saw Bluey sitting on his desk. *The talking lizard wasn't a dream after all!*

"G'day, Alex! How's the head?"

"Uh . . . not bad."

Dangling his stumpy legs over the edge of the desk, Bluey said, "I reckon I should be leaving soon, but do you have any other questions before I go?"

Alex smiled. "Only about a thousand . . ."

Bluey laughed. "Let's deal with the biggest ones first."

Alex picked his brain for the questions he wanted to ask the most. "How old are you?"

"Almost eighty million."

"Eighty million *years*? How's that possible?"

"We civilized reptiles—the few that are left, that is—have devices inside our bodies called microbots. They're tiny machines that fix our bodies when we get hurt, keep us from getting old, and prevent death."

"Is that how you healed so fast yesterday?"

"Exactly."

"That's cool . . . and kind of weird, I guess."

"There's lots of strange things in the world, my friend."

Like talking lizards? Alex joked to himself. "And how come you were in Sweetbriar Park?"

"Just keeping an eye out for new recruits."

"New recruits?"

Glancing upwards, Bluey sighed, "The Scipion Legions are back, my friend."

Hair on the back of Alex's neck stood on edge. "Y-y-you mean . . . um . . . you mean the whole attack could happen *again?*"

Bluey nodded. "We've been finding Sleerans on Earth recently. They're the first creatures to arrive before the Scipions attack."

"Sleerans?"

"Think of a earthworm, give it two muscular arms with sharpened blades, a mouth fill of poisonous fangs, and stretch it fifteen feet long—*that's* a Sleeran."

A chill went down Alex's spine. "They sound scary."

"Sleerans killed *millions* of our citizens the last time around, usually by tunneling under their victims and striking from below."

"Can you guys stop them?" Alex gasped, wondering what he'd do if a monster worm ever came through his basement floor.

"We've captured a few Sleerans and killed about a dozen, but we don't know how many have landed so far."

"Can't you guys call the Army or something? They could probably help you, right?"

Bluey took a deep breath and waved off Alex's suggestion. "Adult humans get panicked too easily. We're trying to keep them out of the picture as long as possible."

"Why? They've got nuclear bombs and other stuff to fight the aliens."

"That's my point! We don't want nuclear war with the Scipion Legions. After all, we want an Earth that can still support life when this is over."

"But what are you gonna do?"

"At the moment, we have other helpers who are more trustworthy."

"What kind of helpers?"

"Animals."

"Smart animals?"

Bluey shook his head. "Most animals aren't too intelligent, but we can control them with implants in our brains called neuro-links. They transmit our thoughts to animals and tell them what to do—sort of like telepathy."

Of all the bizarre stories Bluey had told Alex, this one seemed hardest to believe. *Lizards that control animals with their minds?* Corners of Alex's mouth turned downwards in a subtle frown. "You can't be serious . . ." he trailed off, shaking his head.

"All right then, I'll prove it to you! How many birds do you see in your backyard on a regular day?"

"All at once, or over the whole day?"

"Either number works fine."

"I don't know . . . maybe twenty at one time and a hundred through the whole day."

"Sounds about right. Now go take a look outside."

Alex flung himself off his bed, stumbled through the doorway, and shuffled his feet towards the kitchen. Bluey followed, scrambling up a chair and hopping onto a windowsill. Cool, fresh air blew through the screen while Alex stared outside in amazement.

Uncle Roy's rectangular backyard was completely covered in feathers. Nature lover that he was, Alex could identify several species of bird amongst the crowd. There were brown sparrows, red cardinals, yellow goldfinches, cream-colored doves, grey mockingbirds, and even a few bluebirds. They perched on the bushes, the fence, the ground, and Uncle Roy's power tools. Several turkey vultures and a red-tailed hawk soared overhead. A bald eagle then swooped over the treetops and clutched the rear fence in its black talons.

"Found that one migrating over the city," Bluey declared proudly.

Convinced beyond any doubt of everything the lizard had told him, Alex tried to speak. Unfortunately, his mind was too overwhelmed to form words.

"Are you with us, then?" Bluey smiled.

"Huh?"

Patting his hand on Alex's thumb, Bluey said, "If this invasion grows, the Survivors may need your help. Young people could be the key to saving our planet."

How the heck am I gonna save the Earth? Alex thought to himself before asking, "What should I do?"

"First you'll need to prove you can keep a secret, so don't tell anyone what you've learned until I come back. It'll be soon. Then we'll decide the next step for you."

"Um . . . okay," Alex mumbled, secure in the knowledge that no one would believe his story even if he decided to tell it.

"We've gotta be careful, mate. The fate of the world is in our hands. I reckon you understand."

"Yeah, it makes sense . . . sort of."

"Excellent!" Bluey exclaimed. An instant later, he closed his eyes and the birds took flight. As the clamor of wingbeats and chirps began moving in circles over the backyard, Bluey opened his eyes and smirked, "It's easy once you get the hang of it."

Alex struggled with the stubborn window screen so that Bluey could squeeze under and hop to the ground. Once he was outside, the bald eagle took flight and grabbed Bluey. Seconds later, they were gone. All that remained in the yard was a smattering of bird poop on every surface.

"Uncle Roy's not gonna like this," Alex sighed, opening the back door and moving towards the hose. While washing everything down, Alex wondered what he'd gotten himself into. *I'm gonna help stop an alien invasion?* Nothing in his life had ever seemed so impossible—not even trying to make friends at his new school.

CHAPTER 5

Ghet O'Malley

The next day was cool and breezy. Standing at the bus stop with Katherine and Marie, Alex fixed his gaze on the morning sky.

Katherine swept a curl of hair from her face and huffed, "What's wrong with you?"

"Huh?"

"I asked you to tell Marie why that lizard disappeared."

"You did?"

"Yeah. Are you deaf or something?"

Alex glanced into Marie's expectant eyes and hid the truth by saying, "I took the lizard outside for some exercise and he ran under the neighbor's fence."

"How could it move so fast?" Marie asked. "He had short little legs."

"Alex was just being stupid," Katherine snapped in her best friend's direction. "But I'll bet you saw lots of lizards like that when you lived in Africa, huh?"

"No," Marie grumbled. "And stop talking about Africa like that!"

"Like what?"

"Like it's a country!"

"But I thought Africa *is* a country . . . just like America."

"No it's not! There are fifty-three countries in Africa! And America's not a country, either!"

"Huh?"

Now Katherine's being stupid, Alex smiled to himself as the girls continued their argument and his mind began puzzling over something else—the phone call Bluey made on the night they met. When Alex pressed the redial button on his phone after cleaning Uncle Roy's yard, he discovered that Bluey had called a business known as *atarkya.com*. *Why the heck would a talking lizard call an Internet company?*

Alex didn't have much time to think before a yellow school bus rumbled up the street. Over the engine's growl, a deep voice in the back shouted, "The illegal alien's back!"

Alex slumped into his usual seat and tried to ignore Billy.

Another voice laughed, "It's the lizard lover!"

Alex continued staring straight ahead, bit his lip, and wished he could escape from this everyday misery. Kids had been picking on him ever since he arrived in Philadelphia, singling him out for his Texas accent, his longer-than-normal hair, and the tan skin which suggested his Hispanic heritage. Besides the usual taunts of "illegal alien," Alex was also teased with names like "wheat bread" and "brown sugar"—terms that poked fun at his complexion. Back in El Paso, Alex could blend in quite easily. In this part of Philadelphia, however, he stuck out like a sore thumb.

When the bus stopped at Chester A. Arthur Middle School several minutes later, Billy and his gang lurched out of their seats and pushed towards the front. Pausing for a moment in the middle of the bus, Billy crouched down and snarled into Alex's ear, "I better not catch you in Sweetbriar Park again, you little punk." Grabbing onto the Mexican flag pin which Alex kept on the collar of his jacket, Billy yanked it off and grumbled, "Go live in Mexico if you like it so much."

Alex felt a flash of anger surge through his chest. *That was a present Tío Ramiro gave me!* Though he'd been born in the U.S., the pin helped Alex remember his father and *Tío* Ramiro—both of whom had immigrated from Mexico more than a decade earlier. Closing his eyes and taking a deep breath, Alex cooled his rage. Too small to fight the eighth graders who bullied him, there wasn't much else he could do. Fortunately, Alex's contact with Bluey had given him a boost in self-esteem. *Idiots like Billy DeGrace won't bring me down.*

Two minutes after the bus pulled in front of William Henry Harrison Elementary School, Alex entered Mrs. Anderson's classroom and dropped his backpack on the floor. He then retrieved his homework and placed it on the teacher's desk. Since homework was something Alex had *never* done before, Mrs. Anderson appeared to be at a loss for words.

"Th-Thank you, Mr. Hidalgo," she finally stammered, "I'm impressed."

"No worries," Alex replied. He'd heard Bluey say those words and thought they sounded cool.

"Now let's see what other surprises you're hiding," Mrs. Anderson winked before rising from her seat to begin class.

At recess, Alex decided it was time to make friends with his fellow fifth graders. Most of the boys had been pretty mean ever since he transferred to this school, so Alex usually spent recess watching anthills on the playground or trying to catch grasshoppers at the edge of the sports field. On this particular day, however, he felt a strong urge to forget the past and reach out to his classmates. *After all, Bluey will need me to recruit other kids if the aliens invade.* It was a mission that gave Alex a feeling of importance, as if his actions would have an impact on the entire world.

Exiting the cafeteria after lunch, Alex strode out to the field where a football game was getting underway. By this point in late fall, rules against tackling had been forgotten. When recess aides weren't paying attention, the fifth graders could be as rough as professional players.

When Alex arrived on the crowded field, two boys who'd made themselves captains were already selecting their teammates. Of course, they picked the biggest and fastest kids first. Alex watched Ray Blocker move to the left, greeted by a hi-five from his team captain. Not surprisingly, Jeff Barnes was the second to be selected. Since he'd repeated both kindergarten *and* third grade, Jeff was already growing a dark moustache.

Minutes dragged on and Alex soon found himself among three kids at the bottom of the heap. His heart sank when the other two were split between the teams, leaving Alex standing alone. Jeff Barnes took a step forward, pointed towards the sidelines, and said, "Beat it, wheat bread. We got no place for you today!"

Ashamed and hurt, Alex dropped his head and walked to the edge of the playing field. *So much for my big plans*, he lamented. *They still think I'm a loser.* Wandering to a long, metal bench and slumping into a sitting position, Alex wished he could be invisible. Luckily, though, he wasn't.

"Hey man," a boy at the far end of the bench called over, "I heard you found something weird in the park the other day."

Alex turned to see who was speaking and recognized the boy instantly. Everyone knew Ghet O'Malley. Everyone liked him, too. He made people laugh and was considered by many to be the greatest athlete in fifth grade. Strangely, Alex never saw Ghet playing on the football field. He was also one of the only kids who never made fun of Alex.

Ghet's reddish-blond hair blew in the breeze and the sun shined on his freckled face when he asked, "Was it really a lizard?"

"Yeah, a blue-tongue skink," Alex replied, "How'd you know?"

Ghet folded a page in the book he'd been reading and explained, "News travels fast—especially when somebody stands up to Billy DeGrace."

Alex felt a twinge of pride over the moment when he saved Bluey in Sweetbriar Park. *Are people saying I stood up to Billy?* he wondered.

"Do you still have it?" Ghet asked.

"Nah," Alex sighed, kicking dirt under the bench and watching small clouds of dust circle upwards. "He ran away."

"That was still a brave move, though. I couldn't have done it."

"Why not?"

"Guess I can't live as dangerously as you."

"Huh?"

"I've got this problem with my blood—*two* problems, actually. One's called hemophilia and the other's vonWillebrand disease. Ever heard of 'em?"

"Never."

"Well, if I get a cut or something," Ghet explained, "my body has trouble making the bleeding stop. It can be pretty serious if I get punched or kicked."

"You'll never stop bleeding?"

Ghet laughed. "No, it's not *that* bad. I get three needles a week to keep it in check."

Alex's eyes opened wide. "*Three* needles a week?"

Ghet shrugged as if it were nothing. "I used to charge people two dollars to come to my house and watch me stick myself. A few of them passed out in my kitchen. I was making good money, but then my mom found out what I was doing . . . She wasn't too happy."

Once the recess bell sounded, most kids—including Ghet and Alex—rushed to the blacktop next to the school building. The football players, however, tried to squeeze in one last play before the aides started screaming for them to get in line. Ray Blocker caught a final pass and ran it for a touchdown, clinching victory for his team. As always, the losing team accused the winners of cheating. Both teams shouted at each other all the way to the asphalt.

While marching inside, Ghet tapped Alex on the shoulder and asked, "What are you doing after school?"

"I don't know," Alex replied. *Sure won't be going to Sweetbriar Park.*

"Why don't you come to my house?"

"Um . . . okay." It was the first time a fifth grader in Philadelphia had invited him to do anything.

"You know how to get there?"

"No worries," Alex replied with a smile.

* * *

When Alex arrived at the O'Malley's rowhouse after school, three red-haired sisters were doing their homework in the living room and one of Ghet's brothers was playing a noisy video game. Glancing about the rectangular room, Alex noticed one wall was completely covered with family photos.

"Why do you only have pictures on one wall?" he asked.

"Oh, that's for the fairies," Ghet answered, his tone suggesting that the comment was nothing unusual.

"Fairies?"

"My grandma says that fairies always go past the house on the western side. The pictures are over there to get their blessing. Seeing how we have neighbors on the other side of that wall, though, I'm not really sure how the fairies get over there."

"You believe in that stuff?"

"I don't know. Sometimes . . . I guess."

Ghet's younger sister Zig-zag looked up from her homework and rolled her eyes. When Ghet introduced her, he added, "Her name's really Zig-zag. It's even on her birth certificate. My parents were weird with the names." Moving towards the stairway and making sure the coast was clear, Ghet suggested, "How 'bout I show you my figurines?"

After a shrug and a nod, Alex followed his friend up the cramped staircase.

The O'Malley family was big and their house was small, so Ghet's upstairs bedroom was shared between four boys. Flanked on both sides with bunk beds, an odor of sweat and unwashed clothing hung in the air. Seemingly oblivious to the smell, Ghet reached under a pile of blankets while Alex took a seat on what appeared to be the cleanest bed.

"I painted these myself," Ghet said proudly as he retrieved a cardboard box reinforced with grey duct tape.

A fearsome dragon rearing up on its back legs was the first object Alex saw. Detail on the monster's scales made it look as if they were actually *moving* over the mighty reptile's muscles. "You *painted* it like that?"

Ghet nodded. "This one took me two weeks to finish. You like dragons?"

"They're okay . . . but I was more into dinosaurs when I was a kid."

Arching his right eyebrow upwards, Ghet asked, "How old are you?"

"I'll be eleven in December."

"And that means you're a grownup already?"

"What do you mean?"

"You said you liked dinosaurs back when you *were* a kid. That's past tense, dude. It means you're not a kid anymore!"

"I-I-I guess that I'm still a kid, but it just . . . like . . . um . . . it doesn't feel that way sometimes. Up here, things aren't the same as where I used to live."

"You know what? I've been talking *way* too much. Why don't you tell me something about yourself?"

Alex didn't even know where to begin. "What do you want to know?"

While Ghet held up his second figure—a green dragon breathing red-orange fire—he asked, "How do you like it up here?"

Alex considered the best answer before he spoke. *Should I be honest and say it sucks?* "It's not too bad," he finally mumbled.

"You came from Texas, right?"

"Yeah."

"Why'd you move up here?"

That question made Alex uncomfortable. The story behind their move was something he'd rather forget. It started with Dad's disappearance almost two years ago, continued with Mom's depression and job loss, the eviction from their apartment in El Paso, four weeks spent in a homeless shelter, and ended with their desperate move to Philadelphia on a crowded, smelly bus after Mom begged Uncle Roy to give them a place to live. It was a humiliating experience, and one that Alex didn't want to discuss. "My mom grew up in Philadelphia, so I guess she wanted to live up here again," Alex shrugged, hoping that Ghet would believe his lie.

"You still have family in Texas?"

"Yeah, my *Tío* Ramiro and my *Tía* Elena stayed behind."

"Your *what* and your *what*?"

"*Tío* is the Spanish word for uncle and *tía* is the Spanish word for aunt. They're from my dad's side of the family."

"You're Spanish?"

"My dad's from Mexico, so I guess I'm part Mexican."

"Can you speak Spanish?"

"Nah," Alex grumbled. "No one ever taught me."

"Can't your dad teach you?"

"Nah, he got taken away."

"Taken away by who?"

Another uncomfortable question. "Well, my mom says the government sent him back to Mexico and my *Tío* Ramiro told me that gangsters kidnapped him. I don't really know which story is right."

"Crazy stuff, huh?"

Alex didn't answer. He felt like he'd spoken too much already.

Ghet's last model was that of a wizard in a blue cloak. Arms were outstretched as if to cast a powerful spell. Once the figurine had been returned to its newspaper cocoon, Ghet leaned one shoulder against his bedboard and asked, "What do you think?"

"About what?" In an attempt to keep his mind off his family problems, Alex had allowed his thoughts to drift to Bluey, the microbots, the Sleerans, the neuro-links, and the dinosaur soldiers. He was also starting to wonder if Ghet might make a good recruit in the coming struggle.

"What do you think of my collection?"

"Oh," Alex replied. "It's cool, but I guess I never thought people like you were into that sort of stuff."

"People like me?"

"You know . . . sports guys—like Jeff Barnes and Ray Blocker."

"I'm a sports guy, huh? That's one I never heard before!"

Alex didn't understand. Ghet's reputation as an athlete had been mentioned by many kids at school. "You mean you're *not* into sports?"

Ghet shook his head. "No way. I watch 'em on TV and I *do* swim a lot, but that's all."

"But someone told me you're great at baseball, too."

"Nah, I'm just lucky sometimes . . . My grandma's Irish, after all."

"Huh?"

"One day about two years ago, Jeff and Ray invited me to play baseball. I'd never even held a bat in my hands before, but when it was my turn I just closed my eyes and swung as hard as I could. And you know what happened?"

Alex shrugged his shoulders.

"There was a crack and that darn ball went flying over the kids in the outfield. It landed in the parking lot and broke the windshield of the principal's car."

"Whoa!"

Ghet smoothed back his wild hair with one hand and concluded, "I've used the excuse of getting in trouble to keep from playing sports ever since. I'm pretty lucky that no one's found out the truth—that I can't do most sports because of my bleeding problems. When I can't do certain activities in gym class, the teacher says I'm too good to need any practice. I guess the other kids believe him!"

"You're also lucky kids don't pick on you, huh?"

"They give me trouble once and a while, but deep down, guys like Ray Blocker and Jeff Barnes aren't so tough. I've seen 'em both run from Billy DeGrace."

Alex was amazed. "I didn't know that Billy went after *those* kinds of kids, too."

"Yeah, man. That's how things work. Some guys think it's cool to push other kids around, but they get scared when someone *bigger* comes along."

What Alex didn't know was that a guardian would come who was more powerful than Billy, Jeff, and Ray combined. Bluey and the other Survivors would make his arrival possible.

CHAPTER 6

Ten Thousand Miles

Before Alex knew it, December had come to a close. Passage of more than a month since meeting Bluey led him to doubt he'd ever see his lizard friend again. *Maybe he forgot about me.* After all, Bluey said he'd be back *soon*, which to Alex meant a few days (or a week at most). Unfortunately, Alex didn't realize that *soon* in the mind of an eighty-million year old lizard was quite a bit longer than an impatient boy could imagine.

Winter was settling in and nights were cold, but Alex often spent hours staring through the drafty window next to his bed. If he angled his head the right way, he could glimpse a few stars in a tiny sliver of sky that wasn't blocked by the neighbor's house. Most nights, all he heard was the regular rhythm of his sister's snores. One particular evening in the early days of January, however, a whistling sound passed over the house and an object drifted between Uncle Roy's roof and that of his neighbor, illuminating the frozen ground below.

Wonder turned into fear when Alex remembered Bluey's stories of the monster worms called Sleerans. *Maybe they're gonna land here*, he panicked. Unsure what to do, Alex ducked under the windowsill and pressed himself against the wall.

Minutes seemed like hours while Alex lay there, unmoving, frightened about what might happen next. Scratching sounds told him something was climbing onto the windowsill outside, then a snake-like shadow rose and undulated in the moonlight. *Oh crap, it IS a Sleeran!* A single pane of glass was the only thing that shielded him from certain death. Without moving his head, Alex shifted his eyes around the room for a weapon to defend himself. An unused baseball bat—his only Christmas present—was leaning against the far corner of his room. *Can I get it in time?*

Just as he was trying to muster the courage to rush and grab his bat, Alex heard a muffled tap on the window pane and a familiar voice call out, "You in there, mate?"

When Alex rose from his hiding place, a smallish lizard's silhouette let out a high-pitched squeal and fell backwards. Alex pulled his stubborn window open and looked down.

"Crikey, you scared me," Bluey said, stamping his feet and dusting frost from his body.

Alex chuckled, "You kind of scared me, too."

Checking his surroundings with a quick glance, Bluey whispered, "I need you to come with me, and we'd better move fast."

"Where?" Alex asked. Frigid air gripped his skin and seeped through his clothing.

"We're going south. I'll tell you more when we're flying."

"Flying?" Alex gulped. He'd never been in an airplane before.

"It's the only way to get there, mate."

"How long will I be gone?"

"Twenty hours, I reckon. Are you coming?"

Without answering, Alex darted inside and changed into the first pair of jeans, sweatshirt, and sneakers he could snatch from the messy floor. Grabbing his notebook, he found an empty page and scribbled a note for Katherine which read:

Kat,

I've gone to do something important, but I'll be home this afternoon. Don't tell Mom I'm gone. Keep all this a secret and I'll tell you when the time's right.

Thanks,
Alex

Tiptoeing over to his sister's bed, Alex placed the note on top of her favorite shoes and lifted the covers to assure she was still asleep. After breathing a sigh of relief, he climbed awkwardly through the open window and pulled himself upward. Standing for a moment with his tippy-toes on the windowsill, Alex closed the window and hopped to the ground. Once his eyes adjusted to the moon's bluish-white light, he looked down and realized he'd put a different type of sneaker on each foot. *Guess I won't be traveling in style.*

Bluey's flying machine was sitting in Uncle Roy's backyard. Shaped like an egg and no bigger than a car, it had two sets of triangular wings and a dark windshield around the front. Rounding the rear end of the ship, Alex jumped when it opened straight down the middle, like a clamshell.

"That's the cargo bay—and you're my cargo!" Bluey exclaimed.

Alex glanced between his lizard friend and the cargo bay's bare interior. "There aren't any seats."

"Floor's comfortable enough. You'll be fine."

When Alex stepped inside Bluey's unusual aircraft, his feet made soft noises on the curved floor—like musical notes echoing through the midnight calm.

"Crouch down, please," Bluey urged.

Taking a seat on the floor and looking around, Alex realized the inside was made of a material he'd never seen before. Despite the cold air swirling around, it was warm to the touch. When the clamshell doors closed over his head, Alex could see *through* them. The floor was also semi-transparent. After a series of mechanical noises, the wall in front retracted to reveal a cockpit. Bluey was reclining in a small chair which overlooked the ship's controls.

"Hang on, mate!" he commanded with his head turned to the side.

Alex nodded his head in response.

An engine rumbled somewhere, hidden from view. Seconds later, Alex glanced down and realized he was flying. Darkened trees and rooftops passed under his feet. As Bluey's egg-shaped craft soared higher, street lamps merged into rivers of light and houses took the appearance of miniature toys. The sight made Alex's stomach tighten in terror. Closing his eyes and focusing on his breathing, he worried that an asthma attack would end this adventure before it had even begun.

Bluey swiveled around in his chair and said, "There's nothing to worry about. I've flown *millions* of times."

"Uh-huh," Alex grunted.

"Now let me tell you where we're headed. Do you remember everything I told you?"

Eager to keep himself distracted, Alex opened his eyes and replied, "Yeah, I even wrote it down in a notebook so I wouldn't forget."

"Good boy!" Bluey cheered, winking his eye and sticking up a thumb. "That'll come in handy when we get to South America."

"We're going to South America—the one that's far away?"

"That's where you're going to meet the other Survivors."

"You guys live there?"

"A few live there, but the rest of us just visit to help out."

"Help out with what?"

"With the preparations."

Alex gulped. "Getting ready for the alien invasion?"

Bluey nodded slowly and leaned forward. "It might be coming soon."

A tingling sensation spread over Alex's body, as if tiny pins were sticking into his skin. *This is serious.* "So, y-y-you want me to find people to help fight back?"

"Don't worry about that now . . . Let's first see what today will bring, my friend."

Moments later, Alex remembered a question he'd wanted to ask Bluey ever since they parted ways. "Am I the first person you ever talked to?"

Bluey smiled and shook his head. "No, we've made contact with humans every now and then."

"Huh?"

Placing short-fingered hands on his knees, Bluey said, "If you take a look at human history, reptiles enjoy a special place in legends all over the world. I'm not one to brag, but most of it be traced back to us."

"Really?"

"For starters, just look at how many different cultures talk about dragons."

Alex recalled Ghet's dragon figurines and wondered if there was some sort of connection. It was the first time the crazy events in his life seemed to make sense. *Maybe everything's part of some big plan.* "So you guys are dragons?"

"No, mate. But think for a moment—many stories say dragons were scaly creatures with wisdom and power. Part of the story's true, but then you humans went and exaggerated the rest. That seems to happen a lot among your kind."

Alex scrunched his eyebrows and rubbed his cheek while mumbling, "I guess I still have a lot to learn about you guys."

"You could say that."

"And what am I gonna see today?"

"The place where we're headed is one of two bases that survived the Scipion Legions' worst attacks."

"Have people ever been there?"

"You'll be the first."

Even though Alex was disappointed he hadn't been the only human to make contact with the Survivors, he felt excitement over being the first to see their secret hiding place. "You said we're going to a base—like a military base?"

"No, it was more of a factory in our time, and I reckon it'll be one again."

"A factory?"

Stretching out his short arms, Bluey motioned to the aircraft interior surrounding them and said, "Where do you think we made this?"

"But how? I thought there were only a couple of you Survivors left."

"Most of the processes are automatic—run by computers and robots."

"What? You guys have computers and robots?"

Alex's question seemed to annoy Bluey. "You think *humans* were the first to come up with such things?"

Startled by Bluey's angry response, Alex just shrugged his shoulders and said, "I don't know . . . I guess."

"I told you our civilization was more advanced than yours, Alex...*far more advanced*. We could do things people never dreamed of!"

"Sorry," Alex muttered while searching for a way to ease the tension. "What sort of things could you do?"

Bluey's demeanor became more relaxed. "Remember what I told you about the microbots and neuro-links?"

"Microbots have kept you alive for millions of years and neuro-links let you control animals, right?"

"We use neuro-links to control animals nowadays, but that's not why we first created them. Our original goal was something more ambitious . . ."

"What was it?"

"To escape death."

"How?"

"Do you remember Ketoo?"

"The leopard gecko? He was a scientist, wasn't he?"

Bluey nodded. "After the worst attacks killed most of our population and Scipion Legion death squads continued murdering the Survivors, Ketoo started implanting radio transmitters inside our brains which connected to a supercomputer in South America. That computer was programmed to store our thoughts and personalities in case of death."

"Did it work?"

"It worked once. One of our leaders—a great turtle named Chelonius—got neuro-link implants right before Scipion warriors found him and killed him. At the moment his body died, his mind was uploaded to the computer mainframe through a wireless connection. It's been there ever since."

Alex scratched his head. "So . . . this guy's body is dead, but his mind's alive because it was transmitted into a computer?"

Bluey slapped his knee and exclaimed, "You got it!"

"Cool."

Before long, the two were flying over the grasslands of northern Argentina. Sunlight was starting to seep over the eastern horizon.

"We'll be there soon. No worries," Bluey asserted. "In the meantime, how about I play some new music I downloaded from *atarkya.com* this morning."

That's the website Bluey called, Alex remembered. "Um . . . Bluey?" he went on to ask, "Why'd you call *atarkya.com* from my house?"

While ethereal music of Andean flutes and mandolins began filling his aircraft's interior, Bluey's eyes opened in a show of surprise. He flicked his tongue and chuckled, "Didn't know you were checking up on me, mate."

"I just hit the redial button on my phone after you left."

"Tell you what—I'll let you know about it on the way back."

"Guess it's another long story . . ." Alex sighed.

Bluey clambered back to the pilot chair and yelled, "Enjoy the scenery, mate. I'm about to wake up an old friend!"

The flying machine rolled to the right and descended over a sea of tall, yellowish-green grass. Clumps of bushy *caldén* trees grew up from the plain, their shadows long in the early morning sun. Bluey steered his aircraft into a wide circle over a cluster of trees where the soil was bare and a flock of strange birds strutted nearby. Covered in brownish-grey feathers, they picked at the bare soil with their beaks.

Alex peered through the semi-transparent floor and shouted, "What are those birds down there?"

"Those are *rheas*. They're the South American version of the ostrich."

Glancing at a large hole in the soil, Alex spotted the head of a black-and-white lizard poking out. Upon sighting Bluey's flying egg, it sprang into action and scurried towards the ostrich-like rheas with a brown bag on its side and a reddish cloth hanging from its shoulders. It also seemed to be wearing white pants and black boots. *A lizard wearing pants?* Nowadays, Alex never knew what to expect.

Sprinting on two legs across the patch of dirt, the lizard leaped onto the back of a rhea and hunched down while the bird ran towards a ridge of mountains in the distance. Amazed at how the rhea seemed to be running in a perfectly straight line, Alex asked, "Is that lizard using neuro-links to tell the bird where to go?"

Eyes still facing forward, Bluey replied, "Yeah, he's telling the rhea what to do with his thoughts—in the same way I moved those birds into your backyard."

"Cool."

After several minutes of what appeared to be a race, Alex spotted a flock of pink birds soaring in from the west. "Flamingos!" he shouted as they flew under Bluey's aircraft, interrupting his view of the lizard below.

Two flamingos quickly broke from the flock and Bluey shouted, "Check their legs!"

Sure enough, the black-and-white lizard was dangling from the flamingos' webbed feet. As the long-necked birds beat their wings to climb higher in the sky, the lizard's white pants and shoulder cloth flapped violently in the wind.

Five minutes of flying alongside the flamingos passed before Bluey pulled his airship over more rugged terrain. Without warning, the black-and-white lizard let go of his two pink-feathered friends and plunged downwards. Tail swinging with a helicopter-like motion, he managed to land on the back of a waiting llama. The lizard then took hold of the llama's fur and started charging over boulders and loose pebbles below. While he watched, Alex reflected on how amazing it would be to have every animal in nature available at his command.

As Bluey lowered his altitude and steered towards the entrance of a mountainside cave, Alex noticed that the black-and-white lizard was twirling an unusual weapon in the air. Three red cords in the reptile's fist were attached to three stone balls which spun in a tight circle. Right before Bluey piloted his craft over the cave, the lizard on the llama let go of his contraption. It sailed straight for Bluey's airship and hit the rear with a loud *clang*. Alex jumped in surprise. Bluey just sighed and shook his head.

"What was that?" Alex asked.

"That's Tupi's favorite toy," Bluey explained. "It's an old hunting device known as a *boleadora*. The cowboys around here—who are called *gauchos*—use them to hunt . . . I reckon Tupi fancies himself to be the first reptilian *gaucho*."

"A cowboy lizard?"

Bringing his aircraft to rest on a flat stone near the cave entrance, Bluey nodded and said, "He's quite a character."

Once the bay doors opened, Alex climbed out of the aircraft and stretched his stiff legs for the first time in seven hours. The breeze was blowing warm and humid. Bluey came around and said, "I'll bet you dimes to dollars that Tupi will be right in front of the cave, waiting for us."

Sure enough, the other lizard was reclining on a rock near the cave entrance when Alex and Bluey arrived, looking as if he'd been resting there for hours. A wide-brimmed hat shaded his head and a small cup with a metal straw sat in his hand. With a tilt of his head, the lizard peeked out from under his hat and greeted them with a deep-voiced *"Buenos días."*

Bluey replied with the same words. Alex mimicked what they said.

A broad smile crossed the lizard's face. He flipped to his feet, removed his hat, bowed his head, and said, *"Me llamo Tupinambis, para servirle."*

Unfortunately, Alex didn't understand a word the black-and-white reptile had said. His only response was, "Huh?"

Looking crossly in Bluey's direction, the lizard snapped, "I thought you said this boy's last name was Hidalgo."

"Just because he has a Spanish surname doesn't mean he speaks the language, mate."

The lizard looked at Alex with his head cocked to one side. A forked tongue, pink in color, shot from his mouth and retracted again. *"¿No hablas español?"* he asked.

"Huh? I mean—I'm sorry, but I don't understand you," Alex stammered.

"We'll have to work on that, *amigo*," the black-and-white lizard grumbled in thickly accented English. Taking a sip through his metal straw, he added, "I'd offer you some of my drink, but my cup's too small. Later I'll get a big cup and we can drink *yerba mate* together."

Bluey rolled his eyes and scolded, "Tupi, we have a meeting to get to! We're late enough as it is."

"There's always time for *yerba mate*, my friend."

"You might as well let the boy know your species right away," Bluey huffed. "That way you won't have to prove how *argentino* you are at every opportunity."

The black-and-white lizard smiled at Alex and flicked his tongue once before declaring, "I'm an Argentine black-and-white tegu, *amigo*. Don't forget—Argentine means that I'm from Argentina . . . the greatest country in the world!"

"But no tango lessons for the boy right now," Bluey snapped. "We have to get inside."

CHAPTER 7

Underground

The journey to the Survivors' secret meeting place turned out to be the scariest experience of Alex's life. Inside the cave, he banged his head several times before Tupi suggested he crawl on all fours. Rough stones dug painfully into Alex's knees while creeping through hundreds of feet in total darkness. His body twitched each time an unseen creature fell onto his bare neck or crawled under his shirt.

Just when Alex feared he couldn't survive another minute in the damp, stale air of the cave, his eyes detected a faint light ahead. The sight gave him new strength. As the light became stronger, however, he noticed insects and spiders crawling all over the walls—a sight that almost made him wish he was back in the dark again.

At the end of the tunnel, Alex stepped into a massive cavern where hundreds of lamps attached to steep walls of rock forced him to squint for several seconds. Once his eyes adjusted, he then noticed large boulders along a path which were carved into sculptures—among them giant crocodiles, dignified turtles, and graceful lizards.

One statue in particular caught Alex's eye. It was a dinosaur who stood nearly twenty feet tall, with jaws full of dagger-like teeth and three-clawed hands at the ends of his muscular arms. A crest rose from the great monster's snout and a helmet wrapped around the rear of its head. His chest and midsection were covered in armor.

"Who's that?" Alex asked in a hushed voice, almost believing the sculpture could come to life and eat him if he spoke too loudly.

Tupi took a sip from his cup of *yerba mate* and replied, "That's General Bakura. He was one of our leaders when the Scipion Legions attacked. I carved him myself."

"*You* carved that?"

Tupi nodded. "I carved all of these statues."

"How'd you do *all* of them?"

Shrugging his narrow shoulders, Tupi explained, "I've had millions of years of free time, *amigo*. You can get a lot done."

"What happened to that general?"

"He was killed in the rebellion, like most of the others."

"Rebellion?"

"I reckon you'll learn about it today, Alex," Bluey explained. "But let's get down to the meeting first."

Awestruck by the sights around him, Alex followed the lizards down a pathway which snaked along the cavern walls. In the valley below, seven creatures were gathered on a narrow strip of land next to an underground river. Two of the smallest stood on a stone platform and appeared to be arguing with each other.

When Alex's mismatched sneakers crunched into the pebbles of the riverbank, the two lizards on the platform took a pause and bowed in his direction. One was brown and red with smooth scales and the other looked identical to spotted lizards at the pet store near Alex's house. Bluey introduced them as "Togo the fire skink" and "Ketoo the leopard gecko." Alex recalled the name Ketoo from Bluey's stories.

Bluey and Tupi went on to present the other reptiles in rapid sequence. Talitha was a veiled chameleon whose body had the ability to copy any combination of colors in a matter of seconds—a feat which allowed her to disappear in plain sight. Bity was a plump beaded lizard with scales that glistened like yellow and black pearls. Salvator was a large monitor lizard who was doing his best to keep humans safe from Sleeran attacks, and Suzikha was a crested gecko, orange in color, with pointed scales over her eyes that looked like eyelashes.

Mama Taonga was the last to be introduced. She was a tuatara—a type of ancient reptile unrelated to other scaly creatures in today's world. Though she was little more than two feet long, Mama Taonga carried herself like a queen. As a result, Alex thought a corny greeting like, "Nice to meet you, your highness," might be appropriate. Before he could speak, however, he was interrupted.

"Where's Aira?" Tupi snapped. "She was supposed to be here already!"

Ketoo stepped to the edge of his platform and peered at the underground river's flowing water. "She'll be here, Tupi," he assured calmly. "I know you want to get started, but Aira had to check on a possible Sleeran landing in New Guinea first."

"Relax, Tupi," a voice boomed from overhead. "You came late, too!"

Alex jumped at the sound, then looked upward to see a turtle's face projected on a smooth wall over the river. It seemed like an image one would see in a movie theater, but the face blinked and smiled as if it were watching the action below.

"Is this the boy I've heard so much about?" the turtle asked.

"That's Chelonius!" Bluey shouted.

Recalling Bluey's story of the dead turtle whose mind had been uploaded onto an ancient computer, Alex took a closer look at the massive face above him.

Skin on the turtle's head and neck was dark grey in color, with bright yellow patches on the top and a pinkish hue around his mouth.

"I can hear you, Alex!" the voice proclaimed. "Say something!"

With the words he'd planned to say to Mama Taonga still stuck on his tongue, Alex fumbled, "Oh . . . um . . . nice to meet you . . . your highness."

The turtle's mouth opened wide and laughter echoed throughout the canyon. Several lizards joined in the fun. When he calmed down, Chelonius explained, "I'm not a king, so leave that 'your highness' rubbish for someone else."

Seconds later, a stream of bubbles appeared on the river's surface and a penguin burst from the water. Clinging to it was a grey lizard with black stripes. As soon as the penguin slid onto the riverbank, the lizard leaped, somersaulted in the air, and landed on the stone platform between Ketoo and Togo. When she put her wet arms around the others, Togo appeared to cringe from drops of cold water dripping down his back.

Shaking his head, Bluey looked up at Alex and whispered, "That's Aira. She's an Eastern water dragon. She *loves* to make grand entrances."

"A dragon?"

"Not the kind you're thinking about. That's just a name for lizards Down Under."

"Down Under?"

"Australia, mate."

Togo the fire skink seemed eager to get the proceedings underway, so he looked up at Chelonius and yelled, "Now that everyone's here, what's the plan for stopping this invasion?"

"We haven't made any plans yet."

"Why not? Our enemies are back! The time for action has come!"

"They haven't landed yet, my friend."

"What about the Sleerans? Hundreds of them are here already!"

"But we've been able to take down several dozen," Salvator boasted.

"Wounding Teeth and Swift Runners could come next!" Togo exclaimed. "We've got to stop them!"

"Nine lizards, one tuatara, and one human against an army of battle-hardened warriors—are you *serious*?"

"Diapsid traitors," Togo grumbled. "I'll bet they're back to take the planet."

"We all knew it would happen sooner or later . . ." Ketoo sighed.

"If you hadn't gotten them to believe those crazy ideas," Togo snapped, "we never would've been in this situation!"

"Those ideas were the only way to keep them under control!"

"Lot of good that did . . ."

While Chelonius, Ketoo, and Togo continued their heated discussion, Bluey turned in Alex's direction to whisper, "Diapsids were those dinosaur warriors I told you about—the ones involved in the rebellion."

Before the Survivors' argument continued any longer, Mama Taonga raised her arms and shouted, "Enough!" With a gnarled finger pointed in Alex's direction, she then said, "Ketoo, tell our human friend about the Diapsids and their rebellion."

Everyone became absolutely silent. Only the faintest trickle of water rushing through the cavern could be heard. Nervous energy gripped Alex's insides when all eyes turned on him.

Ketoo looked at Alex and said, "You don't know everything about the last invasion, do you?"

"I-I-I guess not."

"But Bluey told you about the army I created, right?"

Alex nodded. "He said you picked the best dinosaurs and made them smarter and stronger to fight the aliens."

Ketoo lowered his head and closed his eyes, as if he were visualizing a long-forgotten scene from his past. "Two species of dinosaur warriors—the Swift Runners and the Wounding Teeth—were unstoppable in battle. They crushed Scipion Legion forces on Earth, then used captured spacecraft to continue their victories in space. It wasn't long before every Scipion warship in the solar system had been taken.

"Unfortunately, the main key to their success was a religion we created for them—one that led Swift Runners and Wounding Teeth to believe a war god named Unim would reward their bravery with glory after death. That's what made them confront the enemy without fear."

Engrossed as he was in the story, Alex lost some of his shyness and asked, "You *created* a religion?"

Ketoo nodded. "It's not hard to do—just make up some gods, think of a few tricks to suggest they exist, and then push the believers to do whatever you want. With the Diapsids, we had an easy time convincing them to believe this imaginary religion because they began learning it right after they hatched. Those beliefs, however, combined with their devastating success in battle, eventually led Swift Runners and Wounding Teeth to think they were destined to rule the universe."

Alex was starting to wonder what life must have been like during those times. He could picture armies of muscular dinosaurs—brandishing fearsome weapons and covered in body armor—standing on fields littered with the bodies of dead aliens. Being a typical boy, it was a sight he longed to see with his own eyes.

Ketoo continued, "After defeating the Scipion Legions in our solar system, Swift Runners and Wounding Teeth started agitating for war in other parts of the universe. Since victory had made them more bloodthirsty than ever, we decided that sending them off to fight the Scipions would be less dangerous than keeping them here."

"It was the only way to get rid of them," Bluey added. "We hoped their imaginary religion would keep them from turning against us, but it didn't."

"Why not?"

"Because they found power greater than ours."

"Huh?"

"Someone gave them the Zokana Device."

"The *what*?"

"The Zokana Device is a brutal weapon that can burn the surface of an entire planet," Ketoo explained.

"Who gave it to them?"

"It appears the Scipions must have given it to the Diapsids. Maybe it was a way of tricking them into joining the Scipion Legions."

"And once they had the device," Bluey interrupted, "they came back."

A chill overcame Alex's body. *That must've been the time when millions of reptiles were killed.* Gripping his hands tightly together, he asked Bluey, "Is that what you didn't want to talk about at my house?"

"It's the time none of us like to remember, mate—especially when we get to Lord Upadravin."

The other lizards shuddered when Bluey said that name, but Alex didn't understand why.

"Who?"

Ketoo took a breath and said, "A Swift Runner who called himself Lord Upadravin turned his Diapsid followers against us and returned to Earth. He then launched the Zokana Device to destroy our civilization and murder all 'five fingers.'"

Alex looked down at his hand. "Five fingers?"

"Lord Upadravin claimed any creature with five fingers on each hand should be killed to honor Unim."

Another shudder of fear coursed through Alex's body. *They'd say the same thing about people.* "But that god Unim wasn't real, was he?"

"As long as the Diapsids believed in him, it didn't matter."

"How'd you guys survive?"

"Once the Diapsids returned, I loaded my spaceship with reptiles—including the ones you see here—and sped off. With only seconds to spare, we escaped the Zokana Device's path of destruction."

"In a spaceship?"

"Like the one that brought you here today."

"Where'd you go?"

"I buried my ship inside Jupiter's moon Europa, where we were frozen there for two million years."

"Frozen?" Alex asked. "Wouldn't that kill you?"

Ketoo shook his head. "Lots of animals can survive freezing, Alex, even for long periods of time . . . Wood frogs in Alaska freeze every winter, yet come spring they thaw out and hop away."

"People are on that path, too," Bluey added. "Search for the word 'cryonics' the next time you're on the Internet."

"People can be frozen and brought back to life?" Alex gasped.

"Most everything's possible through science, mate."

His mind swimming in this sea of new information, Alex could only think of one additional question. "Will this new war be against dinosaurs or aliens?"

"Probably both."

The thought of seeing live dinosaurs filled Alex with both excitement and terror. *What kind of fighters are they?* he wondered.

CHAPTER 8

The Challenge

On board Scipion Legion Destroyer 3176, Commander Trod had been so busy preparing for the Earth invasion he hadn't even thought about his mutiny plan for weeks. Desperate for rest inside his cramped sleeping quarters, the tired Wounding Tooth removed his body armor and heaped bedding into a crude nest. Curling himself on top of the pile and resting his head on crossed arms, Trod yawned and looked forward to falling asleep. Before he drifted off, however, the intercom on his wall crackled.

"Commander!" a voice shouted through the speaker. "Report to the Throne Room immediately!"

"Understood," Trod replied lazily, stretching out to relax for another minute.

"NOW!" the voice bellowed.

Commander Trod staggered to his feet and a sharp metal *clang* sounded when his head struck the shelf above his nest. Anger flushed through his body along with the throbbing pain. *Enough of this!* Trod raged while strapping his body armor back into place. *The days of Dromeus must come to an end!*

Stumbling into the hallway, Trod cursed under his breath when he realized his helmet was still in the room. He trudged back to his sleeping quarters, grabbed the metal dome with four horns sticking from the top, and dragged his feet towards the elevator. After the doors opened, Trod placed the helmet on his head and noticed a lump had been raised on his cranium. *Dromeus will pay for all of this.*

At the entrance to the Throne Room, Commander Trod was surprised to see two Swift Runners waiting for him. Trod recognized Vice Admiral Hati instantly—no other Diapsid on the ship sported such hideous injuries. The other was Captain Ripu, chief of the admiral's security detail.

"You're moving too slow," Vice Admiral Hati snarled.

"Wounding Teeth are too busy to come running every time Dromeus calls," Trod hissed in response.

Captain Ripu glared at the commander with an icy look of hatred in his yellow eyes, then turned and led the way to Admiral Dromeus.

Trod's mind was foggy from lack of sleep, so bright lights and white walls inside the Throne Room gave everything a dreamy glow. Ignoring Diapsid protocol to bow before the admiral's marble steps, Commander Trod instead straightened his back and glared upwards at Admiral Dromeus.

"How are the preparations going?" Dromeus snarled, flexing the killing claws on his feet.

"Everything's going well."

"That's not what I've heard! Captain Ripu tells me the Savages *still* aren't ready."

"You never gave me the extra workers I requested," Trod growled. "Our numbers are too small to follow your impossible schedule!"

Leaning forward on his silver throne, Admiral Dromeus hissed, "Are you questioning my leadership?"

Even though he'd clearly enraged the admiral by refusing to bow when he entered, Trod decided to push Dromeus further. "I question your strategy for the Earth invasion. It won't work."

Dromeus flashed his pointed fangs and snarled, "Then we'll see how good *your* strategy skills are at the Bloodfest this evening."

"*My* skills?" Trod gulped.

"You will oversee the Wounding Tooth butchers."

"But admiral, I haven't slept for days."

"I care nothing for your troubles, Commander Trod. Lead the butchers or die."

Though participation in the Bloodfest would put Trod's life in danger, he also knew it would take place in full view of the public. *Perfect for a challenge.* "I'll lead the Wounding Teeth, Lord Conqueror," he said. "May our feast be equal to that of mighty Unim."

"May it be so."

Trod saluted all three Swift Runners and marched out of the room. *No time to waste.* Shuffling down the hall and activating the elevator, Commander Trod hoped he'd finally find time to sleep once Admiral Dromeus was dead.

* * *

Two hours later, doors of the Slaughterhouse on board Legion Destroyer 3176 opened to roars from hundreds of Diapsids. Inside, Swift Runners and Wounding Teeth sat on separate benches rising from a stadium-like central oval where twenty Diapsids—ten Wounding Teeth and ten Swift Runners—brandished traditional weapons known as sword-axes. These were the butchers, so called because they were to chop up an unsuspecting dinosaur in a few minutes' time. Admiral Dromeus, scowling and clutching his own sword-axe, took his place on a platform jutting over the fenced-in oval while chants from ancient Diapsid legends began to murmur through the crowd.

Commander Trod was among his fellow Wounding Teeth butchers in the central oval, glaring at his arch-enemy Captain Ripu across the pebble-strewn floor. The sword-axe Trod held was standard issue for all Diapsids, consisting of a metal bar seven feet in length that thickens to a club at one end and flattens into a sharp blade at the other. Clubs are adorned with foot-long metal spikes and blades generally measure four feet in length. Trod knew Captain Ripu would use his sword-axe as a murder weapon if given the opportunity, so he resolved to keep watch on his rival during the Bloodfest.

Doors forty feet in height opened on one wall of the Slaughterhouse and loud trumpeting noises signaled the arrival of the butchers' prey. It was an *Alamosaurus*—a species of long-necked dinosaur that had been taken from Earth before Lord Upadravin's rebellion sixty-five million years ago. Several of the giant beasts were maintained on Legion Destroyer 3176 for both food and combat practice.

A small head passed through the portal first, scaly and maroon in color. Crosswise stripes of yellow appeared at intervals on the neck and four pillar-like legs carried the alamosaur's thirty-ton bulk. Eight Diapsids guides followed the unfortunate creature with long sticks, slapping its hindquarters and prodding it forward. Once the beast's body was trapped within the tall fence of the enclosed oval, the doors closed and the Diapsid guides clambered out of the ring. It was time for the butchers to do their work.

The main job of the twenty combatants within the oval was to weaken the dinosaur and bring its head to rest on the platform where Admiral Dromeus stood. It was then the Lord Conqueror's honor to inflict the final blow and kill the mighty *Alamosaurus*.

Battle drums began thumping from the spectators' ranks and excited energy surged through Commander Trod's team while the fifty-foot long creature swung its long neck from side to side, eyes nearly popping out with fear. Trumpeting noises continued to rush from the creature's nostrils and its tail slashed through the air. Commander Trod took a brief moment to scan the crowd, feel the drumbeats charge his senses, and assure that this was the right setting to issue his challenge to the admiral. *Everything is perfect*, he concluded.

When the twenty carnivores started closing ranks around the panicky *Alamosaurus*, those in the rear crouched low to avoid the creature's whip-like tail. Closer to the front, Commander Trod surged forward and thrust the blade of his sword-axe into the foreleg of the giant beast, prompting a hoot of pain to spill from the creature's mouth. Flicking its long tail instinctively towards the source of the pain, the *Alamosaurus* caught Trod on the back. Protected by armor and charged with bloodlust, however, he didn't even feel it.

Swift Runners attacked in unison. All ten jumped onto the huge beast's side and started slashing with the blades of their sword-axes. Killing claws on their hind feet gave them enough traction to cling to the creature for more than a minute, and each butcher followed his slice with a thump from the spiked end of his sword-axe. Streams of red rushed down the alamosaur's scaly skin and spilled onto the pebbled floor. Moaning in agony, the mighty beast attempted to dislodge the attackers by rearing up on its hind legs. In response, Swift Runners returned to the ground and Wounding Teeth hacked at the leviathan's hindquarters. Tendons and ligaments began snapping with hideous tearing sounds, causing the long-necked dinosaur's back legs to collapse.

Before long, only one of the alamosaur's body parts remained in perfect working order—its tail. The gigantic whip slashed to the right with a deafening boom and then screamed to the left with several tons' force. One Swift Runner was thrown against the perimeter fence by the creature's tail, killing him instantly. Swift Runners in the stands bellowed in anger, clutching their sword-axes and lifting them high over their heads. All seemed eager to jump into the ring and take the fallen warrior's place.

After a quick check of Captain Ripu's position, Commander Trod leaped onto the back of the *Alamosaurus* and ran towards the rear. Drenched in blood, he slipped several times before reaching the base of the tail. With a precise thrust from the long blades on his sword-axe, Trod penetrated the rear vertebrae of the dying beast and severed its spinal cord. Cheers erupted from all sides when the creature's last remaining weapon fell limp.

Taking its final breaths, the *Alamosaurus* groaned and its body slumped to the ground. Diapsids at the front end of the oval used the clubs on their sword-axes to prod its head towards the platform where Admiral Dromeus stood. Lights dimmed to a small circle, illuminating the admiral and his raised sword-axe. The blade of his weapon caught the spotlight's glare. His time to kill had come.

An instant before the admiral's sword-axe fell to chop off the alamosaur's head, Commander Trod surged onto the platform and knocked Dromeus to the ground. Surrounded by darkness, Trod's muscular silhouette then bounded from the platform and grabbed the dinosaur's long neck in his claws. With a roar, he sank his teeth into its throat. Except for a few muffled trumpets from the *Alamosaurus*, the Slaughterhouse had fallen silent.

Commander Trod bit with all of his might, ending the giant beast's life with a sickening crunch of bone. While the beast's head tumbled lifelessly to the floor, hundreds of eyes watched Dromeus return to his feet and Trod straighten his posture. When lights became bright, Trod spat dinosaur blood and snarled, "You have been shamed, Dromeus. Consider that your challenge."

Murmurs of disbelief began to rumble through the stadium.

Baring his fangs, the admiral bellowed, "I welcome the chance to kill you in the tradition of our ancestors, Commander Trod."

Trod wiped drops of red from his face and scowled at the Lord Conqueror with disdain. "When?"

"Twelve days from now. That will give us time to prepare for your death."

"I wouldn't be so sure."

Dromeus flashed a cruel smile and sneered, "Eat, Commander Trod. Enjoy the feast. It will surely be your last."

CHAPTER 9

atarkya.com

When Bluey's egg-shaped airship departed from the Survivors' secret base in South America, Alex found himself back in the cargo hold with arms wrapped around his knees. Bluey set the automatic pilot and hustled to the rear portion of the aircraft.

"Your own vehicle will be better able to fit a good-sized human like yourself," he said.

Alex's eyes opened wide. "You mean that I'll have my own . . . um . . . flying machine?"

"Probably in the next few weeks."

"What do you call this thing, anyway?"

"We call it a Drifter. I reckon it's not the most creative name, but it does the job."

"But I don't understand . . . If you can still build stuff like these spaceships, why didn't you ever bring your civilization back?"

"What do you mean?"

"Once the Scipion Legions were gone, why didn't you start building your cities all over again?"

Bluey shrugged, "By the time we returned to Earth, those reptiles who'd survived the Zokana Device had gone back to being ordinary animals. We took it as a sign to let nature take its course."

"And you never wanted to go back to the way things were before?"

"Sure, but we also enjoyed the peace and quiet . . . until humans came along."

"Huh?"

"Things were great until people started taking over the planet."

Alex was shocked by Bluey's comment. "You don't like us?"

"There's good and bad about humans, mate. Your kind has the intelligence to save all the world's problems, but it usually seems you'll wind up destroying everything first."

"What do you mean?"

"Well, for starters, human governments spend more money on weapons for war than they do in saving people's lives through medical research."

"Really?"

If you don't believe me, you can see the data on *atarkya.com*."

Recalling the promise Bluey made on the way to South America, Alex leaned forward and said, "You said that you'd tell me about *atarkya.com* on the way home, remember?"

Bluey placed his short-fingered hands on his knees and chuckled, "That's the last piece of the puzzle, isn't it? Tell me, Alex, what do you know about *atarkya.com*?"

"Everybody says it's the coolest website. Even my teachers like it."

"And have you ever heard of a man named Sikandar Tendulkar?"

"I think so. Isn't he a super-rich guy in India who's afraid of germs?"

"That's what they say about him," Bluey smiled. "In fact, they say that he does all his work from a sealed apartment in the Indian city of Mumbai. Since he *never* leaves that place, people can only talk to him through telephone or video link."

"Whoa! He's really *that* afraid of germs?"

"You don't get it?"

"Don't get *what*?"

"Think of the voice you heard on *atarkya.com*'s telephone message. It's supposed to be Sikandar Tendulkar, but haven't you heard it somewhere else?"

Alex tried hard to remember the voice on the phone. To his surprise, it was familiar. "Was that Ketoo?"

Bluey laughed heartily and grabbed his belly. "You're a smart one, all right," he managed to blurt between girlish giggles.

"Is there really a guy named Sik . . . Sikan . . . um . . . Tenelker?"

"Sikandar Tendulkar's just a myth—a personality we created because people would expect to see a *human* running our Internet company. All that nonsense about his fear of germs was our way to keep him from public view. When he does an interview on television, we create the video image and Ketoo does the voice. No one suspects the truth about us!"

"But how the heck could *lizards* start an Internet company?"

"All we had to do was patch our South American computer into the World Wide Web and start an online business. Within a few years, *atarkya.com* became a multi-billion dollar company. We even have human employees nowadays, and the CEO for those operations is a man named Ashoka Mehta." Pausing for a moment, Bluey added, "Of course, Mr. Mehta doesn't know his *real* bosses are reptiles . . ."

"But why start a business in the first place?"

"Ketoo got excited about your advances in technology and wanted to guide your development as best he could. Before long, we realized *atarkya.com* would also be a good way to prepare for the coming invasion. Now we have plenty of money to buy whatever we'll need to face the Scipion Legions."

Alex had hoped to continue their conversation, but his eyelids were too heavy to say anything else. Awake for nearly twenty hours without a chance to rest, sleep overcame his body and maintained its hold until Bluey's Drifter landed on the frozen ground of Sweetbriar Park that evening. Frigid air brought Alex back to his senses when the clamshell doors of the cargo bay opened and wind swirled all around.

Bluey hopped in front of Alex and shouted, "I'll have to leave you here, mate."

"What time is it?"

Bluey looked at the aircraft's control panel. "It's seven o'clock."

Alex's eyes opened wide and he felt his stomach sink. *That's later than expected.* "I have to get going," he said, stumbling out of the Drifter. "My mom's gonna kill me."

While Alex's frantic footsteps charged through the darkness, Bluey yelled, "Start looking for people to help us!"

Though he heard Bluey, Alex was too frightened to respond. Instead, he continued crashing over frosty leaves and through dark bushes. By now *everyone* knew he'd skipped school. Cold air stung his throat when he reached the street next to the park.

With only a wrinkled sweatshirt and a pair of jeans to protect him from the cold, Alex turned the corner and hesitated for a moment. A police car was parked outside of Uncle Roy's home. He was even in *bigger* trouble than imagined. Heart pounding like a hammer inside of his chest, Alex slipped through the front gate without a sound, tiptoed along an ice-encrusted walkway, and crept through the back door as carefully as possible. Unfortunately, the door creaked when it shut. *Now I'm gonna get it.*

Seconds later, Katherine's footsteps rushed through the dining room and into the kitchen. She struck her brother on the shoulder with a closed fist and shouted, "Where were you?"

Mom's heavy steps thumped through the dining room immediately afterwards. "You're home! Oh, thank goodness!" she cried. Upon entering the kitchen, Alex noticed her blonde hair was a complete mess and her eyes were puffy and red.

Before Mom could put her arms around him, Alex took a deep breath. The cigarette smell embedded in her clothing was never pleasant. Trying to hold his breath while he talked, Alex squeezed out the words, "Yeah, Mom, I'm back."

"Are you okay? What happened to you?"

"I'm fine. I just went on a little trip . . . It's nothing."

"Where'd you go?" Mom asked, stepping back and looking him over from head to toe.

Searching for a response his mother would believe, Alex leaned forward and peered through the dining room. To his surprise, a police officer was standing there with a note pad and pen. Relief came when Uncle Roy called the officer and he stepped back out of sight.

A full minute of uncomfortable silence passed while Alex pondered what he could say. He obviously couldn't tell the truth—it would sound crazier than any lie he could think up. With his gaze turned towards the linoleum on the kitchen floor, Alex finally stammered, "I . . . uh . . . I tried to get on a bus to go see *Tío* Ramiro."

"You're telling me you left before the sun came up—without a winter coat and without any money—to try to get a bus down to *Texas*? You expect me to believe *that*?"

"I got a ride to the bus station and thought it would be easy to sneak onto a bus headed west. After a while, I just gave up and walked back home."

"Who gave you a ride down to the bus station so early in the morning?"

"Um . . . some creepy old guy offered me a ride." It was a lie Alex hoped would make his mother too angry to continue asking questions.

Mom's face flashed bright red. Shaking her hands in front of her, she screamed, "How could you do something so stupid? You're lucky you're not dead!"

Before any more words were exchanged, Uncle Roy called Mom into the living room to speak with the police officer one last time. As soon as she was gone, Alex glanced at his sister with a wide grin on his face.

"That's not what *really* happened, is it?" Katherine asked, squinting her eyes and putting her hands on her hips.

Alex shook his head and chuckled, "Far from it."

"Well, where were you?"

"Can't tell you now. Mom's gonna lecture me first."

Katherine frowned and punched her brother in the arm again. "I'll be in my room," she grunted.

"It's *my* room too, you know . . ."

True to Alex's prediction, Mom returned and scolded Alex for fifteen minutes before screaming, "Go to your room!" and slumping her head between her arms on the kitchen table. Her round figure heaved as she began to cry.

Without a second thought over the sadness he'd caused, Alex rushed into his room and closed the door. There he found Katherine, arms crossed, pouting on her bed.

"Are you going to tell me *now*?" she whined.

Alex smiled. "Okay, you remember that lizard I saved back in the fall?"

"You mean the one that got away?"

"Yeah."

"I remember you were stupid for letting it escape."

"Well, he needed to get to an important meeting."

"Huh?"

"His name's Bluey. He took me to South America last night."

Katherine's eyes opened wide. "What the heck are you talking about?"

"Just let me explain," Alex urged with hands in the air. He then talked nonstop for thirty minutes and was sure Katherine didn't blink the entire time. Before Alex could finish the story, however, a heavy hand knocked on the door.

Alex's first thought upon seeing Mom enter his bedroom was that she looked *awful*. After a brief fit of coughing and a few gurgling sounds that made both children cringe, she straightened herself, pushed back her hair, and said in a hoarse voice, "Alex, all we got is each other, and I don't want to lose either one of you."

Alex shrugged his shoulders in reply.

Mom continued, "I wish you could understand what I'm feeling, but you probably won't until you have children of your own."

Trying to avoid conversation, Alex mumbled, "Guess not."

"I just can't understand *why* you left last night. I know you miss your *tío*, but why wouldn't you tell me something?"

"I figured you'd say we don't have any money." By this point, Alex almost believed his own lies.

Mom's face got even sadder. "I wish we had the money . . . I try, but things aren't working out. If your father hadn't left us, things would be easier."

It seemed strange that Mom said his father *left* instead of her usual story about the government taking him away, but Alex didn't want to press her on the issue at the moment. His goal was to get Mom out of the room as quickly as possible. "Look," Alex said, choosing his words carefully, "I'm sorry for what I did. You're right, though . . . I probably won't understand what you're feeling until I have a baby of my own."

Mom's mood seemed to brighten a bit. "You're only eleven, Alex. Don't go havin' babies anytime soon!"

Alex and Katherine looked at each other and giggled for a moment before Alex turned to his mother again. "Things will get better, Mom."

"I think he's right," Katherine agreed.

"Well, we can hope, can't we?"

Both children nodded and sat in silence, hoping Mom would get the message that it was time to leave. She did, but not before hugging them both and telling them again how much she loved them. Once the door was shut and her footsteps moved into the living room, Katherine turned to her brother and whispered, "What are the aliens like?"

"I don't think the worst ones *are* aliens. They're some kind of super-smart and super-strong dinosaurs who work for an evil civilization in some other part of the universe."

"Why do they want to attack the Earth?"

Alex shrugged. "Maybe they want it back. That leopard gecko named Ketoo is planning a spy mission to gather more information, but he needs a strong power source to get one of his new ships out to Jupiter."

"They have *spaceships*?"

"They're building them in a factory right now. Ketoo says the only thing he still needs for the trip is uranium."

"What's urine—I mean urininum?"

"The word is *uranium*. It's the stuff that they use to make nuclear bombs. It's really hard to get because it's so powerful and dangerous. Ketoo doesn't want to steal it, but he doesn't think he can buy it, either."

"They have *money*?"

Alex chuckled. "Yeah, Katherine, they have money. Lots and lots of it. You know that website you visit on Marie's computer?"

"You mean *atarkya.com*?"

"Yep. They *own* that site."

"No way!" Katherine squealed with delight.

"Yes way!" Alex exclaimed with the first outburst of enthusiasm he'd shared with his sister in months. "But do you know what the strangest thing is?"

"What?"

"Those lizards only want kids to help them. They don't trust grownups."

"Well I don't trust grownups, either."

As the two continued their conversation, Alex felt relieved that someone understood what was happening to him—even if it was just his sister. Drifting off to sleep after Mom ordered them to turn out the lights, one thing Alex wished more than anything else was that he could see Wounding Teeth and Swift Runners with his own eyes.

CHAPTER 10

Ready for Action

Heavy metal doors screeched open in the Savage Training Area and Commander Trod marched inside. Powerful odors from wild beasts filled the corridor among towering walls fifty feet in height. After a brief search, Trod found his allies in the central staging area.

Lieutenant Titus, who was a Wounding Tooth like Trod, was the first to salute his superior officer and snarl the Diapsid greeting, "*Hracha Kedru Husak Sek.*" The other two followed his lead.

"How's our plan going, lieutenant?" Trod growled.

Lieutenant Titus glanced about nervously before leaning forward and whispering, "The *Triceratops*, *Ankylosaurus*, and *Gallimimus* are responding to our new training. They will be ready in twelve days."

"What about the *Tyrannosaurus rex*?"

Titus shook his head. "One of our favorites has become more aggressive than usual. I cannot keep her from snapping at my trainers. Lieutenant Cyrus was almost eaten right before the Bloodfest."

"She's the biggest one?"

"The alpha female. She doesn't like taking commands from me."

Commander Trod flexed his muscles and snarled, "Let me in with her".

"I don't think that's a wise decision."

"I give the orders, Titus. Let me in!"

Without saying another word, the lieutenant led Trod to the *Tyrannosaurus rex* holding area. Each one of the flesh-eating dinosaurs was housed in a cage bigger than a football field, with gates that were reinforced three times to prevent escape. Roars from the most fearsome predators of all time filled the hall while the group of Wounding Teeth marched towards the largest female's holding pen.

Upon smelling her trainers, the *Tyrannosaurus rex* bellowed and strode towards the gate. She was brownish in color, with faint bands of light orange along the length of her body. Trod grabbed a metal bar from a nearby rack and opened the first set of gates. Stepping through and locking the first gate behind him, he moved to open the second. By the time he came to the third gate, the huge dinosaur was snarling on the other side. Hot breath blasted from her nostrils and foul-smelling saliva dripped from her six-inch teeth.

Trod roared and flung the door open in the face of the *Tyrannosaurus*, catching her on the snout. The enormous predator shrieked with surprise and took three steps backward. Trod leaped through the doorway and slammed the gate behind him. *There's no escape.*

The tyrannosaur came to her senses and her voice thundered a second time. Called "Kusa" by the Wounding Teeth who knew her best, her eighteen-foot height was twice that of Trod's nine-foot stature. Her massive head, almost seven feet from front to back, was about the same length as the heavy staff Commander Trod clutched in his hands.

Kusa the tyrannosaur lunged at Trod with her mouth wide open, but the wily Diapsid struck his metal bar against the ground, vaulted over her vicious jaws, and landed on her back. When Trod jabbed the pole into her side, the tyrannosaur let out a shriek and shifted her eight-ton body to throw him back to the ground. Bringing her head around for a sideways attack, she was blocked by a swing from Trod's metal staff on the bony ridge above her left eye. Shock from the blow drove her to take a few steps in the opposite direction. The ferocious monster growled and stared at Trod while seeming to calculate her next move.

Trod roared again and gave the tyrannosaur commands in the Diapsid language. Kusa curled back her lips and exposed her teeth. Her throat rumbled. Realizing that she was still unwilling to obey, Trod charged at her with his staff raised high. Apparently startled by the Diapsid's boldness, the tyrannosaur bowed her head in submission and lowered her body to the ground. Despite her surrender, Commander Trod still brought the heavy metal staff down on her snout with all the force his powerful arms could manage. The *Tyrannosaurus rex* yelped in pain.

Confident he'd broken her will to fight, Trod climbed onto the cowering predator's back and ordered her to stand. She complied without hesitation. Leading her to the front gate, Trod proudly hopped from the great beast and ordered her to walk away. The once disobedient *Tyrannosaurus rex* did exactly as she was told.

When Commander Trod left the holding area and the third gate clanged behind him, he sneered fiercely at the other Wounding Teeth. "She will not give you any more trouble, lieutenant."

"That was impressive, commander."

Handing his metal bar back to Lieutenant Titus, Trod growled, "That's nothing compared with the challenges ahead. We must be fearless in facing tyrannosaurs, Swift Runners . . . even the Scipions."

Titus checked his surroundings and warned, "Those who speak against the Scipion Legions have a way of disappearing."

"Unim is on our side, my friend. You know as well as I that if we remain with the Scipion Legions, Elektyls will destroy us." Elektyls were a newly discovered alien species the Scipions were starting to use for planetary conquest—once an exclusive privilege of Diapsids and Sleerans. In fact, many Diapsids were worried the Earth invasion would be the last opportunity to impress their alien overlords before Elektyls replaced them entirely.

"But we have been loyal warriors of the Scipion Legions for sixty-five million years!"

"And yet the Elektyls grow more powerful each day."

Lieutenant Titus glanced at his fellow Wounding Teeth with orange eyes full of worry. "Can we stop them?"

Trod pulled closer to his trusted allies, so close that their snouts almost touched. "Now's the time for action, comrades. After I kill Dromeus, we'll take our struggle back to the Diapsid Homeworlds and break from the Scipion Legions. That's the only way our clan will survive."

"Our *clans*," Titus corrected.

"Do not hold out hope for the Swift Runners. They've grown too corrupt to be of much use."

"Are we going to kill *them*, too?"

Trod's scaly lips pulled back in a wicked smile, his two-inch teeth gleaming in the bright light. "One step at a time, my friend . . . One step at a time."

CHAPTER 11

Jean Diop

The sun was bright on the morning after Katherine learned of her brother's secret life. While the two siblings waited together at the bus stop, they spoke in hushed tones, careful not to let anyone hear the subject of their excited conversation.

When Marie arrived and greeted her best friend, Katherine didn't squeal or rush to hug her. She only waved weakly. Once the school bus flashed its red stop sign for the children to board, Katherine stayed behind Alex and sat next to him on a seat where only two people would fit.

Standing in the aisle, Marie said, "Hey Katherine, why don't we find a spot to sit together?"

"Um . . . I can't, Marie. I need to sit with my brother today."

"Then how about a seat where all three of us can go?"

Katherine refused to search for another place to sit. "Why don't you go somewhere else?" she snapped. "I need to talk to my brother *in private*."

Confusion written across her face, Marie shuffled to an open seat farther back and pulled out the novel that she'd been reading. Despite only being in third grade, Marie was on page 598 of *War and Peace*.

Alex's school day was uneventful, but Katherine's was quite the opposite. When Marie tried to sit close to her at lunch, Katherine picked up her tray and moved down the table. At recess, Katherine ran every time Marie tried to approach her. On the bus back home, Marie again sat alone while Katherine whispered back and forth with her brother. When the bus pulled to their final destination and the doors opened, Marie followed Katherine down the rubber-coated steps and asked, "Why do you hate me all of a sudden?"

"I don't hate you, Marie. I just . . . um . . . need to figure some things out with Alex."

"What kinds of things?"

"I can't tell you. It's a secret."

"I don't know why you're being so mean!" Marie shrieked with tears in her eyes, storming down the sidewalk towards her house.

After witnessing the spectacle in silence, Alex turned to Katherine. "What's with her?"

Katherine watched her best friend run away and shrugged, "I guess I wasn't very nice to her today."

"Why not?"

"I was afraid I'd tell her about your lizard friends and the dinosaurs in space if I talked to her."

Alex considered what he knew about Katherine's friend and asked, "Didn't you say that Marie's smart?"

"She's the smartest kid in my class. Why?"

"I guess we'll need smart people to help us in this struggle."

"You mean I can tell her everything?" Katherine squealed.

Second-guessing what he'd just said, Alex answered, "Well . . . maybe not so fast."

"Why not?"

"Didn't you tell me her brother gets into trouble?"

"Marie says he sneaks out of the house and argues with his parents all the time. Sometimes he gets into fights, too."

"Exactly. Let's keep this stuff secret for a little while longer."

"You're no fun," Katherine whined, following her brother back to Uncle Roy's house.

* * *

Hip-hop music was pumping from the second floor when Marie barged through the front door of her home, so she tossed her backpack onto a plastic-covered couch and charged up the stairs to talk with Jean, her older brother. He was fourteen and in eighth grade, but tall and muscular enough to pass for a nineteen-year-old.

Marie banged on Jean's door once, but there was no response. After she banged a second time, the music inside lowered a few decibels.

"Who is it?" Jean yelled.

Marie tried to open the door, but it was locked. She banged a third time and heard her brother shuffle to the door.

Peering through the crack, Jean pulled a cell phone from his ear. "What?"

Tears in her eyes, Marie sobbed, "My best friend won't talk to me."

Jean opened the door and sighed through his phone, "I'll get back to you later, my man." He then took a seat on his unmade bed, put his hands between his knees, and asked, "You talkin' about that girl named Katherine?"

Marie nodded. "She just ignored me the whole day."

"Ain't she the one whose uncle kicked you out of the house a while back?"

"Yes."

Jean shrugged and shook his head. "You gotta accept something, Marie. Deep down, all white people's racist. That's why her uncle chased you. That's also gotta be why your friend ain't talking to you."

Marie crossed her arms and scolded, "You know you're not supposed to be using that street talk."

"Huh?"

"You're always trying to copy those rappers, but Mom and Dad don't like it."

"If you want me talkin' like Moms and Pops, should I start talkin' with a funny accent, too?"

"I'm just saying that you should speak English correctly . . . the way it's *supposed* to be spoken."

"And my friends say I'm tryin' to act white when I talk like y'all."

"There's nothing wrong with saying things the right way."

Jean waved his hand to stop the argument. "I ain't gonna discuss that with you right now, Marie. What I was tellin' you is that white people are racist. They like to pretend they ain't, but it all comes out sooner or later."

"But Katherine's not even *that* white . . . Her dad's from Mexico."

"Spanish folk ain't no better. They all want to keep black people down."

"I said her dad's from Mexico. That would make her *Mexican*, not Spanish."

"Same difference."

"No it's not!"

"And what's that girl's mom? She ain't Mexican, is she?"

Marie paused for a moment, then said, "Her mom's got blonde hair and blue eyes, so I guess she's white."

"And her uncle?"

"He's a fat guy with a brown moustache . . . He's white, too."

"There you go!" Jean exclaimed. "Her mom's and uncle's white. They probably got nervous you was hangin' around their little girl too much—gonna lower their property values or somethin'."

"Who gives you these ideas?"

"Look, I'm just sayin' you're gonna see a whole lot of nonsense if you keep hangin' around white folk. What you need to do is stick with your own."

"Stick with my own?"

"You know . . . hang around black people."

"There aren't any other black kids in my class, Jean! Why's it always black versus white for you?"

Jean shrugged, "That's how the world works."

After a groan of frustration, Marie shook a finger at her brother and snapped, "What if aliens came down to Earth? Do you think they'd care about people's skin colors?"

"Now that's just crazy talk," Jean chuckled.

"Well, my point is that skin color isn't important. We're all people."

Jean snickered at his sister's comment, rose from his bed, and patted Marie's braided hair. "It'll be alright, baby girl," he said with a smile.

Marie batted her brother's hand and shouted, "Stop patting my head! I'm not a dog, and I'm not a baby, either!"

Jean strode towards the door and opened it. "Get moving, Marie. I gotta get ready."

"Ready for what?"

"Gonna get my groove on tonight."

Marie shot her brother an angry, sideways look. "It's a school night, Jean!" she scolded while stepping towards the doorway. "You know Mom and Dad won't let you out!"

"Who says I gotta ask 'em?" Jean replied with a wink before shutting the door in his sister's face.

CHAPTER 12

Battle Dome

The twelfth day after Commander Trod's challenge came with great fanfare. Doors to the Sacred Arena were unsealed and the chamber was cleaned for the coming duel. With separate sections for Wounding Teeth and Swift Runners, the arena was many times larger than any stadium on Earth. Stone benches circled a tall, curved structure in the middle of the floor. This was the Battle Dome—the site where the actual struggle would take place. Except for a detailed mural at the bottom, the Battle Dome's outer shell was completely covered with reflective metal. Spectators were not permitted to see the action inside, but they nevertheless gathered to see which combatant would pass through the Door of Victory upon conclusion of the fight. Of the two warriors who entered, only one Diapsid ever left the Battle Dome alive.

Admiral Dromeus stood next to Vice Admiral Hati on a metal path leading to the Battle Dome. Light glinted off his body armor and his sword-axe gleamed with a newly sharpened edge.

"What have you learned?" Dromeus asked amid excited noises echoing throughout the Sacred Arena.

Hati scanned the area with his functional eye and growled, "Wounding Teeth plan to launch their mutiny when you're inside the Battle Dome."

"Security is on high alert?"

"The highest, sir."

"What about our plan?"

"I planted what you requested inside the Battle Dome."

"On the boulder up above?"

"The very one you showed me."

"Trod will not live to see another day on *my* ship," Admiral Dromeus boasted.

"He doesn't stand a chance, sir."

On the other side of the arena, Commander Trod strutted down the Challenger's Path. He was alone, roaring defiantly and holding his sword-axe above his head. When his orange eyes caught the gaze of Lieutenant Titus in the stands, Titus lowered his head with a single nod and flashed his dagger-like teeth. *Everything is set for mutiny*, Trod concluded from the gesture.

Lieutenant Titus was essential to Trod's plot for mutiny. As soon as the duel began, Titus would leave his post near the Battle Dome and help his underlings release dinosaurs from their cages in the Savage Training Area. After they were led to the Sacred Arena, seven hundred war-hardened Swift Runners would be no match for ninety-six *Tyrannosaurus rex*, one hundred and twenty *Triceratops*, and forty-eight *Ankylosaurus*. Such a devastating attack would make it easy for Wounding Teeth to seize control of the ship once Commander Trod emerged victorious.

Metal scales on Trod's chest armor clinked when he stepped into the Battle Dome. Green moss on the floor was cool and damp, just like the air above it. Beams of light shining from the rounded ceiling made it hard to see through the hazy atmosphere, but Trod's sharp eyes were still able to focus on a bright doorway and black silhouette on the other side. He was looking at Admiral Dromeus.

Heavy doors slid to a close behind the two mortal enemies, prompting Commander Trod to let loose a deafening roar. Sounds of his fury echoed throughout the inner chamber, bouncing off walls of jagged rock set in iron. Trod stretched his neck and flashed a cruel grin while striding towards the center of the Battle Dome. Admiral Dromeus returned his gaze with a look of supreme confidence.

"Present your weapon," Commander Trod snarled.

"I'm your superior officer!" Admiral Dromeus raged. "Present *your* weapon!"

Trod turned the flat side of his sword-axe towards the admiral in a traditional salute. Instead of returning the gesture, Dromeus came at the commander with a sideways chop that whistled through the humid air. Trod dodged the attack with little effort, but hadn't expected the admiral's counterstrike with the spiked end of his club. Trod saw the deadly mace racing towards his legs and leaped backwards. Missing his mark, Dromeus spun in midair and slashed Trod across the cheek with a metal hook strapped to his tail.

"First blood is mine!" Admiral Dromeus bellowed.

Ignoring the pain, Commander Trod growled and focused on the admiral's next move.

Metallic clangs from sword-axes echoed through the Battle Dome as each Diapsid lunged at the other with murderous energy. Trod took a swing at Dromeus, but the admiral blocked the sword-axe blade with the thick bar of his weapon. Dromeus then spun and brought his own blade across Trod's chest. Fortunately, the cutting edge couldn't penetrate Trod's armor and left only minor scratches. Trod kicked upwards in response, catching Dromeus in the groin and sending him several yards backwards. Landing on his feet—but apparently startled by his rival's strength—Dromeus began shuffling towards the far wall.

"Coward!" Trod roared, pursuing the admiral with his sword-axe in attack position.

It wasn't until Admiral Dromeus had backed into rocks on the rear wall that Commander Trod finally caught up with him. Trod's next move was a low swipe with his blade, a reverse in momentum, and a stab at the admiral's right shoulder. In response, Dromeus twisted his body and kicked his killing claws to drive Trod away. The admiral then scrambled up the wall's jagged boulders with amazing speed and escaped his attacker's sword-axe a second time. Trod's weapon threw sparks as it glanced off solid granite.

Trod began scaling the stone where Dromeus had taken refuge, proud that he'd managed to force his rival into retreat so quickly. Placing his hand on the boulder where Dromeus stood, Trod was startled to see the admiral's sword-axe sail over his head and make muffled clangs on the ground below. Instead of filling Trod with a sense of victory, however, the sight filled him with dread. *Something is wrong.* An instant later, the face of the boulder exploded and Commander Trod was thrown to the ground. Landing heavily on his back, he looked up and spotted Dromeus clutching a mobile blaster in his hands. The inside of Trod's left arm was burned from the blaster's discharge, but it wasn't a direct hit. If it had been, the commander's arm would be gone.

"*Ragana katrak!*" Commander Trod snarled in the Diapsid language equivalent of "Cheater!"

"You cannot defeat me!" Dromeus bellowed from a slab of rock still attached to the wall. He then leaped from his perch with right leg recoiled for a strike.

Trod saw the move and tried flipping to his feet, but Admiral Dromeus knocked him back to the ground. One of the admiral's killing claws caught him in the left forearm, tearing his flesh to the bone. Another killing claw was pressed into Trod's throat, stabbing the gap between his jugular vein and windpipe. Unbearable pain prompted the commander to swipe at Dromeus with the club end of his sword-axe.

Force from Trod's swing thrust Dromeus against the stone wall with a *crack*. Long metal spines penetrated the admiral's left side, snapping his ribs and puncturing one lung. Commander Trod scrambled to his feet and positioned himself to slice the admiral's throat with the blade of his sword-axe, but Dromeus coiled his broken body and pushed his shoulder into Trod's chest with all of his might. The commander was knocked back several yards before sliding to a stop amid rattles of body armor.

Admiral Dromeus tried to roar, but an awful gurgling was the only sound that escaped his mouth. He limped towards the commander and pointed his laser gun, but the mobile blaster merely clicked when he pulled the trigger.

Trod returned to his feet. "You didn't recharge!"

The admiral's yellow eyes widened with the apparent realization that he should have pumped the handle of his mobile blaster to fire a second time. Hastily recharging his weapon while still struggling to breathe, Dromeus began stepping backwards in a desperate attempt to recover his sword-axe. The mobile blaster in his claws then made a screech, signaling it was ready to fire.

Trod had been bounding towards Dromeus, but he dove to the floor when the admiral's mobile blaster recharged. Throwing his sword-axe at Dromeus to block the shot, the commander's weapon exploded in a greenish blast of laser fire. Landing face down in the moss, metal fragments pierced Trod's neck and right arm. Streams of blood trickled to the ground as he struggled back to his feet.

Flexing the handgrip to ready his weapon a third time, Dromeus stooped to lift his sword-axe from the mossy floor. "A Wounding Tooth will *never* be admiral!" he wheezed.

Left with few options to stay alive, Commander Trod sprinted towards Admiral Dromeus. The move seemed to catch Dromeus off guard, for he seemed unsure whether to use his mobile blaster or sword-axe against the attack. When the commander came within striking distance, Dromeus thrust the blade of his sword-axe towards Trod's legs, stabbing him in the right thigh. Though Trod stumbled from the injury, momentum from his seven hundred pound bulk couldn't be stopped. He slammed into Dromeus and sent him to the ground, then removed the admiral's sword-axe from his leg and took it in his hands.

Dromeus aimed his mobile blaster while sprawled on the floor, but Trod dove forward with the sword-axe and sliced through the admiral's arm before he could fire. Returning to a standing position on his left leg, Trod saw the admiral's severed hand twitching in the moss—unable to fire the mobile blaster still clutched within its claws.

Bleeding heavily and unable to put weight on his right leg, Trod propped his body against the admiral's sword-axe and snarled, "Your trickery was unable to save you, Lord Conqueror."

Shallow breaths indicating that death was overtaking him, Admiral Dromeus only managed to respond, "Swift . . . Runners will *not* . . . fail!"

"Enough!" Commander Trod bellowed, shifting his weight and raising the admiral's sword-axe high. He slashed the blade across the throat of Admiral Dromeus, who died seconds later in a spasm of violent shaking.

Exhausted and sore from the hardest duel he'd ever fought, Commander Trod removed the admiral's mobile blaster from the green-scaled arm on the floor. *This weapon will be useful in our mutiny.* Using the Lord Conqueror's sword-axe as a crutch, he then ambled towards the Door of Victory in agony. His right leg was badly injured, as was his face, neck, and left arm.

Once metal panels on the Door of Victory slid open in front of him, Commander Trod heard nothing but silence—no sounds to suggest a Wounding Tooth uprising, nor that his Savage dinosaurs were killing and eating Swift Runners. Tossing the admiral's sword-axe to the floor and sliding three fingers onto the handgrip of his mobile blaster, Commander Trod pressed his body against the wall and hopped through the open doorway. When warm, dry air of the Sacred Arena blew on his striped skin, Trod's body froze in shock.

Lieutenant Titus lay in a pool of blood in front of the Battle Dome, and the hulking figure of Captain Ripu stood with a foot pressing on his corpse. Killing claws on Ripu's feet flexed menacingly, but his face was one of absolute calm.

"Quite an awkward situation, wouldn't you say?" Captain Ripu grunted, his yellow eyes staring down at the claws on his left hand.

"What do you mean?" Commander Trod hissed in reply.

Glancing upwards, Ripu growled, "Take a look around, commander." His tone suggested confidence—as if he had Trod and the others right where he wanted them.

Commander Trod surveyed the Sacred Arena with a painful twist of his neck. Nearly every Swift Runner in the stands had his sword-axe drawn across the throat of a Wounding Tooth, and not a single Savage dinosaur could be seen. "*Ketu seeta ratasa*," he cursed.

"You must have known that Swift Runners would *never* bow to a Wounding Tooth admiral," Captain Ripu sneered.

"I suspected there might be trouble."

"And that's why you sent your supporters to unlock the Savages, wasn't it? You thought your tyrannosaurs and *Triceratops* would be able to finish us Swift Runners off!"

Commander Trod chose not to answer.

"We've known about your mutiny plans for a long time," Ripu said while removing his foot from the body of Lieutenant Titus and bringing it one step closer to Trod.

The commander stood his ground and flexed his muscles. He pointed the mobile blaster at Captain Ripu and roared, "Another step and I will destroy you!"

"Your weapon isn't charged," Ripu scoffed.

Tossing the mobile blaster aside, Commander Trod bared his teeth and raged, "I could still take you down before your followers reach me!"

"*His* followers?" another voice bellowed from outside Trod's field of vision. "You seem to have forgotten who's now in charge of this ship!"

The commander turned and spotted the misshapen form of Vice Admiral Hati limping towards the Victory Pavilion. Instead of the sword-axe he usually clutched in his right arm, the one-eyed Swift Runner was carrying a mobile blaster.

"Wouldn't you say your situation is impossible?" Captain Ripu growled coldly.

"I have defeated Dromeus!" Commander Trod raged. "I should be the new admiral!"

When he was close enough to speak without raising his voice, Vice Admiral Hati hissed, "Captain Ripu and I cannot let that happen. Tradition forbids it. The rank of admiral has *never* been bestowed upon a Wounding Tooth. I will be the ship's new leader."

Dizzy from blood loss, Commander Trod dropped his head and grunted, "Then what happens to us?"

Vice Admiral Hati glared at Trod for a moment with his functional eye, as if he were considering the possibility of immediately ending the commander's life. Taking a deep breath, he said, "Tensions between our clans continue to grow ... more so than at any time in the last sixty-five million years. You know as well as I that the Scipions have recently granted powers of invasion to the Elektyls, and we worry that one day they will rise up and exterminate all Diapsids."

Commander Trod's body relaxed slightly, relieved there was at least one concern he and Hati shared.

Vice Admiral Hati continued, "Since the death of more Wounding Teeth on board this ship will lead to further conflict between our clans, I believe we should work out an agreement."

"What sort of agreement?"

"You and your fellow Wounding Teeth will take the Savages to Earth and establish a base. When you are in position, we'll support the invasion from above."

"But we only have five hundred warriors. That's not enough for a ground force."

Pointing to the bloody corpse of Lieutenant Titus with his sword-axe, Captain Ripu snorted, "You only have four hundred and ninety-nine warriors, commander."

Trod dropped his shoulders and started sliding towards the ground. "That's not enough," he hissed.

"Then you'd better be creative," Hati replied. "It's your only option to stay alive."

His field of vision now collapsing to a small circle directly in front of him, Commander Trod tried to scan the faces of his fellow Wounding Teeth and consider his options. If he managed to conquer territory with a few hundred warriors, it would certainly send a message that his clan was capable of great things. *This might be another way to bring us power.* With a groan, Trod decided to accept the vice admiral's proposal before he lost consciousness. "You must provide us with invasion discs, mobile blasters, and particle beam cannons. That's the only way we'll be successful."

"Of course," Captain Ripu agreed. He then turned to face the crowd of Diapsids with a wicked smile and ordered, "All Swift Runners shall release the Wounding Teeth immediately!"

"You insult me, Ripu!" Vice Admiral Hati roared. "I'm in charge—not you!"

"My apologies, vice admiral."

"All Swift Runners shall release the Wounding Teeth immediately!" the one-eyed vice admiral bellowed. Glancing back at Commander Trod, he snarled, "Heal your wounds, prepare your forces, and be ready to invade Earth within thirty-six days."

"Better make it twenty-four," Captain Ripu suggested.

Hati's only response was a deep growl.

Commander Trod didn't hear any more of the brewing power-struggle between Vice Admiral Hati and Captain Ripu. Instead he slumped to the ground and slept for many days, giving his body time to strengthen for the most anticipated event in all Diapsid history—their return to planet Earth.

CHAPTER 13

PravaPort Game System

On a cold night near the end of January, Alex found himself on a tattered chair in front of the living room television. Uncle Roy's flabby body covered most of the couch, Mom was sitting on a plastic chair to his right, and Katherine was sprawled on the carpet with a blanket over her legs. Even though no one was actually *speaking* to each other, it was nevertheless a rare moment of family unity.

At that moment, Alex wished he didn't have a sense of smell. Uncle Roy's unwashed feet were only a few inches from his head, making him sick to his stomach. Desperate to escape from the stress of a looming invasion, however, he tried his best to suppress his gags and focus on the television program.

The evening's show was *Ultimate Icon*, a talent competition where unknown people desperate for a moment of fame embarrass themselves by singing and dancing in front of a national audience. No one really tuned in for the performances, though; they watched to see a panel of judges insult the contestants. One of the judges was internationally famous for his cruelty.

While a heavyset man with crossed eyes wailed through the television's speakers, the kitchen telephone rang. Alex looked at the others, but no one moved a muscle. The phone rang a second time, and still no one acknowledged the sound. When a third ring rattled through the air, Alex grunted in frustration over everyone's laziness and trudged through the dining room to pick up the receiver.

"Is this the Hidalgo residence?" a familiar voice asked on the other end.

Alex moved towards the kitchen table and whispered, "Ketoo, is that you?"

"Bluey said you're a smart one, and I see he's right."

Leaning back and checking the dining room, Alex made sure that no one could hear him before asking, "So . . . what's new?"

"Good things. We now have uranium, so I'll be flying up to check on the Scipion Legion warship in a day or two."

"Wow!" Alex shouted, forgetting he needed to keep quiet. Lowering his voice, he asked, "Where'd you find the uranium? I thought it was really hard to get."

"The less you know, the better," Ketoo responded in his characteristic Indian accent. "Right now I'm calling to speak with your mother."

"My mom?"

"That's right, my friend. Tell her that Sikandar Tendulkar is on the phone for her."

Without another word, Alex ran into the living room and said, "Mom, someone named Sikandar Tendulkar is on the phone for you."

"Can't it wait, Alex?" Mom grumbled, still staring at the television screen. "He's probably a bill collector or some jerk who wants to sell me something."

"No Mom. This call's *really* important."

After Mom rose from her sagging chair and shuffled through the open doorway, Katherine looked up and Alex winked at her.

Ultimate Icon was almost finished by the time Mom got off the telephone. In the closing minutes, the well-groomed host was torturing remaining contestants over who would be the next to go home. Uncle Roy had already fallen asleep and was interrupting the television chatter with regular snores when Mom strolled into the living room with a slight spring to her step. It was as if she wanted to be happy, but wasn't quite sure how to show it.

True to her nature, Katherine was the first to speak. "Who was *that*?" she asked.

Mom stammered, "Th-th-that was some guy who wants to give me a job."

Alex tried his best to pretend he didn't know the story behind Sikandar Tendulkar. "That guy had some sort of accent," he said. "Did he say where he's from?"

"He's from some city in India and runs an Internet company called atarkie-dot-com or something."

"You mean *atarkya.com*?" Katherine squealed.

"You know about it?"

"It's like . . . the coolest website *ever*, Mom!"

"Well, the whole thing sounds strange, but that guy wants me to go to Center City tomorrow and look for some new office building that's just been built."

Alex wondered if the Survivors had set up an office in Philadelphia just to give his mother a job. *Would they really do all that to help me?*

"Why does the whole thing sound strange?" Katherine asked.

"Well," Mom explained, "it's a computer company, and I don't even know how to turn the suckers on! I told that to Mr. Teniker—"

"Tendulkar," Alex corrected.

Mom continued, "I told Mr. Tendulkar I don't know anything about computers, but he told me it wasn't a problem. Then he said something about you two, which was the weirdest thing of all."

"What do you mean?" Katherine gasped.

"He told me I should take this job because it would be good for Alex and Katherine. I don't remember telling him your names, but he seemed to know both of them right away."

"Oh . . . I told him our names right before I passed the phone to you," Alex lied.

Mom shook her head and sighed, "He also said I'll need to quit smoking and eat healthier to get their medical insurance. Now how the *heck* would he know I smoke?"

"I told him that, too," Alex blurted, face turning red out of fear of being discovered.

Mom narrowed her eyes and stared at her son for a moment before scolding, "You don't need to go blabberin' about all my bad habits to the rest of the world, Alex."

Eager to finish the conversation, Alex rose from his chair and yawned, "I'm going to bed now." Turning towards his sister with a sly grin, he added, "You should go, too."

The two siblings immediately rushed into their shared bedroom, then Alex shut the door and whispered to his sister, "Ketoo."

"The leopard gecko?"

"Yep."

"So they really *do* own *atarkya.com*?"

"Told you it was true."

* * *

The next morning, the house seemed to shake when Mom screeched, "ALEX AND KATHERINE! RISE AND SHINE!"

Both kids hated that call, especially in the middle of winter when they felt cozy and safe under their covers. Slowly and painfully, Katherine crawled out of her blankets, pulled up her socks, tied back her hair, and stumbled to the kitchen. Alex followed a few seconds later. As usual for most meals, their mother was frying something at the stove with a cigarette dangling from her mouth.

"I thought Sikandar Tendulkar said you need to quit smoking," Alex snapped.

"Well good mornin' to you, too," Mom grunted in reply.

Watching his mother bring a sizzling pan full of scrapple to the kitchen table, Alex tried to resist thinking about all the ashes he must've eaten from times when Mom smoked over his food. "Don't you think Sikandar Tendulkar will take back his job offer if you're still smoking?" he asked.

"He's not gonna be there today. I'm supposed to talk with him over a computer or something."

"But there must be people in that office who could tell if you're smoking."

"I'll worry about quitting after I find out how much they're gonna pay me and what I have to do."

"The doctors keep saying it's bad for my asthma," Alex persisted.

Mom tossed her cigarette into the sink, where it landed with a hiss in the dirty water. "You happy now?" she mumbled while dishing scrapple onto her children's plates.

Katherine said, "This job might be a big deal, you know."

"I guess," Mom sighed. "But I don't think they're serious about givin' me work."

"Why not?" Alex asked as he picked through greasy rectangles of scrapple on his plate. They were brownish-grey in color and made of every part of the pig he'd rather not eat. Glancing at Katherine, Alex was relieved to see she was similarly grossed-out.

Mom leaned against the counter and explained, "The whole thing sounds too good to be true. How is it that they're gonna give *me*—a high school dropout—a job with this big-time computer company?"

"Stranger things have happened," Alex chuckled. *Like my life these past few months.*

Katherine looked up at her mother and whined, "Can't you get us some cereal or something?"

"Cereal's too expensive, honey. I can get this scrapple real cheap. It's protein, right? That's good for you."

"I wish we were vegetarians. This stuff is gross."

The two managed to force down a few mouthfuls of salty pig scraps before proclaiming they were full and escaping to the bus stop. Once they boarded the school bus, Marie walked past Katherine without saying a word.

"You're still not talking to each other?" Alex whispered to his sister.

"*She* won't talk to *me*," Katherine clarified.

Several minutes later, when the bus pulled in front of Chester A. Arthur Middle School, Alex felt someone yank hard on a lock of his hair. There was then a *snip* and the tension released. Confused about what had happened, he looked up and noticed Billy DeGrace glaring at him. Alex's body tensed in horror.

Clutching a handful of Alex's hair—which he'd clipped with a pair of scissors—Billy sneered, "It's about time you cut that hair, you friggin' lizard lover."

Alex was too frightened and confused to say anything.

"It makes you look gay," Billy added as he swaggered to the front of the bus. Members of his gang followed, laughing and pushing other kids. Before offloading, Billy flashed his scissors and said, "*All* your hair comes off if I see you in Sweetbriar Park again!"

Tears welling in his eyes, Alex stared down at his clenched fists while the bus rolled forward again. Sweetbriar Park was usually too cold to visit in the wintertime, but he'd recently made a few trips there to escape the never-ending arguments between Mom and Uncle Roy. Unfortunately, Billy and his goons always seemed to be in the park as well, smoking stolen cigarettes and chasing anyone who dared enter their territory. *Now I'll have nowhere to go,* Alex despaired. *Why does something bad happen when it feels like my life should be getting better?*

Katherine put a reassuring hand on her brother's shoulder. "Don't worry, Alex. We'll have other places to go."

"I know, but it bugs me that Billy thinks he can get away with that kind of crap."

"Someday he'll pick on the wrong person."

"Maybe he already did."

"No, Alex," Katherine scolded in her almost-motherly tone. "Don't do anything stupid."

The bus pulled to a stop in front of William Henry Harrison Elementary School moments later. Checking the spot where Billy had clipped his hair, Alex asked his sister, "Do you even know why I grew my hair long in the first place?"

"I figured you were too lazy to get it cut."

Alex shuffled into the aisle and shook his head. "No, it was a promise I made to myself when we left Texas. I wasn't gonna cut my hair until we saw *Tío* Ramiro again."

"Maybe we can drive down and see him if Mom gets this new job."

Recalling the possibility of receiving his own "flying egg" from the Survivors sometime soon, Alex's mood lightened when stepped into the cold January morning and chuckled, "Maybe we can go there ourselves."

* * *

That afternoon, when Katherine and Alex arrived home from school, they'd barely made it through the front door before they started tripping over bags of clothing and gadgets scattered throughout Uncle Roy's living room. Greeted by huge hugs from their mother, Alex noted that she seemed happier than they'd seen her in years. *She also didn't reek of cigarette smoke.* When Mom began handing out new clothes for them to try on, however, Alex quickly grew to hate the words, "I just want to make sure that it fits."

Not much later, Uncle Roy came down the steps and began to shout about the noise and the mess. Her self-confidence apparently refreshed, Mom handed him a large wad of money and ordered him to shut up.

"What'd you do . . . rob a bank?" Uncle Roy asked once he'd counted the bills in his hand.

Loudly munching on a wad of nicotine gum, Mom replied, "I might as well have. That Teniker guy wired me fifty thousand dollars and says that he's gonna pay me a starting salary of two hundred thousand a year!"

"The guy's last name is Tendulkar, Mom," Alex corrected. "You should say his name the right way if you're gonna work for him."

"I'd hardly call it *working*, Alex. All I have to do is click buttons on a computer for a couple hours each day."

"But I thought you didn't understand computers," Katherine said while trying to squeeze her feet into a new pair of pink boots.

"Oh, these are easy," Mom replied. "I don't think I'm gonna have any trouble."

"Just don't make the Survivors angry," Alex mumbled under his breath.

"What did you say?"

"I said . . . um . . . that surviving is happy."

Uncle Roy pocketed Mom's money and said, "Maybe you can pay some rent now, huh? It's been over a year that *I've* had to pay all the bills."

"Don't worry, Roy," Mom grumbled. "I'll make it up to you."

Once Uncle Roy trudged back upstairs, Alex spotted a large box with his name on it. "What's over there?" he asked excitedly.

"Oh, that's something Mr. Teniker said you'd like."

"It's Tendulkar, Mom. The man's name is Sikandar Tendulkar."

"Aw heck, I'm never gonna get his name right." Popping another piece of nicotine gum into her mouth, she added, "I'm not gonna be seein' him anyway, so it doesn't matter that much."

"Why won't you see him?" Katherine asked.

"They were tellin' me at the office that he never leaves his apartment over there in India because he's scared of germs. What kind of man is *that* afraid of getting sick?"

Alex laughed out loud, but quickly caught himself and pretended it was his reaction to what was inside the box. He needed to make sure Mom didn't find out the truth—that Sikandar Tendulkar wasn't a man after all. The owner of *atarkya.com* was a ten-inch leopard gecko named Ketoo.

"What is it?" Katherine asked while Alex freed a heavy object from its bubble-wrap cocoon.

It wasn't long before Alex figured out the gift from Sikandar Tendulkar was a brand-new video game console. A handwritten note inside read:

Alex,

This video game system is called the PravaPort. Try it out and let me know what you think. You might learn something important from these games, so take them seriously. As for me, I will be making my long journey very soon!

All the best,
Ketoo

Alex stared at the message for a moment and wondered how a lizard who wasn't much bigger than his hand could hold a pen in order to write. Deciding such a detail wasn't important, he rushed to connect his new PravaPort to the living room television. *Just what sort of game,* he wondered, *would super-smart reptiles create?*

CHAPTER 14

New Recruit

Alex's PravaPort was only in the living room for a few days before Uncle Roy forced him to move it into the basement. Though he feared Sleerans might attack him underground, the PravaPort's new location meant Alex could use it whenever he wanted. Even better, Ghet could sneak through the basement door and play from time to time. When word of the video game system grew, several of Ghet's friends also came over, making Alex feel more popular. Ray Blocker and Jeff Barnes even asked if they could come over a couple of times, but Alex always found an excuse not to let them in.

The flight simulator game Ketoo had sent, called *Drifter Defense*, was incredible. Everyone who played felt like they were soaring high above the clouds, landing on exotic worlds, and defending the Earth from a global alien invasion. It was while playing *Drifter Defense* one day when Alex decided to ask Ghet a question. Since a late winter snowstorm had closed school for the day, the two had been playing on the PravaPort for several hours and were finally growing bored with it.

"Hey Ghet," Alex blurted, "Do you ever think we could be attacked by aliens?"

Ghet didn't take his eyes from the screen, but still answered, "Nah, I don't think so."

"Why not?"

"If aliens can travel to other planets, then why haven't they landed on Earth yet?"

"What if they did, but it happened a long time ago?"

Ghet paused the game and turned to face Alex. "Where are you talking about?"

"I know some people—well, not exactly people—but they told me the Earth was invaded once, and it's gonna happen again."

"You're kidding me, right?"

Alex thought about stopping right there, telling Ghet it was a joke and that he should forget about it. Still, there was a feeling of urgency gnawing inside him. *The invasion could come any day.* "You remember that lizard I saved in Sweetbriar Park?"

"The blue-tongue skink?"

"Yeah," Alex answered. "It was actually a Survivor from an alien attack sixty-five million years ago."

"How do you know?"

"He told me."

"It talked?"

"Yep. There are about ten of Survivors in all. One of them sent me this PravaPort."

Ghet's face couldn't hide his disbelief. "You're telling me a *lizard* gave you this game system? I thought you said the owner of *atarkya.com* sent it to you."

"Well," Alex replied after a long pause, "I didn't say a *human* sent it to me. It was a leopard gecko named Ketoo. He disguises himself as this Indian guy named Sikandar Tendulkar. My mom thinks he's her boss."

Ghet pushed back his reddish-blonde hair and laughed heartily. Catching his breath, he chuckled, "I saw four leopard geckos at the pet store last week. Do you think one of them can give me a sweet video game system, too?"

Alex shook his head. "The Survivors are the only ones that are smart. Other reptiles are just animals."

"I've heard some crazy stories, Alex, but this one takes the cake."

Alex was stunned Ghet didn't believe him. *Katherine believed me right away.* While thinking of a way to prove everything to his friend, thin wooden panels covering the basement entrance rattled with a knock. Alex hopped from his seat and pushed on the flimsy door. Opening it a crack, cold winter air poured into the sparsely furnished room. A voice hissed, "Come on, Alex, open up!"

"Hey, we were just talking about you!" Alex exclaimed when he recognized Salvator standing outside. *What better proof is there than the Survivors themselves?*

Ghet heard the voice and leaned forward to see what was going on. Alex's long hair whipped around in the frigid breeze and hinges screeched when a gust of wind caught the basement door and slammed it against the outside wall. Amid the swirl of tiny snowflakes in the fading twilight, a figure could be seen. It was wrapped in a heavy woolen cloak that was flapping in the tumultuous air. The strange apparition stepped carefully through the door with a hood over its head and helped Alex pull the door shut.

Seconds later, strong, scaly hands with large claws reached from inside the cloak and folds of tan cloth parted to reveal a monitor lizard's body patterned in grayish-brown scales. After removing his hood, Salvator flicked his forked tongue and joked in Ghet's direction, "You can breathe now, my friend."

"Um . . . uh . . . um," Ghet stammered, voice trembling.

Alex glanced over and observed that Ghet was ghostly pale with fright. "Relax. This one's friendly. His name's Salvator."

"He's one of those . . . Sur-Survivors?" Ghet managed to force through his lips.

"I see you've already heard of us," Salvator hissed through a toothy grin.

"What brings you out on a day like this?" Alex asked his reptilian friend.

"Decided to take a break from hunting Sleerans to come and visit."

"Sleerans?" Alex gulped.

Salvator swept the cloak from his shoulders and laid it on a chair before waving his hands and hissing, "Nothing to worry about. They aren't anywhere nearby." Besides a brown loincloth and dried palm leaves wrapped around his feet, Salvator was practically naked. Hopping onto the folding chair next to Ghet's recliner, he laid back, put his hands behind his head, and smiled, "We also brought some real nice cargo for you."

Starting for the door, Alex exclaimed, "What's out there?"

"Hold on a second," Salvator commanded with a raised hand. "It's not going anywhere. Bluey and I just came from the other side of the world, you know. Let him get in here before we tell you."

Less than a minute passed before frantic tapping could be heard on the basement door. Alex ran to let Bluey in.

"Crikey, mate! I don't know how you Yanks live in this cold!" Bluey griped after hopping inside. He then turned towards Ghet and asked, "Who's this? A new recruit?"

After an awkward silence, Ghet managed to ask, "Y-Y-You're the lizard that Alex saved in the park, right?"

"The very one!"

Apparently refreshed after only a few moments of relaxation, Salvator leaped from his chair and suggested, "Why don't we take a look at what we brought for you, Alex?"

Shrugging his shoulders and keeping a straight face, Alex tried to play it cool. Of course, there was nothing he wanted to see more than what the lizards had out back.

The two reptiles led the way and Alex followed close behind. Ghet managed to stumble out of his chair a moment later to see where everyone was going. Salvator pushed the basement door open and moved out into the empty, snow-covered backyard. The night sky was a reddish-purple color, just as it was most days when it snowed in the city.

"Beautiful, isn't it?" Bluey asked his human companions.

Since the backyard looked pretty much the same as always (plus the fact that he couldn't see anything special waiting for him), Alex didn't respond.

Scanning his surroundings, Salvator asked, "What do you see out here?"

"Um . . . a lot of snow, I guess," Alex replied with disappointment in his voice, pulling his arms tight around his body. In his rush to get outside, he'd forgotten to put on a jacket.

"Nothing else?"

"Not that I can tell."

"How about your friend?"

Everyone turned to see what Ghet would say.

"I don't see anything," he mumbled.

Bluey flicked his tongue and said, "Make a few snowballs and throw them into the middle of the yard!"

Alex and Ghet did what they were told and hurled lumps of snow as hard as they could across Uncle Roy's backyard. To their amazement, the snowballs burst in midair—as if they'd hit an invisible wall. A metallic *clang* could be heard each time ice struck the mysterious object, and it wasn't long before both boys began to walk towards the area where the camouflaged vehicle sat.

"Careful, now!" Salvator urged.

The two stretched their arms in front of them and shuffled to the middle of the yard, where their hands found a large, round object that felt warm and hard.

After a few moments of watching the boys try to figure out what they were touching, Bluey asked, "Alex, do you remember that Ketoo was a scientist in our civilization?"

"Yeah."

"Well, this is one of his best ideas. It's a covering for our Drifters that copies the colors of whatever happens to be behind it, making them completely invisible. Ketoo used this camouflaging skin to travel to Jupiter and back without anyone noticing."

Ghet looked at Alex and whispered, "What's a Drifter?"

Salvator strode behind Ghet and gave him a pat on the back. "It's a spaceship, my friend."

Surprised by Salvator's touch, Ghet jumped and banged his head on an invisible wing. A gong-like sound echoed in the backyard.

"Are you okay?" Salvator asked nervously. "I didn't mean to scare you."

"Yeah, I'm alright," Ghet mumbled, rubbing his head. "I took my factor medicine today, so I don't have to worry too much about bleeding inside my head."

"Factor medicine? Do you have hemophilia?"

"Hemophilia *and* von Willebrand disease," Ghet explained. "Lucky me, huh? What are the chances of a person getting *both* bleeding disorders?"

"About one in 500,000," Bluey and Salvator replied in unison.

Ghet checked where the wing ended with an outstretched hand, shook his head, and sighed, "I still can't believe all this is real."

Salvator checked his surroundings and hissed, "Will a flight inside Alex's spaceship help prove everything?"

My spaceship? Alex asked himself. *This Drifter's for me?*

Before Alex could repeat his question out loud, Ghet exclaimed, "Let's go!"

"Then climb on in!" Bluey responded with a smile.

"Climb where?"

Alex was similarly confused.

The lizards guided the boys around the invisible spacecraft and Bluey shouted, "Alex Drifter! Rear door open!"

What happened next was a sight unlike any other. Three feet above the ground, where there seemed to be nothing but frigid air, a bright line cracked its way across an expanse of empty space and widened into a rectangle. Squinting in the bright lights of the Drifter's interior, Alex could see a large cargo bay and cockpit. After clambering inside, he noticed it was a bigger version of Bluey's spaceship. *Perfect for an eleven-year-old pilot.* Ghet and Salvator followed Alex into the cargo bay, then Bluey hopped in and the door closed behind them.

With a quick glance around the Drifter, Alex spotted a front viewing screen for flying, another screen for computer navigation, and a chair with controls identical to his PravaPort Game System. It was then Alex realized that the video game *Drifter Defense* would be a great way to train an entire army of young fighter pilots who'd be ready to face the Scipion Legions in case of an invasion. *That must be Ketoo's plan when they start selling it in stores.*

Ghet was the first to break the silence. "Smells like a new car in here."

Bluey chuckled and exclaimed, "Take your seat at the helm, Alex!"

While Salvator, Bluey, and Ghet took seats in the cargo bay, Alex eased himself into the pilot's chair and felt it conform to his body shape. A greeting flashed across the main screen, accompanied by a woman's voice through the ship's speakers.

"Good evening, Alex Hidalgo. It's nice to meet you."

Alex shouted back to Bluey, "Is this thing *alive?*"

"Sure seems like that, doesn't it? This Drifter runs on the best artificial intelligence in the world. If you want, the computer can do most of the flying. Of course, she can also obey your commands when you give them."

"How do I do that?"

"At the moment, she'll only respond to a command that's given with the key words 'Alex Drifter.' If she doesn't hear those words, she won't do what you tell her. Give it a try, won't you?"

"Um . . . okay. Alex Drifter, lift off!"

"Vertical ascent seems to be the safest route," the computer responded.

Alex didn't quite understand, but he agreed, "Okay, go ahead."

Nothing happened. After a few seconds' pause, Salvator leaned forward to say, "Remember, Alex, the computer only responds to a command that has 'Alex Drifter' in it."

Darn it, I already forgot something. Pushing back his hair with one hand, Alex said, "Alex Drifter, vertical . . . um . . . liftoff . . . or whatever you called it."

Seconds later, the spaceship's occupants were pulled downwards by the invisible hand of gravity. The feeling of flying his own spacecraft made Alex nervous, excited, and confused—all at the same time. *I just hope we don't crash . . .*

Alex's first flight was a simple one. He spent several minutes steering on his own, passing between the Liberty Towers in downtown Philadelphia and soaring high over the Benjamin Franklin Bridge. One building, known as the Cira Centre, was flashing with a rainbow of nighttime colors. *City sure looks pretty from up here*, he thought. Before long, however, Alex realized it was suppertime. A few extra minutes in the air wasn't worth the punishment Mom would give if he arrived late.

Approaching Uncle Roy's house, Salvator instructed Alex to touch down on the roof. The flat, rectangular patch of snowy white on the housetop seemed a perfect fit for the Drifter. After the egg-shaped object's landing gear came to rest soundlessly on the roof, Salvator said, "We called this spaceship 'Alex Drifter' because it was an easy name to remember. Of course, you can give it any name you want."

"Really?"

"It's *yours*, Alex," Salvator replied.

The new pilot picked his brain for the best possible name. Dozens that crossed his mind were quickly eliminated. Sitting in silence, Alex began to worry what would happen if Uncle Roy discovered the spaceship. *He might try to fly it.* In order to avoid losing his Drifter, Alex decided to give it a name his uncle would hate.

While Bluey and Salvator told Ghet about the Sleerans, Swift Runners, and Wounding Teeth, Alex remembered two words his uncle despised. Uncle Roy used to play guitar in a rock band, but he lost his job one night when he punched a guy who was yelling "Free Bird!" nonstop. The incident ended Uncle Roy's music career forever.

"Alex Drifter!" Alex commanded, "Your new name is Free Bird!"

"Understood, Alex Hidalgo."

"Free Bird, just call me Ale," he ordered. Alex missed hearing the nickname *Tío* Ramiro used to call him.

"Understood Ale."

Everyone reluctantly left the warm interior of the Free Bird and stepped back into the icy chill of the winter evening. Salvator and Bluey told the boys to stay put and leaped from the roof, returning a minute later in Bluey's Drifter. Alex and Ghet each grabbed a wing of the Drifter and it lowered them back to the ground.

When the boys touched down, Bluey opened his door and shouted, "Listen, Alex. This Drifter is a big responsibility. Make sure it doesn't get you into trouble."

"Um ... okay ... no problem," was all that Alex could manage in reply.

Bluey propped an arm on his chair and turned to Ghet. "You know what? I don't think we actually introduced ourselves earlier. My name's Bluey ... and I reckon yours is Ghet O'Malley."

Ghet smiled. "The very one!"

"Sorry again about your head!" Salvator hissed from Bluey's cargo bay.

Bluey flicked his tongue. "Now mate, please keep today's events a secret. We're not ready to reveal ourselves to the world quite yet."

"Oh, I can keep a secret—no problem," Ghet replied, his breath making swirls of vapor in the icy air ... as if his words had been given physical form in the winter evening.

As the spacecraft's door started to close, Bluey said, "We'll get to work on another one of these Drifters for you, too."

"Awesome!"

Right before the door clicked shut, Bluey shouted, "Cheers, mates!" and his vehicle disappeared with a sound of whooshing air.

Immediately afterwards, Alex turned to Ghet with arms crossed. "You *do* believe me now, right?"

Ghet laughed, "I'll believe *anything* that you tell me from now on, buddy!"

Nodding with satisfaction, Alex decided it was time to invite Ghet to the next All-Survivor Conference. Since they were about to face an invasion by the greatest warriors in the known universe, the Survivors had been developing a plan.

CHAPTER 15

The Resistance Grows

When Alex told his sister that more children should go to the next All-Survivor Conference, Katherine knew right away who she wanted to invite. By this point, however, she and Marie hadn't spoken for almost seven weeks. One day in late winter, amid the bustle and chatter that always filled the school cafeteria, Katherine finally worked up the courage to ask Marie for forgiveness. Stepping out of the lunch line with vegetable lasagna, sliced carrots, and little carton of milk on a tray, Katherine took a deep breath and walked towards her former friend.

"Hi, Marie," she said softly while moving to sit down.

Marie placed her novel *Moby Dick* on the table, rolled her eyes, and whined, "What do *you* want?"

"I'm sorry for being mean to you," Katherine sighed.

"Why have you been ignoring me?"

Katherine glanced at her friend and shrugged, "I wasn't *trying* to be mean . . . I just needed to talk to my brother about some things we needed to keep secret."

"What kinds of things?"

"Um . . ." Katherine hesitated while tugging on a lock of her curly hair. "I needed to talk about . . . um . . . these talking lizards and this . . . alien invasion . . . thing."

"What?"

Katherine tried her best to explain what she'd learned from her brother in the past month and a half—including several stories about riding around in Alex's invisible spaceship. Conversation between the two girls carried over into recess and after school, so all the hard feelings between them had evaporated by the time the bus dropped them off that afternoon. Before making a run for her house, Marie hugged Katherine and asked, "When can I go for a ride?"

"Huh?"

"When can I ride in your brother's spaceship?"

"Oh yeah!" Katherine shouted. "I almost forgot! Alex wants more people to go to the next lizard meeting. You want to go?"

"Sure would! When is it?"

"Alex said that the lizards could plan it around your schedule—if you're available sometime in the next week or two."

Marie's perfectly white teeth gleamed in a smile. "You were going to plan the meeting around *me*?"

"Yeah. I mean . . . you're still my best friend, right?"

Marie nodded and said, "My parents have to go to some conference in New York next weekend and they won't be home until real late. Jean's supposed to watch me, but I guess I could tell him I'll be at your house."

"Why don't you bring him along?"

"Oh my goodness!" Marie laughed. "That'll teach him a lesson!"

"What do you mean?"

"I asked Jean a few weeks ago what would happen if aliens invaded Earth and he said it was crazy talk. I can't wait to see his face when I tell him it's true!"

"Well my brother says most of them aren't aliens—they're dinosaurs that have been living in space. I guess that's kinda the same thing, though."

"Sounds like a complicated story . . ."

"And I haven't even told you about *atarkya.com*!"

* * *

Saturday came quickly. Everyone knew to meet in the middle of Sweetbriar Park at 7:00 AM. Spring was just around the corner, but the morning was still cold. Marie and her brother Jean were blowing into their hands when Ghet showed up in the clearing and asked, "You both here for the trip?"

Jean just nodded his head and looked away, but Marie waved in greeting and replied, "We sure are. Are you a friend of Alex?"

"Yep. My name's Ghet O'Malley."

Jean half-smiled with his head cocked to one side and said, "A white boy named Ghetto, huh? Now I've heard *everything*."

Ghet shrugged his shoulders and joked, "Maybe I'll be a great rapper someday."

Dressed in a long coat and baggy jeans, Jean pulled his head back and griped, "There ain't no good white rappers, kid."

Before Ghet could respond, a rush of air blasted overhead and the rear door of Alex's camouflaged Drifter opened out of thin air. Upon hearing Katherine greet them from inside, Ghet and Marie rushed into the warm interior. Mouth open in amazement, Jean checked his surroundings and followed the other two. Without time to waste, the cargo bay doors of the Drifter closed and the vehicle surged towards the south.

Passing over the Amazon basin an hour later, Bluey's spacecraft caught up with the children and the two Drifters soared along the Andes Mountains.

Even close to the equator, many of the highest peaks were covered in snow. On the other side of the mountain range, the Drifters passed over a narrow stretch of the Atacama Desert. Right before they dove under the rolling waves of the Pacific Ocean, Marie shouted she could see penguins on the coast. Jean argued it couldn't be true, but Bluey's voice came over the radio to explain that Marie must have seen Humboldt penguins. In the unique landscape of South America, penguins indeed waddle along stretches of the world's driest desert.

Dozens of feet below the ocean surface, the two spaceships entered a tunnel carved by robots produced in the Survivors' underground factory. Shipboard computers of the Drifters guided them through the twisting entryway as it snaked upward. Katherine began to get queasy from the constant rocking motion of Alex's spacecraft and screamed she was going to throw up. While everyone frantically began searching for a plastic bag, Katherine vomited on the floor. To everyone's surprise, a dozen mouse-sized robots crawled out of an opening under Ghet's seat and cleaned the mess in a matter of seconds.

"There's something I never saw before," Alex shrugged.

It was the first of many surprises that day.

Moments later, the Drifters surfaced on the underground river that passed through the cavern of Chelonius. Alex recognized the place instantly. Stepping out onto the pebbled riverbank with unsteady legs, all five children were greeted by the gathered lizards.

Ketoo the leopard gecko called the meeting to order and invited the humans to sit on a semicircle of rounded rocks. Rising on his stone platform to his full height of six inches, his face then became serious. "My friends, I believe that it will only be a matter of *days* before the first invasion forces arrive."

Eager to prove his closeness with the reptiles, Alex asked, "What did you find when you went to Jupiter?"

Ketoo clutched his wrists behind his back and explained, "I found one ship from the Scipion Legions orbiting Jupiter, and it looks like they're planning something big."

"Now let's get to the plan!" Togo the fire skink interrupted.

"Okay, Togo," Ketoo sighed with hands raised in resignation. "Speak your part."

Togo hopped onto the stone platform and proclaimed with a broad grin, "Talitha and I have been hiding a secret from the rest of you. We aren't the only Survivors." Turning to the massive turtle projected on the rock wall above, he asked, "Chelonius, would you please show the videos?"

In a matter of seconds, both the lizards and children began to gasp and mumble over the images moving across the rock wall. Large creatures with long necks and small heads could be seen waddling through a stretch of dense rainforest. They ambled about on two powerful legs and clutched simple tools with strong arms and long claws. Alex thought they looked like dinosaurs, but before he could ask a question, Jean blurted, "Those things *Mokele-mbembe* or somethin'?"

Togo's eyes opened wide when he heard the question. "What do *you* know about the *Mokele-mbembe?*"

"It's a creature people say lives in central Africa. They say it's big and has a long neck . . . I thought it was just a legend."

"Many legends are based on facts, my friend," Togo said with a wink and a nod.

Ketoo leaned back on the stone where he was sitting and asked, "Are those Sickle-claws?"

Talitha the chameleon stepped close and patted Ketoo on the back. "They sure are." Scanning the confused faces of the children with her turret-like eyes, she went on to explain, "We used to think those dinosaur warriors who rebelled against us—the Swift Runners and Wounding Teeth—had exterminated all other species of dinosaur, but it appears one of Ketoo's genetically-enhanced species, which we called Sickle-claws, somehow managed to survive."

"But how could they have stayed hidden for *so long?*" Ketoo wondered aloud.

"Your guess is as good as mine."

Shortly thereafter, Togo asked Chelonius to project another set of videos onto his rock wall. These showed Sickle-claw archers firing arrows into solid blocks of stone. After a moment of hushed awe, Togo went on to explain, "If the attacking Wounding Teeth and Swift Runners still ride on *Tyrannosaurus* or *Triceratops*, our Sickle-claw archers should be able to take the dinosaurs down with only one or two arrows. They have excellent aim, and their uranium-tipped arrows can penetrate the thickest armor."

Alex raised his hand to speak. He felt silly doing so, but years of conditioning told him it was the right thing to do. "Excuse me, but did you say the dinosaur soldiers will ride on *Triceratops* and *Tyrannosaurus rex?*"

Togo nodded. "In our last war against the Scipion Legions, we trained Wounding Teeth and Swift Runners to ride on several different dinosaur species. We thought our soldiers would be more frightening if we mounted them on *Triceratops*, *Tyrannosaurus*, and *Ankylosaurus*. Not only did they scare the aliens, but they also kicked butt!"

As a hunting band of Sickle-claws butchered a hippopotamus in yet another video, Katherine leaned towards Alex and whispered, "They're gonna *kill* the dinosaurs?"

"Don't start your vegetarian preaching right now," Alex scolded. "Those dinosaurs are gonna kill *us* if we don't stop them."

"But maybe there's another way."

"You don't know what you're talking about."

"Yes I do! Killing animals is wrong!"

"What's going on?" Togo snapped with his arms crossed, apparently upset the siblings' argument had interrupted his presentation.

Alex looked towards the fire skink and said, "My sister's just being silly—she says the dinosaurs shouldn't be killed."

Togo ran a stubby hand down the smooth scales of his stomach and explained, "We plan on capturing the Swift Runners and the Wounding Teeth, but we'll need to weaken their forces first. Killing the dumber dinosaurs might make it easier to save the smarter ones."

Glancing at his pouting sister, Alex was conflicted over whether to say more. He didn't want to offend the lizards by criticizing their battle strategy, but he also didn't want to deal with Katherine's whining if he kept quiet. With his face twisted into an expression that said he'd rather not speak, Alex nevertheless sighed, "My sister thinks that even killing the dumb animals would be wrong... she's a vegetarian."

Ketoo frowned. "I don't like the idea of killing the dinosaurs, either."

Without warning, Tupi the black-and-white tegu leaped to his feet and shouted, "¡*Amigos!* I have an idea!"

Since Tupi's exclamation had been completely unexpected, everyone jumped in surprise.

"*Perdóname*," Tupi apologized before running over and whispering something into the earhole of Bity the beaded lizard. The thick-bodied reptile with yellow and black scales nodded her head in response.

Tupi flicked his pink tongue and suggested, "Bluey and I will take the children up to the surface while Bity explains my idea to the rest of you." Looking up at Katherine, the tegu winked and said, "I think we solved your problem."

"What do you mean?"

"Let *us* discuss it first," Bity implored. "We need to decide if it'll work."

While Bluey, Tupi, and the five children started climbing the path that led to the eastern tunnel, Alex put a hand on his sister's shoulder and whispered, "You may have just spoken up for the animals, but I bet you don't love *all* of them."

"What do you mean?"

"You're not gonna like the way out of here."

Sure enough, Katherine whimpered and whined for the entire journey through the narrow tunnel that led to the surface. Periodic screams echoed through the chamber as one crawling creature or another touched her hands or fell into her hair. She kept shouting about wanting to go home, but Alex urged her to be patient. He had a feeling he knew what was waiting for them on the grass-covered *pampas* above.

A bright sun beat down when five humans and two lizards left the cave and looked out over rocky landscape bordering a sea of yellow-green grass. Bluey, always giddy about new surprises, turned to the others and asked, "What do you see out here?"

"Nothin'," Jean replied.

"I guess I see rocks, grass and a blue sky," Katherine said.

"This is the most beautiful countryside I've ever seen!" Marie squealed. "Mother Nature is always the most amazing artist!"

"This all sounds familiar," Ghet chuckled.

"And *I* see a lizard who's repeating his same old routine," Alex quipped.

Winking at Alex and flicking his blue tongue, Bluey yelled, "Drifters, visible!"

Immediately afterwards, four spacecraft appeared several yards away.

When she spotted the egg-shaped ships, Katherine screamed, "Aliens!"

Tupi darted in front of the children with arms raised. "No need to worry! "They're not alien ships! We made them, and they're for you."

Jean, Marie, Ghet and Katherine all seemed to be at a loss for words.

"But before we begin," Bluey's voice cut through the humid air, "I want you to understand you'll need to call your ship by name before you give it a command."

Katherine asked, "What do you mean?"

"Katherine Drifter, turn pink!" Bluey shouted.

When her ship changed color less than a second later, Katherine squealed with delight. She then took a good look at her spacecraft and said, "Actually, I like purple better."

"Katherine Drifter, turn purple!" Bluey commanded. The spacecraft obeyed instantly.

"Not *that* kind of purple! I like lavender."

"Katherine Drifter, lavender!" Bluey grumbled, his tone reflecting increasing frustration.

Katherine crossed her arms and complained, "*That* doesn't really look lavender to me."

Sighing loudly in anger, Alex scolded, "Kat, you have your own spaceship, and you're going to complain about the *color*? Maybe the Survivors should take it back!"

"Sorry, Mr. Bluey," Katherine mumbled, looking downwards and kicking loose rocks on the ground.

"That's okay," Bluey replied in a reassuring tone, clasping his short-fingered hands in front of him. "But the most important thing you must do is keep these things hidden. Drifters can hover for long periods of time, so it might be a good idea to keep them over your backyard or your roof."

"How am I gonna hide *that* big thing?" Jean asked.

"Drifters, camouflage!" Bluey shouted. All four ships instantly disappeared. "Just don't forget where you left them," he added with a smile.

Tupi showed each child to his or her spacecraft and ordered the shipboard computers to fly a scenic route over his beloved Argentina. As they soared off, a fifth Drifter appeared where the others had been. Alex instantly recognized his own *Free Bird*. The cargo doors opened and Ketoo scrambled out. Once he'd climbed onto a rock near the spot where Alex was standing, he said, "Your Drifter is ready, my friend."

"Ready for *what*?"

"I just installed enough uranium fuel in the *Free Bird* for our voyage."

Alex took a seat on the rocky soil and looked into Ketoo's greenish-grey eyes. The cat-like pupils inside had contracted to mere vertical lines in the bright sunlight. "Where do you want me to go?" he asked nervously.

"When we escaped the Scipion Legion attacks sixty-five million years ago, I saved the eggs of four dinosaur soldiers. They've been hidden in Europa's ice ever since."

"Europa?"

"The moon of Jupiter where we were frozen."

"Wow!" Alex exclaimed. "And the eggs are still up there?"

Ketoo sat on the rock and clutched his hands around his knees. "Those eggs were my greatest invention, Alex. The second generation was going to be even *better* than the first. I think we'll need their support in this new struggle."

"You're going to hatch them?"

"Yes, my friend, I think it's time."

"Won't it take a while for them to grow up?"

"No, they'll be fully grown in six months."

"But what if they go bad—like the Wounding Teeth and Swift Runners?"

Ketoo waved off Alex's question. "We'll be more careful this time. Will you join us for the recovery mission?"

"You mean . . . fly out to Jupiter with you guys?"

"We need all the help we can get."

"Is it safe?"

With a look of supreme confidence, Ketoo replied, "There's nothing to worry about. Our spaceships will be camouflaged the entire time."

Alex pondered his readiness to travel farther than any human had ever gone before. "I'll go," he finally said while asking himself, *Oh crap, what am I doing?*

Ketoo smiled. "And there's one other thing I'd like to ask."

"What?"

"Would you like to have a new brother?"

"I don't think *that* will happen," Alex mumbled, glancing over his shoulder to see if the other Drifters had returned. "My mom hasn't seen my dad in more than two years."

"I'm talking about an *adopted* brother . . . or maybe a sister."

Looking up at the cloudless sky, Alex shrugged and said, "I guess so."

"Great! We want two of the hatchlings to be raised by humans."

"Huh? You mean I'm going to adopt a *dinosaur*?"

"Precisely."

Alex thought for a moment and replied, "I'll see what I can do."

With that last comment, an artificial breeze began blowing on the two friends. Four Drifters returned to their landing positions.

Katherine hopped out and shrieked, "Where's a bathroom around here? I gotta go!"

Tupi, who'd been riding with Marie to practice his French, darted over to Katherine's spacecraft and showed how the pilot chair on her Drifter could tilt upwards and reveal a toilet. After screaming again that she needed privacy, Katherine shut the cargo bay doors and her Drifter became invisible. Alex just shook his head and sighed. *Katherine always makes a scene.*

As the day's excitement came to a close, the other Survivors surfaced from the cave and bid farewell to their new friends.

When Jean looked over the assembled group of humans and reptiles, he mumbled, "*Dag*, I guess we're all in this together."

"What do you mean?" Ghet asked.

"Well, I've been used to seeing things in black and white, but that ain't gonna work here. Black people, white people, brown people, and lizards—we all gonna need to work together to save this planet. If we just keep lookin' out for our own, we're dead."

"Let's keep that in mind when the invasion comes," Ketoo advised.

"How long 'til those dinosaurs land?"

"All signals indicate they'll be here in six days."

Alex shuddered with the realization that the end of the world and life as he knew it could come by next Friday. All he could hope was that he was ready to face the dangers ahead.

CHAPTER 16

Invasion

When Alex's mother arrived at her office on Monday morning, an image of Sikandar Tendulkar greeted her from a video screen and asked, "Mrs. Hidalgo, have you heard about *atarkya.com*'s Young Leaders' Conference?"

"No."

"We're planning on having a seminar this Friday in Baltimore, Maryland. Why don't you send Alex and Katherine?"

"No way, Mr. Tendulkar. My son isn't doing well in school. He can't miss classes."

Sikandar Tendulkar paused for a moment and leaned back in his virtual chair. "This conference will build his self-esteem, so it might help bring his grades up."

Mom sighed, "How much is it gonna cost me?"

"It's free. The only requirement is that Alex bring four children with him."

"Well, Alex doesn't have too many friends . . . As far as I know, he mostly hangs around one kid with reddish hair and freckles. I guess that he could take his sister, too. That'd make three."

"What about Katherine's friend Marie?"

Alex's mother narrowed her eyes. "How do you know about Marie?"

The image on the screen fumbled for an answer. "Oh . . . um . . . I-I-I think your daughter told me."

"But you've never talked to my daughter, have you?"

"Maybe I called your house one time and she answered the phone."

"Okay, Mr. Tendulkar," Mom relented, "Alex and Katherine can go. I'll get in touch with Marie's parents and Ghet's mother, too."

"Don't forget to invite Jean."

"Who's Jean?"

"That's . . . um . . . uh . . . Marie's brother."

"And how would you know a thing like that? I didn't even know Marie had a brother!"

The computer face of Sikandar Tendulkar appeared to be worried. "You must be forgetting things, Mrs. Hidalgo. Are you feeling okay?"

Mom shrugged her shoulders. "All this work must be messin' with my memory or somethin'."

Sikandar Tendulkar smiled. "I'll send you the permission forms immediately. The children will leave early on Friday morning."

Rising from her swivel chair, Mom went over to the fax machine and picked up Sikandar Tendulkar's paperwork. Of course, there wasn't *really* a Young Leaders' Conference that Friday. It was all an elaborate scheme to get the everyone out of school for the first Diapsid invasion.

* * *

When Friday came, all five children were picked up from their homes by limousine at 6:30 AM. It was Katherine's idea to travel in style, and Ketoo was happy to oblige. An hour later the limousine pulled into a rest area on Interstate 95 and the five darted off into a nearby forest. There they found their invisible spaceships, which had followed on automatic pilot. Disguised as Sikandar Tendulkar, Ketoo then called the limousine driver and offered to wire him $10,000 if he'd wait for everyone to return that evening . . . if they returned at all.

Once the Drifters set course for southern Africa, Katherine called Marie on her radio and asked, "Hey Marie, aren't you happy to be going back home?"

"What do you mean?" Marie's voice replied.

"Well, Ketoo said we're going to Africa. Aren't you African?"

A loud and angry sigh rattled through Katherine's speakers and Marie griped, "Katherine, I've told you before I'm from Senegal, which is about *four thousand miles* from where we're headed. We aren't going to be anywhere close to where I used to live!"

"Oh . . ."

Everyone else remained quiet for the rest of the journey. They were too anxious over what was to come. Before they knew it, the children were soaring high over the plains of southern Zimbabwe. A cluster of white houses adorned with colorful lines and shapes passed below.

In the style of their forefathers, *Matabele* people who lived in this community covered their homes with roofs of dry grass. Young men kicked a tattered soccer ball on the outskirts of town, but they were forced to stop their activity and turn down their radio when they spotted danger approaching.

Near the soccer field marched a bull elephant—an animal known for its potential to destroy entire villages. Fortunately for everyone involved, the beast walked up a ridge of hills on the village's eastern side and descended to the vast plain below.

What came next was even more peculiar. A black rhino came charging through the cornfields, paused in the middle of town, snorted, and galloped over the hills to the east. Next, zebras trotted around the village and moved towards the grassy flatlands on the other side. Several more elephants followed the same path, as did a family group of giraffes and more than twenty wide-lipped white rhinos. Not a single villager—not even the oldest of the elders—could recall such an unusual movement of animals through the area.

Moments later, the ground rumbled with the arrival of several hundred wildebeest, a large flock of ostriches, scores of buffalo, and dozens more elephants. Most people retreated into their huts to avoid being trampled by the thundering hooves marching eastward. Roars of lions and leopards, hisses of cheetahs, and barks of wild dogs became audible amongst the commotion.

Though villagers were astonished by this unusual gathering of animals, the topic was forgotten once spacecraft began screaming through the midday sky. A few brave souls climbed onto their roofs and spotted hundreds of flying saucers racing towards them . . .

* * *

In the lead invasion disc, Commander Trod ordered his forces to the selected landing site. His mission was to secure the area and release the Savage dinosaurs that accompanied him. After herds of *Tyrannosaurus rex*, *Triceratops*, *Ankylosaurus*, *Gallimimus*, and *Alamosaurus* began marching across the African plains, Trod would lead his warriors to destroy Zimbabwe's capital and seize control. In a matter of weeks, the entire southern part of the continent would lapse into chaos while more nations fell to the commander's conquering army.

Slowing his invasion disc over a ridge of hills, Commander Trod was surprised by the gathering of animals below. They numbered in the hundreds, maybe even thousands. *More food for the tyrannosaurs*, he smirked while steering his spacecraft over the village. Trod then placed fingers on his blaster controls and attempted to fire a shot at houses in the center of town. Terrified people below ran in all directions to escape, but nothing happened. Roaring over the village and turning back for another try, the blasters failed a second time. "*Ketu seeta ratasa*," he cursed, returning over the eastern hills and searching for a spot to land on the plain.

Four hundred invasion discs and twenty-four transport vehicles landed behind Trod's spacecraft a mile distant from the village. The commander strutted down his disc's access ramp and stretched in the blazing sun—the same star that had warmed his ancestors sixty-five million years earlier. Sunlight felt good on his skin, soothing the fresh scars on his face, neck, arm and thigh. Armor glinted all around as nearly five hundred Wounding Tooth warriors stepped from their ships into the noontime glare.

Inspired by the vast fields of green in front of him, Commander Trod lifted his sword-axe high and roared, "Earth will be ours!"

After a cheer from his minions, shrieks, moans, and grunts from hundreds of dinosaurs started filling the humid air. They were being unloaded from Diapsid invasion discs and box-shaped heavy transport vessels. Commander Trod released a massive *Tyrannosaurus rex* from his own cargo bay and tightened her body armor. Roaring as she sniffed the air, the tyrannosaur's senses were overwhelmed by the smell of animals to the west. Having gone without food for two days, the formidable predator was *very* hungry.

Climbing onto the back of his *T. rex*, Trod patted the enormous beast through a gap in her body armor and lurched forward. He then rode to the closest heavy transport vehicle and watched four Wounding Teeth struggle with a resistant *Alamosaurus*. On command, Trod's *Tyrannosaurus* let out a deafening roar, which prompted the long-necked herbivore to leave its cage and trudge forward into the sunlight. Her massive, maroon-and-yellow striped body seemed strangely out of place on the African savannah.

Confident everything was going according to plan, Commander Trod hopped down and strutted towards one of the lieutenants who'd been helping unload the thirty-ton *Alamosaurus* from its holding pen.

"Lieutenant Genghis," he growled, "the weapons systems on my invasion disc don't seem to be working."

"Not to worry commander," the lieutenant sneered, exposing his dagger-like teeth. "We have enough mobile blasters and particle beam cannons to tide us over. I'll check your ship as soon as that human village is destroyed."

Trod nodded with a sinister grin and said, "I'd like to see what you've brought."

Lieutenant Genghis obeyed instantly, darting up the access ramp into the boxy spacecraft. Upon rounding the corner of the *Alamosaurus* holding pen, however, he froze. Not a single weapon could be seen—not even one mobile blaster. Orange eyes wide with shock, the lieutenant rushed back into the open and met Commander Trod with a worried expression on his face. "Commander, our weapons are gone!"

"What? Where could they be?"

Scrambling onto his tyrannosaur, Commander Trod called the remaining transport ships over his handheld communicator. The answer was the same each time—all had been stripped of weapons. *Captain Ripu did this*, Trod realized. *He wanted this mission to fail.*

Once he'd returned to his invasion disc, the commander discovered another problem—he didn't have enough fuel to return to Jupiter. *The power cells have been drained.* Trod punched his vehicle's control panel in anger and roared, "Ripu has stranded us on Earth!"

* * *

In the *Matabele* village, a young man crept slowly towards the ridge and looked over the wide grassland on the other side. A few boys followed him. Unfortunately, their eyes couldn't detect the camouflaged Drifters that had been sitting on the hill. The young man in the lead screamed and fell backwards when his head hit an invisible wing with a loud *clang*.

Villagers started running to help the injured teen, but soon after a voice shouted, "Watch out!" in *Sindebele*, the local language. More than half of the community screamed, ran, or fainted when they turned to see a sight like nothing they'd ever seen before.

From a spot high above the frightened masses, the voice urged everyone to remain calm. A mighty beast accompanied the sound, standing more than twenty feet in height, with a small, narrow head that was adorned with a beak. Its neck arched upwards and two massive arms ended in three-fingered hands. Every finger sported a long, curved claw and greenish feathers covered most of its body. The monster waddled on two bird-like feet and a long tail swished behind. This was a Sickle-claw, the only type of dinosaur from Ketoo's army that survived the Diapsid rebellion sixty-five million years ago.

Those villagers with the sharpest eyes noticed a miniscule red-and-brown lizard sitting on the Sickle-claw's shoulder. It was Togo, and he was the one who'd actually been speaking. The fire skink advised everyone to return to their homes. Powerful warriors had arrived to defend their village.

A loose formation of two hundred Sickle-claws followed behind their leader. Grunting and honking with goose-like calls to each other, they clutched twelve-foot longbows in their hands and carried quivers of specially made arrows slung over their shoulders. The dinosaur archers marched with gazes fixed towards the east—where they would face the Wounding Teeth for the first time in more than three hundred thousand generations.

Alex, Katherine, Ghet, Marie, and Jean stepped from their camouflaged Drifters once the Sickle-claws reached the ridge of hills where they'd been waiting. Togo hopped down from the lead archer's shoulder, flipped through the air, and landed on a rock. Motioning for the humans to sit with him, he went on to announce, "Since we'll have the home field advantage in our battle today, the Survivors have decided you should get some experience guiding the animals with your minds."

"How the heck we gonna do *that*?" Jean snapped, nervously checking the Diapsid lines over his shoulder.

"Ketoo injected neuro-links into each of you this morning," Togo reminded them. "You can use them to control animals with your thoughts. We Survivors will look after the rhinos, elephants, ostriches, and lions, but the remaining animals may be divided among yourselves." Putting his stubby hands to his sides, Togo seemed eager to see which animals each human would pick.

Jean smiled. "That's easy. I'll take the leopards."

"And I'll take the zebras!" Katherine shouted.

Marie spoke next. "I'll take the giraffes."

Everyone turned to see what Alex would choose, but he was caught up in thoughts over the significance of this moment. *Dinosaurs are back on Earth, and I'm supposed to fight them?* This was all a far cry from the miserable life he'd lived just a few months earlier. Upon realizing that all eyes were on him, Alex shrugged his shoulders and said, "I don't know what's left . . ."

"How about the buffalo?" Togo suggested.

"Uh . . . sure."

Just as everyone began to stand, Ghet raised his hand and yelled, "Hey, you're forgetting about me!"

"Why didn't you speak up sooner, Ghetto?" Jean quipped with a smile.

Togo scanned the plains for another type of animal. "There are *hundreds* of wildebeest down there. Can you handle them?"

Ghet thumped his chest in mock pride and exclaimed, "Call me 'Lord of the Wildebeest!'"

"Now remember," Togo shouted while moving into position, "If you sense any danger, get into your Drifters and leave. *Do not* try to be heroes. There will be time for that later on."

Seconds later, thunderous booms began echoing across the plain from the Diapsid lines. Sickle-claw archers squawked with excitement. Ketoo climbed onto a rock next to the children and took a deep breath.

Alex looked down at his leopard gecko friend and asked, "What's that noise?"

"Battle drums," was Ketoo's nervous reply.

CHAPTER 17

Ranid Surprise

It wasn't long before Alex had adjusted to his mental powers over the animals. All he needed to do was imagine the herd of buffalo walking to the left and they'd begin strolling in that direction. If he thought that half of the creatures should move left and the other half right, they would obey. He could even look at one individual and give it a command just by thinking. The other children were having similar success with their own chosen creatures. Jean seemed to be having a particularly good time watching the leopards leap, sprint, and roar under his command.

Booms from the Diapsid battle drums became stronger as the minute passed. Togo directed the Sickle-claw archers to draw arrows from their quivers and load them onto their twelve-foot longbows. Marching forward, they prepared to make an initial volley into the Diapsid lines.

* * *

His sharp eyes peering at the forces assembled against him, Commander Trod assessed his chance of victory and concluded the battle would go to the Diapsids. Even without their advanced weapons, his warriors were impossible to defeat. Bowing his head and saying a short prayer to Unim, the Diapsid war god, the Wounding Tooth pointed his sword-axe towards the mammalian lines and roared, "*Triceratops* cavalry, prepare to charge!"

One hundred and twenty *Triceratops* riders howled and prodded their seven-ton steeds to advance towards the ridge. Rumbles from hundreds of feet thumping the ground combined with the rhythmic *clank, clank, clank* of body armor made a horrifying noise. *Triceratops* cavalries were famous across the known universe for their strength and power.

Lieutenant Genghis, the Wounding Tooth who was leading the cavalry, lowered his sword-axe as his dinosaur galloped across the muddy grassland. Upon sighting the Sickle-claw archers take aim with their first volley of arrows, he warned the others and ducked behind the bony frill of his *Triceratops* for protection. Seconds later, arrows met their mark with the loud *pang* of metal piercing armor. Returning to his upright position, Genghis looked both right and left and noticed that most of the *Triceratops* had been hit. Long, needle-like shafts stuck from faces, shoulders, and necks of their three-horned steeds, but since none of the animals appeared to be seriously injured, the charge continued.

Halfway to the ridge, the entire herd of *Triceratops* groaned and unexpectedly tumbled to the ground. Since his dinosaur was the first to fall, Lieutenant Genghis went flying over his beast's three-horned head and landed with a hard thud on the reddish soil. His armor rattled as he rolled to a stop.

Pushing himself to his feet and gasping for air, the leader of the *Triceratops* cavalry scanned the landscape for some clue as to what had happened. Every last *Triceratops* appeared to be dead on the battlefield, and their Wounding Tooth riders were wiping dirt from their armor while searching for lost sword-axes. Genghis scraped a coating of damp soil from own chest plate and gasped when he spotted a herd of buffalo and wildebeest charging at him. Sounding the alarm, the lieutenant sprinted away from the onslaught of thundering hooves and sharp horns. After taking a few steps, something struck him in the back. *It's an arrow from the Sickle-claws*, he realized. A feeling of warmth radiated from the point where the needle had penetrated his tough hide.

Lieutenant Genghis roared in shock when hundreds of colorful creatures suddenly appeared in the tall grass around him. No bigger than grasshoppers, these tiny warriors had four legs and moist skin that glistened in the bright sun. All of them carried small, thin tubes and raised them to their lips in unison. Puffs from the creatures' throats then sent tiny pinpricks into the great warrior's skin.

Numbness overcoming his arms and legs, Lieutenant Genghis felt a tingling sensation seize his torso and spread upwards into his head. Determined to force his leg to take another step, the powerful Diapsid collapsed and his world went black. Drifting into unconsciousness, the lieutenant heard muffled chirps of victory in his ear holes. The bodies of one hundred and nineteen other Wounding Tooth warriors soon followed Genghis to the ground as they, too, crumpled on the field of battle.

* * *

Inside of his Drifter, Tupi the black-and-white tegu called Togo on his communicator and said, "It looks like the tyrannosaurs will move next, so let's send elephants through the middle to distract them. Sickle-claws can form diagonal lines along the ridge to get clear shots."

"Agreed," Togo responded from the shoulder of the Sickle-claw leader. He could see the *Tyrannosaurus rex* forces breaking into two groups that were beginning to strut in his direction. The huge carnivores moved like enormous birds, rocking their heads back and forth with each step. After he'd passed the order to the Sickle-claws, Togo cheered back through his communicator, "Things are going even better than I expected!"

"Children are doing well, aren't they?" Tupi's voice responded.

"Couldn't be better."

Little did they know the Wounding Teeth were about to reveal a surprise of their own.

* * *

Commander Trod quickly improvised a new type of weapon upon discovering that his mobile blasters and particle beam cannons were gone. Recalling primitive weapons he'd seen Pachan soldiers use in their bloody campaigns against the Ko-Kak Federation, he used a wooden pole and spike from his sword-axe to fashion a spear eight feet in length. Along with a throwing handle he'd constructed from spare parts taken from his invasion disc, Trod managed to make a weapon that could fly far and hit its target with deadly accuracy. He then taught his underlings to do the same.

Watching the *Triceratops* cavalry and their riders fall a half-mile distant from his position, Trod split his *Tyrannosaurus* team and started leading them around the edges of the battlefield. Convinced nothing could stop such an assault, Trod prodded his *Tyrannosaurus rex* into action. The gigantic predator growled and stepped forward, her powerful legs making rhythmic sounds while she accelerated. *Clank, thump. Clank, thump.*

Once his armored tyrannosaur reached a speed of twenty miles per hour, Commander Trod loaded one of his newly fashioned spears into its throwing handle. Arching his right arm back, his eyes scanned the enemy lines for a target. Dozens of other Wounding Teeth in the *Tyrannosaurus* team did the same.

With a powerful voice, Trod shouted, "Get the elephants!" and released his weapon. A deadly swarm of spears soared across the field.

Half the elephant herd crumpled to the ground in a matter of seconds. Trumpets and moans of dying animals filled the air, accompanied by the cheers of Wounding Teeth.

"We've weakened their lines!" Commander Trod bellowed while giving a victory slap on his tyrannosaur's hindquarters.

Instead of quickening her pace, however, the mighty predator roared and jerked her head from side to side. Behind fallen bodies of elephants and *Triceratops*, two diagonal lines of Sickle-claws were raising their bows and aiming at Trod's *Tyrannosaurus* team. The Diapsids were out in the open and completely unprotected.

Bowstrings slashed the air with loud *twangs* and needle-like arrows whistled over the grasslands, striking their targets with such impact that many Wounding Teeth were thrown from their saddles. Trod was torn from his seat when an arrow slammed through the body armor on his stomach. Crashing to the ground on his back, he saw the profile of his *Tyrannosaurus rex* against a backdrop of blue sky. The dreadful beast was sniffing the air as she nervously scanned the landscape. *Something's spooking her*, Trod realized.

A burning sensation radiated from the site where the needlelike arrow had pierced Commander Trod's flesh and started pumping yellowish liquid into his body. Yanking the strange needle from his belly, Trod's attention quickly shifted back to his tyrannosaur. Deep bellows of panic sounded in her throat when tiny, fast-moving shapes began scampering in her direction. They hopped through the grass from one blade to another, flashing brilliant colors while they moved. As soon as he could focus on one of the miniscule creatures, Trod recognized them. *They're frogs.*

Alarmed by the movements in the plants below, the powerful *Tyrannosaurus rex* roared and turned away from her master. Her three-toed feet squished in the damp soil and she began throwing her head and tail wildly through the air, tiny arms flailing in distress. Trod lifted his head high enough to see brightly colored spots moving around the tyrannosaur's neck and between gaps in her body armor. He wondered what the little frogs could possibly be doing to such a giant predator, but when a dozen of the tiny creatures appeared on the grassy sheaths in front of him, Trod no longer had time to think.

Flipping to his feet, Commander Trod stared at the amphibian warriors with both curiosity and confusion. *Why are they here?* No more than two inches long, their skins glistened with reds, yellows, blues, greens, and many colors in between. Raising a clawed hand to flick the frogs from his path, Trod hesitated when he noticed they were holding thin tubes to their lips. Less than a second later, tiny pinpricks jabbed Trod's hands, arms, feet, and neck. His left arm fell limp, noises grew muffled, and his vision got blurry. Commander Trod staggered onwards to save his tyrannosaur, but the mighty dinosaur collapsed before he could reach her. Trod then followed her to the ground while little frogs croaked in victory.

* * *

The rest of the battle went to the Survivors and their allies in a matter of minutes. Battle drums fell silent when gigantic, turtle-like ankylosaurs and their Wounding Tooth riders were paralyzed, along with a flock of long-legged, purple and yellow striped dinosaurs known as *Gallimimus*. Before long, nothing moved on the Diapsid side of the plain.

Once the mission was complete, Ketoo called everyone to gather around the rock where he'd been standing. As Alex, Katherine, Marie, Jean, and Ghet tried to find seats on top of the hill, vultures began circling in the skies above and cackling hyenas could be heard in the distance.

"Togo, could you keep those animals off the dinosaurs?" Ketoo requested. "There's enough poison out there to kill every creature within a hundred-mile radius."

Slouching on a rock and visibly saddened by the deaths of more than fifty elephants, Togo closed his eyes. Vultures remained in the air and the hyenas didn't come any closer.

Katherine was the next to speak. "You guys *killed* those dinosaurs, even when you promised you wouldn't!"

"Most of them are still alive," Ketoo assured. "Half of the tyrannosaurs died before we could shoot them with our microbot solution, but the others will be back to normal in a matter of hours."

Alex decided to get some clarification. "What's this about microbots? I thought those Sickle-claw arrows had some sort of tranquilizer inside."

Ketoo shook his head and opened his mouth to speak, but Aira the Eastern water dragon interrupted before he could answer. "Those arrows," she explained, "contained a yellow solution that was full of life-saving microbots. We didn't know if tranquilizers would work against those beasts, so the only option was to poison them with massive amounts of neurotoxin."

"Where'd the poison come from?"

"Wait a few seconds and you'll see," Aira replied with a smile.

Moments later, thousands of poison dart frogs began hopping into the oval of gathered friends. Their leader—golden-yellow in color with black marks on its arms and legs—bowed in front of Ketoo. The leopard gecko returned the greeting and cheered, "Long live the Ranid Warriors!"

Stepping from his invisible Drifter, Tupi translated Ketoo's exclamation to "*¡Que vivan los guerreros ranas!*" so the tiny amphibians would understand the cheer in Spanish, a language more common in their part of the world.

Since the frogs seemed to understand Tupi's words, Alex decided it might be a good idea to learn some Spanish for himself. It was, after all, the language both his father and *Tío* Ramiro seemed most comfortable speaking. "How do you say smart in Spanish?" he asked.

"*Inteligente.*"

"And those frogs are . . . um . . . *inteligente?*"

Tupi flicked his pink tongue and nodded. "It's another secret we've been keeping. Only Bity and I knew about them . . . until recently."

"But how can frogs be smart?"

"Intelligent species can appear anywhere, mate," Bluey chimed in while taking a seat on the soil. "Remember you humans aren't as special as you've always thought."

"But *frogs?*"

"Intelligence usually arises from danger—think fast or you die," Tupi explained. "These frogs live in the rainforest, where they need to protect their tadpoles, find food, and remember where their territories are. Besides escaping danger with their poisonous skin, they also use their brains."

"Wow."

Salvator the monitor lizard straightened his muscular body and gazed over the grasslands below. Clouds were gathering on the horizon, signaling the approach of afternoon rains. "We'll need to move those bodies soon, Ketoo," he advised, flicking his tongue in the direction of the fallen dinosaurs.

"We'll load them onto their ships as soon as the rains come," Ketoo responded.

"Elephants can help you . . . those that are still alive, at least," Togo grumbled.

Ketoo nodded and declared, "Everything must be out of here by nightfall. No evidence of this battle should remain."

"Why not?" Alex asked. "Now that the Wounding Teeth are landing, shouldn't we get some sort of message out to the people of Earth?"

"We have a plan of our own, my friend," Ketoo assured. "And the time isn't right to alert humanity."

"But won't the guys up in that spaceship launch another invasion?"

"Not as long as we keep them wondering about us."

"Wondering about *who?*"

Ketoo held up one of his tiny hands and wriggled the fingers. "We know Diapsids don't like reptiles with five fingers, so once warriors on the Legion Destroyer realize how swiftly their Wounding Tooth soldiers were defeated, they'll probably hold back from a second invasion until they figure out how to defeat us."

"What about that weapon they have—the Zokana Device?"

"It's a risk we'll have to take, my friend. If they do fire it, nothing would be able to stop it, not even all of the human armies in the world."

That doesn't sound good, Alex reflected before asking, "Well what are you going to do with all these dinosaurs in the meantime?"

"They'll be kept safe, Alex. Don't worry."

Silence returned to the group, prompting Jean to rise from his seat and brush himself off. Marie saw him stand and asked, "Where are you going?"

"I'm gonna check out that village over there," he said, pointing towards the west. "I wanna see how my brothers and sisters live way down here."

"You'll need a translator!" Togo shouted as he scampered behind the towering young man.

Marie skipped after her brother on the western side of the ridge, but Katherine and Alex cautiously stepped down the hill's eastern side. An eerie silence had fallen over the plain; only the rustle of wind through the tall grass could be heard. When they recalled the epic battle that had raged less than an hour earlier, the lack of sound haunted them.

True to her character, Katherine didn't let the silence last long. "What do you think they're gonna do with the dinosaurs?" she blurted.

With a sigh of frustration over his sister's inability to keep quiet, Alex shrugged his shoulders and snapped, "I have no idea, Kat."

"Are they gonna kill them?"

"Obviously not, or they wouldn't have gone through all that trouble to save 'em."

"Do you think that there's gonna be a war?"

"I sure hope not," Alex replied. Peering out on the fallen dinosaurs as raindrops began to fall, he added, "I don't think we can win against a whole *army* of those monsters."

"What'll happen to us?" Katherine gasped.

"I guess it'll be *our* turn to go extinct."

* * *

When night began to fall, a bucket of cold water splashed over Commander Trod and jolted the mighty warrior back to consciousness. With vision blurry and a pounding headache to boot, Trod groaned and tried to focus on the figures in front of him. When he realized the cavernous room where he sat was rocking gently to the left and right, he concluded someone must have dragged him inside a Diapsid heavy transport vessel and taken off.

"Wake up, you overgrown turkey!" Jean shouted in a deep voice. "We got some questions to ask you!"

"What do you want, *human*?" Trod snarled in reply, curling his lips to expose fearsome teeth.

"You need to learn a little respect!" Jean snapped, pointing a weapon in the commander's face.

Furious orange eyes looked upward while Commander Trod growled and tried to stand. With arms and legs chained to the floor, however, he couldn't move. Glancing down the barrel of the weapon Jean was holding, Trod noted its shape was vaguely reminiscent of a mobile blaster. Colored yellow with orange and red attachments, it connected to a round, green tank via blue tubes. *This must be some sort of gun that five-fingers have made for humans*, the commander concluded before deciding he'd rather *not* find out what sort of damage such a weapon could do. "Ask your questions," he grunted.

Seemingly unable to control his jitters, Jean hesitated to say anything more. In a frantic search for someone to help him with the interrogation, he then turned to Salvator and asked, "Now what?"

The grayish-brown monitor lizard patted his human companion on the arm and said, "I can take it from here."

"All right. I got your back, my man."

"Man?"

"Lizard . . . you know what I mean."

Stepping towards Commander Trod, Salvator pulled back the hood of his woolen cloak and hissed, "My friend, listen to me. We defeated your forces, but we allowed you to live. If you respect us with the same peaceful intentions, I'm sure we can reach an agreement that will benefit both our societies."

"I will not deal with five-fingers!" Trod raged. "Your kind is worthless!"

Crossing his thick arms and flicking his forked tongue, Salvator asked, "Why would you think such a thing?"

"Five-fingers enslaved my ancestors before Lord Upadravin freed us from your cruelty. Our god Unim says we should never trust your kind again!"

Salvator leaned forward. "Let me be clear. We could have killed all of you on that battlefield today, but we didn't. We want to help you. Please tell me, why are you here?"

"To retake our home planet!"

"And who gave you permission to invade?"

"The Scipion Legions!"

The very name of that dreadful regime made the other lizards shudder. Alex, Ghet, Katherine, and Marie were also watching the conversation unfold, but at a safe distance.

Salvator scratched his neck for a moment and closed his eyes while asking, "Can you tell me how it's possible that the most powerful warriors in the known universe came to attack our planet with nothing more than spears?"

Trod's eyes narrowed in anger. "Swift Runners betrayed us, five-finger. They took our weapons and drained our power cells."

Salvator clasped his hands behind his back and asked, "But you'll still trust Swift Runners more than five-fingered lizards who spared your lives?"

Commander Trod considered his options. If his forces were still on Earth when the full invasion began, Captain Ripu would surely accuse him of treason. Such a charge was punishable by death. On the other hand, Trod had been told since his earliest days that five-fingers were not to be trusted. In order to avoid making an immediate decision, he grumbled, "I must speak with my lieutenants."

Salvator stepped back and nodded at Jean, who raised his weapon and shouted, "We ain't got time for this nonsense! You with us or you against us?"

"I could crush you with my bare hands," Trod raged. "Do not threaten me!"

Copying his posture from the tough guys in his favorite movies, Jean hollered, "That's it! You're outta here!"

The rear door of the heavy transport vehicle opened on Jean's command and a strong wind whistled through the cargo bay. When Trod heard the sound of splashing water outside, his body froze in horror. Despite their fearlessness in battle, most Diapsids were deathly afraid of drowning.

Jean pointed his weapon at Commander Trod's chest and told him to look down. In the vast expanse of ocean below, tall waves were whipped by driving rains and stormy tempests. Both the darkening sky and the water were steel grey in color. Hideous forms of sharks and whales thrashing near the surface added to his panic. Trod roared and tried to pull away from the nightmarish scene, but the chains holding him were too strong. "I'm with you!" he bellowed. "Just keep me from falling down there!"

Appearing to be satisfied with the commander's answer, Salvator gave the order to close the cargo bay door. Winds and spray stopped their lashing as soon as the spaceship's hatch locked itself with a loud *clang*.

Everything became quiet while Commander Trod caught his breath and pondered his fate. *I shall give these five-fingers a chance to prove themselves*, he resolved, *but I'll kill them if they dare trick me*. Growling in Jean's direction, Trod then snarled, "Once you release me, I'd like to teach that miserable *human* some manners!"

"Oh, that's it! I've had enough of this chicken-head!" Jean screamed, cocking his weapon twice and pulling the trigger.

"No!" Marie shrieked at her brother. "Don't do it!"

Commander Trod roared forcefully in the face of death, but it wasn't long before he realized the gun's only discharge was a stream of water. *It's just a child's toy*. Observing how Jean and the others were laughing over the incident, he decided it could be considered *funny*—a human term Trod didn't understand very well. Reflecting further, he decided one trick wasn't enough to warrant killing his new allies . . . *at least not yet*.

CHAPTER 18

Counterstrike

Alex, Katherine, Jean, Marie, and Ghet made a brief stop in South America after their encounter with Commander Trod over the Atlantic Ocean. They traveled with a fleet of spacecraft carrying hundreds of unconscious dinosaurs in their cargo bays. Apart from a multitude of new stories the *Matabele* villagers could discuss within the confines of their tiny town, nothing was left behind in Zimbabwe. The huge formation of spaceships—many flying on automatic pilot—passed over the coastline late at night and low in the sky to avoid being detected by Brazilian military radar.

Still chained to the floor, Commander Trod was asleep, but everyone else on the heavy transport vessel peered through the ship's windows at the blackness below. They were approaching a base the Survivors had recently established in the same secrecy that accompanied all of their activities.

Over the past few months, Ketoo (disguised as Sikandar Tendulkar of *atarkya.com*) had purchased a gigantic swath of land in the Brazilian state of Bahia with the help of Ashoka Mehta, *atarkya.com*'s human CEO. A massive workforce was then organized to build walls—fifty feet tall and ten feet thick—around the compound. Of course, the workers never learned why an Internet company was building a park in the midst of the *sertão* scrublands, but when complete, the parcel of Brazilian territory was a perfect place to resettle hundreds of dinosaurs and their Wounding Tooth riders.

After landing, groggy beasts struggled to their feet and trudged out of the spaceships while Alex and his friends bid farewell to the Survivors and headed home in their Drifters. The egg-shaped spaceships had automatically flown from Africa and were waiting for the five on a field where Wounding Teeth were gathering to hear about Commander Trod's new plan.

At four o'clock in the morning, the limousine driver who'd waited all day at the rest stop in Maryland was awakened by Jean's fist banging on the driver's side window. Alex and the others returned to Philadelphia in the car and the invisible Drifters followed.

The next day was a Saturday, so no one bothered to wake Alex that morning. Stumbling into the bathroom at three o'clock in the afternoon, he brushed his teeth and glanced at himself in the mirror. *Did everything I saw yesterday really happen?* he wondered. It all seemed too fantastic to be true. When he heard Katherine trying on new clothes in the living room, Alex pushed back his long hair and trudged in to ask her what she remembered. Spotting his sister singing in a pink satin dress and a tiara, however, Alex forgot his question and instead chuckled, "Aren't you a little old for that?"

Startled by her brother's question, Katherine snatched the sparkling crown from her head and snapped, "I just wanted to see what it would look like—that's all." Betraying her embarrassment, her face flushed bright red.

"Mom bought that stuff for you?"

"Yeah . . . she said she felt bad she couldn't get it for me when I was a little girl."

"Now she's trying to make up for her mistakes, huh?"

"Something like that."

Alex paused to think for a moment. "Why don't you call your Drifter *The Princess*?"

"What?"

"You said that you couldn't think of a name for your spaceship, right?"

"Uh-huh."

"Just call it *The Princess* and get it over with!"

"*The Princess* . . . hmmm . . . I like it!" Katherine squealed.

Seconds later, Alex's face became serious. "How about we do some old-fashioned kids' stuff today?"

"What do you mean?"

"Well, instead of trying to save the world or flying around in our spaceships, why don't we just ride our bikes?"

"Um . . . okay."

"Let's go to Sweetbriar Park."

Katherine's eyes opened wide. "Don't you remember? Billy DeGrace said we couldn't go back there."

"I'm not scared of him," Alex boasted with a self-assured tone. "I mean . . . look at what we saw yesterday."

"You mean the dinosaurs and stuff?"

"Yeah, and after all that, you're gonna be scared of one little eighth grader at Sweetbriar Park?"

Katherine just shrugged in reply.

"We can't be afraid for the rest of our lives, you know."

"I guess not."

Moments after the two had changed into more appropriate clothing, Alex and Katherine sped off towards Sweetbriar Park. The air of late winter blew cool, but crocus and daffodil blossoms in the neighbors' yards were throwing forth purples and yellows to signal spring's approach. Bike chains rattled when both kids jumped from the curb and pedaled down the street. The woods were only a few minutes away.

Unstrapping his helmet on the narrow path that led to the center of Sweetbriar Park, Alex moved past the bushes where he'd first saved Bluey and froze when he noticed a figure glaring down from the nearby dirt pile. It was Billy DeGrace, sitting on an expensive mountain bike he'd stolen from some poor soul over the winter.

Billy was alone, but that didn't stop him from shouting, "I told you *never* to come back here again, you illegal lizard lover! Don't you understand English?"

Anger flushing through his chest, Alex's mind flashed with scenes of abuses he'd suffered from Billy and his gang over the course of the past year. *Now's the time to fight back.* "I'm sick of your crap, Billy. I have a right to be here!"

"No you don't—you're a friggin' Mexican! You should be thrown out of the country!"

"I was born in Texas, not Mexico!"

Throwing his bike to the ground, Billy stepped forward and sneered, "I don't care. This is still *my* territory, and you don't belong here."

"Says who?"

"Says me . . . You wanna make something of it?"

With fear starting to temper his anger, Alex wasn't sure if he wanted to make something of it or not. Compared to Billy, he was small and thin. On the other hand, the very reason he came to Sweetbriar Park was to stand up to Billy once and for all. Reassuring himself with the thought that his tormentor was *nothing* compared to Commander Trod, Alex straightened his posture and said with outstretched hands, "Look, man. Why don't you just avoid a whole lot of trouble and leave us alone?"

"Because I don't feel like it," Billy replied in an icy voice.

As soon as he felt Katherine's hands clutch the back of his jacket, Alex huffed, "Stay out of this, Kat."

Billy growled, "Yeah, brat. Keep out of this and maybe I'll even let you run away."

"Come on, Alex," Katherine whined, tugging on her brother's jacket. "Let's get out of here."

Without warning, Billy lunged forward and grabbed Alex by the collar, tossing him to the ground. Katherine yanked on her brother's jacket in an attempt to keep him in place, but Billy used his other hand to shove her away with little more than a flick of the elbow. "Now I'm gonna teach *both of you* a lesson," he snarled while stepping towards her with clenched fists.

Blinded by anger, Alex scrambled to his feet faster than he ever thought possible and yelled, "Don't you dare touch my sister!"

Alex was struck hard on the shoulder when he came within range of Billy's arms and slid on a patch of mud hidden by fallen leaves. Twisting his body and landing on his back, Alex felt his heart sink. *I'm in real trouble now*, he thought while preparing for the pain he was about to endure. Billy crouched down to land another punch, but Katherine grabbed his arm. Reacting on sheer instinct, Alex then kicked upwards, catching his rival between the legs. Billy let out a hideous groan and fell to his knees.

Since Billy was momentarily weakened, Alex grabbed his sister by the arm, helped her onto her bike, and raced out of Sweetbriar Park as fast as his feet could pedal. He didn't speak the whole way home, but did manage to glance over his shoulder a few times to make sure Katherine was still following. Mind full of panic, Alex felt his lungs tighten upon arrival at Uncle Roy's house. Pulling an inhaler from his pocket, he took a seat on cement steps that led to the porch. Katherine put down the kickstand on her bike and sat beside him.

"Thanks, Alex," she said, putting an arm around her brother.

"Thanks for what?"

"For getting Billy before he hurt me."

Alex took a second breath through his inhaler and pondered his fate. *They're gonna get me . . . Billy and his goons probably even know where I live.*

"Well, you sure taught *him* a lesson."

"No I didn't. He's gonna come after me first chance he gets."

"Didn't you win that fight?"

"That wasn't a fight. I just pulled a dirty move and kicked him in the nuts. No one would *ever* think that's tough."

"Well, you had to do *something*, right?"

"I should've stayed away from Sweetbriar Park in the first place." Overcome with a feeling of hopelessness, Alex put his head down in his arms and took a deep breath.

"Why don't we move away? Mom can afford it now."

Still staring at the cement steps below him, Alex paused to take another breath of medicine and said, "Mom's too afraid about losing her job and Uncle Roy keeps bugging her about rent money. She's not saving much."

"Like *he* was ever much help to us."

Mind focused on his safety, Alex mumbled, "Maybe I can ask Ghet's older brothers to keep an eye on me . . ."

"Can't your lizard friends help?"

Alex shook his head. "I don't want the Survivors to find out what happened. If they did, I might not be allowed to fly with them next week."

Apparently delighted to change the subject, Katherine went on to ask, "Where are you going?"

"I'm not really sure if I'm allowed to say," Alex shrugged. He then sat in silence to let his sister's impatience build. Despite his tense situation, it was fun to tease Katherine.

"Aleeeexxxx . . ." Katherine whined.

Relenting to his sister's complaint, Alex asked, "You remember that planet report you told me about?"

"That stupid thing? I still didn't even pick my planet."

Alex nodded with a sly smile and whispered, "I'll make it easy for you. Choose Jupiter."

CHAPTER 19

Retrieval

By the time Monday came, Alex decided to stop riding the bus to school, since that was one place he was sure to see Billy every morning. He instead began riding his bike to William Henry Harrison Elementary, hoping witnesses on the sidewalks might keep the bullies from attacking. Once the school day ended, Alex would sneak over to the O'Malley's house and wait until Ghet's teenage brothers could walk him home. Billy and his friends were intimidated by the older O'Malleys, who were muscular and fair-skinned like Celtic gods. With a new baby in the house (girl number six, child number eleven), the brothers usually seemed happy to accompany Alex wherever he wanted to go. "Sure beats changing diapers!" they'd always cheer.

After enduring the first week without incident, Alex put earthly worries aside and climbed into his Drifter for the greatest adventure of his life. On Saturday evening, the *Free Bird* left Uncle Roy's roof and soared east to join a fleet of Survivors over the Atlantic Ocean. All ten spacecraft then left Earth's atmosphere and accelerated to speeds unimaginable by human technology.

Though he was nervous about the journey, Alex's jitters calmed a bit when he looked through his front viewing screen. A surge of emotion rose in his heart when he saw millions of stars shine with a brilliance that can never be seen from solid ground. *They look like diamonds,* he thought. *Space is more beautiful than I imagined.* Despite his momentary sense of wonder, however, Alex jumped in surprise when a voice rattled over his speakers.

"We should be there in less than two hours," Ketoo said. "But as soon as we cross the orbit of Mars, we'll have to maintain complete radio silence so that warship doesn't hear us."

"How are you holding up, Alex?" Bity the beaded lizard's voice buzzed through the communicator.

"So far, so good," Alex answered, imagining what the thick-bodied, yellow-and-black lizard must look like piloting her own Drifter. It was a welcome diversion from the sudden realization that he was racing away from his home planet at more than 40,000 miles per second. Everything he'd ever known was now millions of miles away . . . *what the heck am I gonna do if something goes wrong?*

"Besides Ketoo, none of us have ever traveled this far before," Bity added.

"You're not making me feel any better, you know," Alex replied, trying his best to sound upbeat. Ever since he'd learned that Bity spent most of her time in Mexico, he'd felt a special connection with her. *Maybe she can even help me find my father.*

When the *Free Bird* stopped its accelerations and began cruising, Ketoo's voice sounded one last time. "Mars is approaching, so I'm shutting down the radios. See you when we get there."

With the close of the final message, Alex found himself enveloped in silence. He checked the rear view of his ship and was shocked to see Earth as a mere speck orbiting a shrinking Sun. Eager to keep himself distracted, Alex unbuckled his harness and stretched his legs. He panicked when he floated out of his chair, but quickly remembered that weightlessness was a normal part of space travel. After several minutes of moving in zero gravity, Alex thought it best to return to his seat and get some rest. It was past his bedtime, and he would need to be alert for the mission ahead.

More than an hour later, rumbling noises startled Alex back to consciousness. Slowly remembering where he was, Alex realized it was the crab-like retrieval robot in his Drifter's cargo bay that had been making the sounds. An entry hatch opened to reveal the robot's metallic interior and the shipboard computer commanded, "Get in, *Ale*."

Surprised by the order, Alex looked through the front screen of the *Free Bird* and saw colorful bands of Jupiter's clouds spanning the entire sky. Every brown, white, and tan strip was filled with turbulent activity that added to planet's immense power. In the lower portion of the screen was a smooth, icy surface—as if a giant cue ball were floating through space. When his eyes adjusted to the moon's brilliance, he noticed long cracks filled with darker material between patches of white. *That must be Europa*, Alex surmised while unstrapping his harness and floating clumsily to the cargo bay.

A feeling of dreadful claustrophobia overcame Alex when the robot's top hatch closed over his head and the cargo doors opened. It felt like being stuck inside a suit of armor . . . floating through space . . . hiding from bloodthirsty dinosaurs . . . *five hundred million miles from the nearest humans!* Since Ketoo had designed the robot to move with Alex's body, sensors on his legs would operate the machine's legs and his hands would control the robot's claws.

Once he'd cleared the spacecraft, bay doors on the *Free Bird* closed and a small engine propelled Alex's camouflaged robot gently towards Europa's surface. Alex was too frightened to look while drifting through space, but when the machine's four spiky legs touched upon the ice, he opened his eyes. On one side of his robot's viewing screen, the sky was pitch black and studded with stars. On the other, the imposing sphere of Jupiter was all that could be seen. Gravity's downward pull was noticeable on Europa, but it was far weaker than what one would feel on Earth.

Nine reddish blips quickly appeared on Alex's screen to indicate positions of Survivor robots on the surface—all were camouflaged and carefully creeping across the ice.

Moments later, a yellow light flashed above the Survivors' blips. When Alex focused on the illuminated message, his stomach contracted and his heart skipped a beat. Yellow letters were spelling out, "FOREIGN CRAFT DETECTED." Three points of light were approaching from the right side of Jupiter, their shapes suggesting a trio of massive boomerangs. Reflecting dim sunlight with a reddish-purple glow, they were heading towards the ten robots on the Europan surface. *Can they see us?* Alex gulped.

As the Swift Runner spaceships, known as Nychus Fighters, became larger and larger on the view screen, Alex regretted joining this mission. He even wished he'd never saved Bluey in the first place. To Alex's great relief, however, the fearsome boomerangs passed overhead and continued their flight around Jupiter. Nothing indicated that Swift Runners were aware of the Survivors below. *Okay, we're safe . . . but I wish this robot had a bathroom!*

After the enemy spacecraft rounded the far side of Jupiter, legs on Alex's robot automatically collapsed inward and brought it to rest on four skate-like legs. Taking a deep breath as his retrieval robot began sliding forward, Alex clutched his hand controls with all of his strength. Thrashed against the insides of his machine with no time to prepare for the jostling, Alex's jaws cramped with tension as he picked up speed.

All ten robots were soon skating towards the curved horizon, clearly marked by brilliant white against inky black. In between prayers he'd make it back to Earth in one piece, Alex noticed a rhythm to the way the Survivors' blips moved on his control screen. *They're definitely searching for something.* Then, without warning, the robots gripped the surface and rumbled to a halt. Alex felt his body lurch forward, as if he'd been in a car that slammed on the brakes. *They must've found what they're looking for.*

Blips from three machines, belonging to Ketoo, Bluey, and Tupi, pulled their legs together and began sinking beneath the surface. Three others, labeled Suzikha, Bity, and Aira, did the same. All six descended rapidly. One additional robot, labeled Togo, followed closely behind. Lowering his control screen, Alex could see seven plumes of hot vapor billowing out into space. With metal skins that could heat to extreme temperatures, the machines were melting their way through Europa's ice crust. Three remaining robots, including the one that belonged to Alex, kept watch on the surface. Alex kept his eyes fixed on the sky and hoped nothing unexpected would happen.

Two hours later, Ketoo's robot surfaced with a capsule that looked something like a metal trashcan. The recovery mission complete, ten camouflaged robots blasted from Europa with puffs of plasma and returned to their waiting Drifters. Inside the *Free Bird* once again, Alex exited his robot and floated back to his seat with greater skill than before. After a much needed bathroom break, he fastened the buckles on his seat and felt a slight jolt to the left when the spaceship turned for its first acceleration.

* * *

Alex stumbled from his Drifter outside of Ketoo's laboratory after his return trip to Earth. Exhausted from the journey, Alex nearly collapsed when his body didn't readjust to gravity's strong pull. Low oxygen levels at the high altitude didn't help, either. He was in the Himalaya Mountains, somewhere between China and Nepal. Winds were blowing hard, making it difficult to see the mountainous landscape all around. Pulling his thin jacket against the bitter highland breeze, Alex crawled into a small tunnel and followed his lizard friends through the darkness.

Once inside, Alex stood on the balcony of a cavernous room while Ketoo, Aira, and Salvator worked below. The interior was similar to the cave in South America, prompting Alex to wonder why the lizards had carved such large rooms underground. Before he could ask anyone about this observation, however, Ketoo made an announcement that erased all other thoughts from his mind.

"It's all set," he said. "If they're still alive, these eggs will hatch before midnight."

CHAPTER 20

The Hatching

Next stop on the homeward voyage was El Paso, Texas—the place where Alex lived before moving to Philadelphia. Though he wasn't sure how to convince his *Tío* Ramiro and *Tía* Elena to raise a pair of dinosaur warriors, Alex knew he'd have more success with his family in Texas than with Mom and Uncle Roy.

Touching down that evening on a clearing of dusty pine needles, Alex immediately sensed something was wrong. The trailer park where his *tío* and *tía* lived wasn't any different from when he'd left it, but Alex was stunned to see only his *tío*'s silhouette on the trailer's tiny porch. *Tía* Elena wasn't anywhere to be seen.

Stranger still was the fact that his *tío* didn't seem to notice when Alex stepped through the portal of his invisible spaceship and walked over to the porch. *Tío* Ramiro's eyes remained fixed on the ground.

"*Tío* . . . I'm here," Alex said softly, hoping for a response.

When the old man looked up and their eyes met, Alex was unnerved by what he saw. *Tío* Ramiro's eyes were red and wet, as if he'd been crying for a long time. His face, once rounded and beaming with energy, was now thin and framed by a sparse beard. Dark skin on *Tío* Ramiro's hands was loose-fitting and wrinkled. Even the ever-present cowboy hat on his head seemed to be drained of life.

Alex waved a hand in the air and asked, "Don't you remember me?"

Staring at the figure before him, *Tío* Ramiro muttered, "*Ale?*"

His brown eyes catching the last rays of the setting Sun, Alex pulled an empty lawn chair to his *tío*'s side and asked what had happened. This wasn't going to be the happy reunion he'd been looking forward to.

Tío Ramiro took a deep breath and turned his gaze back towards the wooden planks of his tiny porch. "It's your *tía*, Ale," he sighed. "She's gone."

Shocked by his uncle's words, Alex blurted, "Gone? What do you mean?"

Tío Ramiro's hands trembled and tears began to drip onto the floor. "She died, *Ale* . . . She died real fast."

Not breathing for several seconds as a wave of sadness overcame his body, Alex finally whimpered, "How?"

"One morning she was cooking breakfast and her arm stopped working . . . then she couldn't talk. The ambulance came, but she was already dying."

"What was it?"

"The doctors told me that she had a stroke . . . a major stroke."

Alex wasn't quite sure what a stroke was, but it sounded bad. "When did this happen?"

"Two weeks ago."

"*Two weeks ago*? Why didn't anyone tell us?"

Tío Ramiro straightened his posture, wiped his eyes, and leaned back in his chair. "I think your cousin tried calling and the man who answered said he'd give you the message."

"That must have been Uncle Roy," Alex replied, shaking his head. "He never told me."

With a face showing his confusion, *Tío* Ramiro asked, "If you didn't know, then why'd you come down here?"

"Long story, *tío*."

"You're here by yourself?"

"Yep."

"How? I'm sure your mother's worried sick about you!"

Alex waved him off. "Mom was away this weekend on business and doesn't have the slightest idea what I've been doing."

Tío Ramiro shifted his position in order to get a better look at his nephew. Apparently relieved to find an escape from his sorrow, he said, "One time your mother called me and said you snuck out of the house to come down and visit me. Don't tell me you did *that* again."

"Um . . . not exactly."

"Well, how'd you get down here?"

Alex started his story at the beginning—when he saved Bluey in the park—and didn't stop until he'd described his journey to Jupiter the previous evening. By the time he's explained everything, the only light illuminating the two was from a bare bulb over the porch.

When Alex was finished, the shadowy silhouette of *Tío* Ramiro asked, "This sounds dangerous, *Ale*. I think you should be more careful."

"You mean—you *believe* what I told you?"

"I will if you give me proof."

Alex looked towards his landing site and shouted, "Free Bird, visible!" A truck-sized spacecraft instantly materialized several yards away. "Is that proof enough?"

Mouth open in surprise, *Tío* Ramiro just nodded his head.

"Can you help me?" Alex asked while clearing his throat.

"How?"

"Could you adopt some children? I'll even send you money to help out."

"Adopt kids?"

"Well . . . not exactly kids . . . not *human* kids, at least."

"What are you talking about?"

Alex leaped from his seat and charged through the Drifter's open door to retrieve a box Ketoo had entrusted to him. Opening the greenish-brown case with extreme care, he revealed two softball-sized eggs to his *tío*. One was white and speckled with brown; the other was a brilliant shade of sky blue.

"What are those?" *Tío* Ramiro gasped.

"Eggs," Alex replied, setting the case on the porch. "Two we brought back from Jupiter."

"Dinosaur eggs?"

"Sort of . . . they'll be special dinosaurs that can walk and talk."

"Talking dinosaurs?"

"Yep, and they're gonna help save the Earth," Alex said while moving to close the case. He stopped, however, upon hearing a muffled squeak resonate from inside the speckled egg.

Tío Ramiro scrambled out of his chair and hunched over the box to get a better look. "What's happening?" he asked with the wondrous eyes of a child.

The egg rolled inside of its foam nest and a crack opened down the middle. Jumping from the case, it landed on the porch with a crunching sound. *Tío* Ramiro shouted in surprise when the speckled egg leaped a second time and struck him on the nose. A small green fist then burst through the eggshell, its skin glistening with moisture. Another hand quickly crashed through the surface an inch away and the top of the egg shot off with a splitting sound.

Inside, a strange little creature squirmed to rid itself of the remaining eggshell. With a head that seemed too large for its body, the hatchling had a curved, bony ridge along the top of its skull and a sharp beak. Once free, the pint-sized dinosaur stared at the old man with its dark eyes, stretched its stumpy arms, and yawned. *Tío* Ramiro poked at the hatchling with his index finger and received a tiny hug in return. They both smiled.

Alex watched the entire scene unfold before interrupting, "Looks like you're stuck, *tío*. These little guys imprint on the first face they see."

"What?"

After noticing that energy had returned to *Tío* Ramiro's eyes, Alex explained, "Dinosaurs and birds always think the first object they see is their mother. It's called *imprinting*. Now you're his mommy!"

Tío Ramiro flashed a near-toothless grin and asked, "Is it a boy or a girl?"

"I think this one's a boy and the other's a girl."

"I don't know if I can handle being a parent again," *Tío* Ramiro sighed.

"C'mon," Alex whined in response, "you don't want to break the little guy's heart. And besides," he added with his best salesman's pitch, "they'll both be full grown in a few months."

"That fast?"

"They were designed to grow quickly."

"Then I guess every second counts!" *Tío* Ramiro exclaimed while lifting the infant dinosaur in his palm. The creature's big eyes, full of wonder at the new world around him, darted every which way.

When Alex checked on the egg still in the box, he was shocked to see only a few blue shell fragments and a trial of azure specks leading to his *tío*'s feet. An even tinier dinosaur, this one clothed in matted feathers, was leaping and chirping in a desperate attempt to get her new "mother's" attention.

"Now you have a new son *and* another daughter!" Alex laughed.

Holding the female dinosaur in the porch light's glare, *Tío* Ramiro said, "She looks like a bird . . . with fingers . . . and teeth—*sharp* teeth."

"Well, she *is* a dinosaur."

"What are their names?"

"Ketoo told me the green one is called a *Yinlong*. It's from China. The purple one is a *Rahonavis* from Madagascar."

Tío Ramiro's was apparently too excited to hear the dinosaurs' full names. "Yin and Rahona? That's what we call them?"

"I guess so," Alex shrugged. "They're *your* kids now."

Not long thereafter, news came over Alex's shipboard radio that two other dinosaurs—named Stygi and Euplos—were hatching in Ketoo's laboratory. Talitha the chameleon then announced her new nickname for the hatchlings, calling them the "Zeus Crew." The name sounded catchy, especially since Zeus was the Greek counterpart of Jupiter. Not one of the hatchlings was interested in this decision, however. They just wanted something to eat.

CHAPTER 21

Hospital Room

Once he'd assured that Yin and Rahona would be comfortable in their new home, Alex returned to Philadelphia. The next afternoon, when Mom returned from her trip, he asked her to begin sending money down to El Paso. Happy to help out, Mom didn't even ask why *Tío* Ramiro needed the cash, nor how Alex knew what had happened to *Tía* Elena (which was probably for the best). Regular payments began the next morning.

With all of the excitement in his life—not to mention relief over surviving the voyage to Jupiter—Alex's scuffle with Big Billy seemed like a distant memory. *He's probably forgotten about me now.* As a result, Alex stopped worrying about the bullies and started taking risks.

One day in the middle of April, *Tío* Ramiro called Alex to ask for more money. Yin and Rahona had tripled in size in less than two weeks and were continuing to get hungrier each day. "Eat and poop is about all they do," Alex's *tío* sighed while explaining why he needed to buy more groceries as soon as possible. There wasn't time to wait for Mom's next money transfer.

After a check of his wallet, Alex realized he could cover the dinosaurs' food for at least two days. All he needed to do was wire it down to Texas. There was, however, a problem—it was 3:30 in the afternoon and no one could protect him if he made a trip to the bank. Weighing his responsibility to take care of Yin and Rahona over the danger of traveling through his neighborhood in broad daylight, Alex chose duty over safety.

Upon reaching the first traffic light on his bike, Alex decided the quickest way to the bank was cutting down an alley two blocks away. *Nobody's there, so there's nothing to be afraid of,* he assured himself while turning onto the narrow cement path and looking through the brick canyon flanked by large trashcans. Alex took a deep breath, gulped, and moved forward. Cars and trucks were zooming along a busy street on the other side. If he could make it that far, he'd be safe. Unfortunately, Alex didn't go more than a hundred feet before a broomstick jabbed through the spokes of his front tire. Lurching over the handlebars, he landed face first on the cracked pavement below. The impact knocked him unconscious, which was probably for the best. Billy and his gang circled around, planning to teach Alex a lesson he'd *never* forget.

* * *

Alex awoke in a hospital bed two days later. Billy and the others had been ruthless. They broke his nose, four of his ribs, his left arm in two places, and fractured his skull. He also suffered bruised kidneys, a ruptured spleen, and deep cuts on his arms, legs, and face. On the afternoon when Alex's broken body arrived at St. Theresa's Hospital, the doctors weren't sure if he'd live through the night. Even when he managed to pull through, everyone believed Alex would be scarred and mangled for the rest of his life.

Opening his bloodshot eyes in the cool, quiet hospital room, Alex tried his best to remember what had happened. He was lying on a bed with white sheets covering his lower body and all sorts of electronic gadgets attached to his arms and chest. A small wooden table on his right held a vase full of flowers and multicolored balloons swayed in the sterile air. Shades on the widows were closed, but Alex could tell it was nighttime from darkness seeping around the windows' edges. Both his mother and his sister were sleeping on a couch next to his bed, looking like they hadn't changed their clothes or brushed their hair in a long time.

Since his left arm was in a splint and connected to an IV, Alex used his right hand to reach up and feel his head. It was throbbing, as was the rest of his body. When he began to feel thick bandages instead of skin, Alex cried out in a panic, "Mom!"

Alex's mother awoke instantly and hopped from the couch. "You're awake," she whispered, leaning down and touching his bandaged head. "Oh, thank God!"

"What happened?"

"You got hurt real bad, honey." Tears welling in her eyes, she paused to wipe her face and asked, "Who did this to you?"

"Nobody saw anything?"

Mom shook her head. "The police told me an old lady found you in an alley. No one else was around."

Mind struggling to remember the events of that horrible afternoon, Alex knew he'd blacked out, but also remembered hearing someone yell, "If you snitch on us, your mom and your sister die." Certain that Billy was dangerous enough to carry out such a threat, Alex decided to keep quiet about his attackers. He looked to the other side of the room and mumbled, "I don't know who did this . . . I . . . I don't remember anything."

"Your sister said some boy named Billy must've done it. She told me you two had a fight in Sweetbriar Park."

"Um . . . no," Alex replied, struggling to keep Mom from learning the truth. "Billy and I made up a few days ago. He said he wasn't mad at me anymore."

"Well, the police stopped by his house, just in case. They didn't find anything, though." Pausing for a moment to take her son's right hand, Mom's voice trembled, "I'm so sorry about this, Alex."

"Why are *you* sorry?"

"Well," Mom explained after a deep breath, "If you'd stayed in Texas instead of moving up here, maybe you wouldn't have gotten hurt so bad."

"But if I'd stayed in Texas, I wouldn't have met the Survivors," Alex mumbled, not realizing he'd only meant to *think* those words.

"The *whats?*"

Oh crap! Alex cringed. *How am I gonna explain this one?*

"What are the Survivors?"

Alex decided to speak quickly to throw her off course. "Well, there's a group of talking lizards that gave me a spaceship, and now they're trying to keep the world from being invaded by dinosaurs . . ."

"Are you feeling okay?" Mom asked with a face full of worry.

"Huh?"

"You're babbling . . . maybe you're even hallucinating. Should I get the nurse?"

"Nah, I'm alright." Breathing a sigh of relief, Alex still knew he'd have to tell her about the Survivors sometime soon. *I can't keep everything hidden for much longer.* Shifting his legs under the crisp sheets, Alex went on to ask, "You still like working for *atarkya.com*?"

Mom's exhausted face brightened a bit. "Oh, it's great. I haven't shown up for work in two days, but Mr. Tendulkar called me this morning to say I shouldn't go back to work until you're better.

"He knows what happened to me?"

"I told him this morning. He seemed real worried about you—even though he never met you. What a great man . . . I'd probably marry him if he wasn't so weird."

Alex giggled. *If only she knew the truth.* He then pictured a scene where his mother actually *did* marry a little leopard gecko. The mental image made him laugh even harder. His broken ribs ached, but he couldn't help himself.

Katherine, of course, slept through everything. Being the heaviest sleeper the world has ever known, she didn't speak with her brother until the next morning. Before she left with Mom to get washed up for school, Alex warned her to keep quiet about Billy DeGrace. *It's the only way to keep everyone safe.*

Around noontime, the nurse fed Alex a few spoonfuls of hospital-flavored macaroni and cheese, checked his vital signs, and left. Alone and unable to do much in his bandages and casts, Alex decided to take a nap. After he closed his eyes and his mind began to drift, the sound of a woman's voice startled him back to wakefulness. The mysterious person spoke for several seconds before Alex pinpointed the source of the chatter. It seemed like someone was speaking right next to his bed, even though he couldn't see her.

Moments later, Alex's eyes detected the faint outline of a chameleon on his metal bed frame. *It's Talitha*. She was talking with Ketoo on her handheld communicator, babbling away like one of Ghet's older sisters on a cell phone.

"Yes, Ketoo," she sighed, "I'll report everything to you immediately after I'm done." Once her body was completely visible, Talitha turned and smiled in Alex's direction. Rolling her eyes in their turrets, she attempted to stop Ketoo's nonstop chatter several times before finally shouting, "Goodbye, Ketoo!" and clicking her communicator shut. She then straightened herself and sighed, "Are you okay? We didn't know about your injuries until your mother spoke to Sikandar Tendulkar yesterday morning."

"I guess Katherine should've called."

"Well none of that matters now," Talitha assured, waving one of her vice-grip hands and changing to a darker shade of green. "Ketoo's been working on something special for you. That's why I'm here."

"Huh?"

"She said we have something for you!" a voice boomed from the computer monitor to the right of his bed.

Alex tried his best to turn his head and look at the screen. To his surprise, there was a little turtle waving on the monitor. The voice belonged to Chelonius, but the image was something quite different. Big eyes, bright colors, and a broad, gleaming smile gave the turtle a comical appearance.

"Like the new look, Alex?" Chelonius asked with a tinge of sarcasm. "Ketoo and your mother gave me an online makeover. I'm now 'Zippy the Turtle.'" Shaking his cute little head, he added, "I was a dignified reptile for more than a hundred million years, but now they've turned me into a cartoon."

"Why'd they do that?"

"It's my new avatar for *atarkya.com*'s website. I suppose *this* was the best they could come up with."

"How'd you get into the computer here?"

"This hospital's record-keeping programs run on *atarkya.com* software. Since I'm stuck in the system, I can go anywhere *atarkya.com* goes."

"Cool."

Without another word, the turtle's appearance morphed into a more recognizable form. It was the same face Alex had seen on the cave wall in South

America. "That's better," Chelonius sighed, "Ketoo can't keep me looking like some freak from a *manga* series all the time!" After a chuckle, his face became serious. "Now Alex," he said in a low voice, "Tell me—do you remember what microbots are?"

"They're the devices that keep the Survivors healthy, right?"

Chelonius nodded. "Ketoo thinks he has a design that'll work in mammals."

"Wow! I guess a lot of people will want to keep their dogs and cats alive forever . . . Maybe even hamsters."

Both Chelonius and Talitha burst into laughter at Alex's comment before Chelonius explained, "You're a mammal, too, my friend! These microbots are for *you*."

"For me?"

"Yes."

"And they'll fix me up—like they helped Bluey when he got hurt?"

"Only if you're willing to accept our rules."

"What do you mean?"

While Talitha crept up Alex's IV tube in order to insert microbots directly into his bloodstream, Chelonius asked, "Are you angry with the boys who did this to you?"

"Well, yeah," Alex replied. "Shouldn't I be?"

"To be angry is natural, Alex. It's a very primitive emotion—a throwback to the time when we were *all* savage animals. Since these microbots will give you incredible power, you must learn to control these darker emotions. You can *never* take revenge on Billy DeGrace for what he did to you."

"Why not?"

"People always forget that revenge usually ends up causing more problems than it's worth."

"How so?"

"No matter how much you feel he may deserve to be punished, you'll eventually feel guilty for harming another human being. Not to mention legal problems you'll have if they catch you."

I doubt I'd feel bad about teaching that jerk a lesson, but I sure don't want to get in trouble with the police, Alex thought before asking, "Well, what should I do?"

"Learn from this incident, my friend, and vow to *never* act like those bullies. In time, you may even try to *forgive* those boys."

Alex realized the time and energy he'd use in a quest for revenge would be better spent doing something else. *And besides, was Billy really worth all that attention anyway?* Nodding his head, Alex said, "All right, I'll do my best to control my feelings."

Chelonius smiled. "Then we'll make you as mighty as Commander Trod . . . and maybe even more so!"

"Really?"

"Just wait and see what those microbots can do."

With that, Chelonius morphed back into his goofy caricature, bid farewell, and disappeared from the screen. Turning invisible and heading for the door, Talitha also said goodbye. Unbeknownst to Alex, completed microbots had already been pumping through his body for several minutes. It wasn't long before Alex began to sense their power.

CHAPTER 22

Moving Day

Though the doctors couldn't explain his recovery, Alex walked out of St. Theresa's Hospital two days after he awoke from his coma. No more broken arm, ruptured spleen, or bruised kidneys. Everything healed without a scar—even the deep cuts on his face. Alex said he felt like a million dollars . . . maybe even a billion. With a body that now worked better than new, Alex vowed to use his powers for good. Still, it *was* entertaining to think what he'd do if he ever met up with Billy again (even though Alex knew his attackers were off limits—something for which they should've been *very* thankful).

Mom returned to work at *atarkya.com* a day later and was surprised to learn Sikandar Tendulkar had bought her a farm in the country. Alex and Katherine were overjoyed by the news, especially when they were told *Tío* Ramiro would be coming to live with them. Of course, Alex had some serious explaining to do when it came to what *Tío* Ramiro was bringing with him. In the month since hatching, Yin and Rahona were now the size of human toddlers.

While movers took everyone's belongings from Uncle Roy's house, Alex and Katherine lounged in the basement with Jean, Marie, and Ghet—all of whom were fascinated by Alex's microbot stories. Besides his ability to heal from any injury in a matter of minutes, Alex had become both quick and incredibly strong. On the outside, though, he still looked the same—scrawny and a little on the small side. The only difference was his hair, which had been clipped short in the hospital.

After Alex explained how he could throw a football in a perfect spiral for more than a hundred yards, he recounted news he'd heard from Bluey about the Wounding Teeth in South America. Put mildly, things weren't going well. Alex summarized the Survivors' growing worry with a warning. "Fighting might break out among the Diapsids if they don't find some way of keeping their aggression under control."

Jean tried to lean forward on the bean bag where he sat, but his six-foot, five-inch height made him look like some sort of uncoordinated spider while struggling to bring his head up to speak. "Didn't you say that dinosaur park is in the state of *Bahia*?" he finally asked.

"Yeah," Alex replied. "That's where Ketoo said it was."

"Well, why don't y'all teach those warriors *capoeira*?"

"What the heck is that?" Katherine blurted.

"It's a Brazilian martial art that comes from African traditions," Jean explained. "I'll bet y'all didn't know there's more black people in Brazil than in the United States."

A look of surprise on her face, Marie asked, "Where do you learn this stuff, Jean?"

"You know those times when I sneak out of the house?"

Marie crossed her arms. "When you make Mom and Dad worried out of their minds?"

"Yeah," Jean smiled with a look of mischief, as if he actually enjoyed giving his parents the extra stress. "Where do you think I go?"

"I always thought you were in a gang or something . . ."

"Nah—not any more, at least," Jean replied, shaking his head. "Nowadays I go to the African Diaspora Center in north Philly. They got great programs most nights, including *capoeira* lessons."

"How come you never told Mom and Dad about this?"

"Somethin' just drives me to keep secrets from 'em," Jean shrugged. "Maybe it's hormones . . ."

Eager to learn how he could help the Wounding Teeth, Alex interrupted, "I liked your idea about that Brazilian . . . um . . . fighting thing. What's it called?"

"*Capoeira*," Jean replied. "It's like a dance for tough guys."

Ghet's watched beeped before anyone could speak again. "Dang!" he shouted, "It's my turn to watch the baby. I gotta go." After smoothing back tussles of reddish-blonde hair, Ghet pushed up his sleeve and removed a band-aid from inside his elbow joint.

"Ewww . . ." Katherine whined.

"You can come over next time I stick myself!" Ghet joked, tossing the bandage into a nearby trashcan.

"Maybe Ketoo can get you some microbots," Alex suggested. "They could probably cure your bleeding problems."

Ghet shook his head. "Thanks, but no thanks," he said. "My mom's always on my case about needles. What would she do if I didn't need them anymore?"

"Just a suggestion," Alex replied.

Bidding everyone farewell, Ghet headed for the basement doors.

"Take it easy, Ghetto!" Jean shouted as Ghet darted into the fresh, springtime air.

Turning back to Alex, Marie asked, "How big are the hatchlings?"

"They're all the size of a turkey . . . maybe bigger," Alex answered, pulling out his cell phone to show the latest pictures *Tío* Ramiro had sent from Texas.

"Four turkeys are gonna save the world?" Jean laughed. "I gotta see that!"

* * *

New Nottingham, Alex and Katherine's new hometown, was beautiful. The air was clean, the forests were clean . . . even the dirt seemed cleaner than Uncle Roy's home in Philadelphia. On the farm itself, one hundred acres of cornfields, pasture, meadows, and wooded retreats awaited exploration. On the day that they arrived, Alex and Katherine set out to see what they could find and didn't return home until after dark. *Now that Billy's far away, we can finally enjoy the woods again!*

Alex told Mom about his secret life the day after they moved, then *Tío* Ramiro and his two adopted "children" came to New Nottingham in Alex's spaceship a few days later. Mom was speechless upon meeting the juvenile dinosaurs, but warmed up when she learned that Yin and Rahona weren't too different from ordinary children. Of course they couldn't go to school like Katherine and Alex, who were forced to begin classes at Rolling Hills K-8 School in early May.

On his first day, Alex took a seat in his new classroom next to a pretty girl with light brown hair and sparkling blue eyes.

"Hi," she said with a smile, "what's your name?"

"I'm Alex . . . Alex Hidalgo," he stuttered. Despite his nervousness, Alex tried to pronounce his last name correctly. True to Spanish intonation, he didn't make any sound for the "h." It sounded like, "*EE*-dal-go."

The girl wrinkled her nose. "Where's *that* last name from?"

"Mexico, I guess."

"Oh really?" the girl squealed. "My babysitter's Spanish, too!"

"She's from Spain?"

"No," the girl responded, rolling her eyes, "I think she's from Guatemala."

"Then that would make her *Guatemalan*, wouldn't it?"

"Whatever," the girl snapped, tugging and twisting her long hair. "So what does your dad do? Is he like . . . a landscaper or something?"

Alex sighed and ran a hand over his closely cropped hair. "All Mexicans aren't landscapers, you know. They can be doctors, lawyers, university professors . . . all sorts of things."

"Hmmm . . ." the girl mumbled, though she didn't seem to be paying attention. She was instead waving at a clique of friends who'd come in through the door. Loud conversation erupted among them shortly thereafter, leaving Alex to his own thoughts until the late bell rang.

Sitting back, Alex decided he wasn't going to let the blue-eyed girl's snub bother him. He had new confidence in his abilities and didn't feel the need to seek other kids' approval. *Soon I'll be more powerful than any of them can possibly imagine!*

CHAPTER 23

Roda Capoeira

A hum resonated through the humid air of the Sikandar Tendulkar Nature Preserve one afternoon in late May, startling a flock of ostrich-like *Gallimimus*. Darting off at speeds exceeding forty miles per hour, their squawks soon mingled with distant sounds of buzzing insects and croaking toads. Five humans then stepped from their invisible Drifters and approached a gathering of Wounding Tooth warriors.

Armor clanking as he strode across the field, Commander Trod stretched out his clawed fingers to shake hands with the new arrivals. Alex was greeted first, followed by Katherine, Marie, Ghet, and Jean.

"We meet again," Trod growled upon shaking Jean's hand.

"Um . . . yeah . . . um . . . I guess so," Jean replied.

"You remember me?"

Jean nervously chuckled, "Um . . . how could I forget?"

"Join us," the mighty commander implored, motioning towards a *capoeira* match with his muscular arms.

Following Trod to the gathering, Alex was astounded by the action before him. Two Wounding Tooth lieutenants were in the center of a dusty ring, flanked by warriors banging an array of instruments. A few held steel-stringed bows they struck with sharpened sticks, producing a distinctive *twang*. Several others beat on cowhide drums. Still others shook rattles that appeared to be made from dinosaur teeth. The two lieutenants in the middle of the circle slid their feet across the dirt in a rhythm that matched the musicians' beat perfectly.

Jean gasped when three heavy claws clamped down on the back of his neck.

"I'm told we should thank you for introducing us to *capoeira*," Commander Trod growled into his ear.

"Uh . . . yeah," Jean stammered, keeping his eyes fixed on the action. "I thought of it."

Sharp teeth only inches from Jean's face, Trod snarled, "The Survivors also tell me you know some moves."

"I know a few."

Commander Trod released Jean's neck and bellowed, "Halt!" When the music stopped and the lieutenants in the ring ceased their combat, he rose to his full height and announced, "Lieutenant Tarik, I want to see your skills against a human—the one they call Jean Diop."

All eyes turned to the tall, dark-skinned boy in the rear of the crowd. Jean flashed a timid smile and shrugged, "All right, then . . . Just don't hurt me."

Jean moved into the ring and shook hands with his opponent before crouching into the starting stance. When Diapsids in the musical ensemble began playing their instruments, he started shifting his weight from one foot to the other in circular steps that kicked dust behind. Bows with steel strings twanged, drums thumped, and rattles clicked. *Twang, twang, thump, click. Twang, twang, thump, click.*

"I'll let you take the lead, *mestre*," Jean shouted to Lieutenant Tarik over the commotion, *mestre* being the Portuguese term for "teacher."

Without hesitation, Tarik flipped onto his hands and swung his legs around in a great circle. Jean feigned back and twisted downwards, nearly losing his head as Tarik's claws passed within inches of his neck. The lieutenant landed on his feet in perfect form and shifted his momentum into a roundhouse kick clear over Jean's head. Though Jean kept his feet moving to the beat, it was clear Tarik's agility had unnerved him.

Lieutenant Tarik crossed the entire circle in two cartwheel leaps, clawed feet and tail flipping over his body both times. In an attempt to save face, Jean tried swinging a leg under the lieutenant during his second vault. Unfortunately, Tarik saw the move at mid-flip and thumped his snout into Jean's chest. Flying backward across the circle, Jean hit the ground hard. His struggle to breathe sent Marie and Katherine rushing to his side for help.

"Cheap shot!" Alex yelled from the back once it was clear Jean had the wind knocked out of him.

Tarik stood straight and scanned the crowd with a wicked grin. "I forgot how weak humans are. Even the largest is *nothing* compared to a Wounding Tooth!"

Convinced it was time to teach these intergalactic know-it-alls a lesson, Alex remembered what Chelonius had told him about the microbots. "Some of us might be more powerful than you think," he boasted with a self-confidence he'd never felt before.

Lieutenant Tarik bared his pointed teeth. "Is this a challenge, monkey-boy?"

"Monkey-boy?"

"I see no difference between you and those fruit-eaters in the trees," Tarik scoffed, pointing towards a group of spider monkeys lounging in the nearby forest.

Second-guessing whether his microbots would give him the strength necessary to take on such a fearsome warrior, Alex attempted to back down from the challenge by saying, "The only problem is that I don't know any *capoeira* moves."

Tarik's throat rumbled. "Not a problem," he snarled. "We can test your skills with the pound-stick."

"Pound-stick?"

Strutting over to a pile of timbers several yards from the *capoeira* circle, Commander Trod lifted a pair of wooden staffs and thumped them on the ground. Each one measured eight feet in length and five inches in thickness. Without concern for anyone's safety, Trod carelessly tossed one of the poles in Alex's direction. Microbots inside his muscles reacted to grab the heavy staff, which looked as if it had been cut from the trunk of a small tree. Wood inside was green and damp, making the pole flexible and strong.

"That's a pound-stick," Lieutenant Tarik hissed. Turning to his superior officer, he asked, "Commander, where is my weapon?"

Trod marched forward with a pound-stick in his claws. "No, lieutenant," he growled. "I will take *this* monkey boy myself."

Alex clutched his pole with white knuckles, his heart pounding and breathing strained. Without microbots keeping watch over his body functions, he'd surely have had an asthma attack by now.

Commander Trod strutted into the circle and the drums began thumping again. Chanting resumed among the crowd, but the language was different. Wounding Teeth in the throng had switched to their own manner of speaking. The blood ritual about to commence was a Diapsid invention.

"No, Alex!" Katherine shouted. "He'll kill you!"

Stepping away from the action, Lieutenant Tarik turned to her and said, "We don't fight pound-stick to the death. The game is over when one of the contenders is knocked onto his back."

"Quick, Alex!" she screamed again, "Lie down on your back!"

Alex shook his head and stared at his opponent with calculating eyes. "Is that the goal, commander? Are we supposed to hit each other until one of us falls?"

"Ketoo said you're wise for a monkey boy," Commander Trod replied. "The game will be over when you fall," he added while taking his first swing.

Microbots had sharpened Alex's senses to the point that he could almost see things before they happened. He saw the commander's first swing as if it were in slow motion and used his own staff to slap Trod's weapon away. A loud *crack* from the impact sent most spectators several steps backwards.

Commander Trod's next move was a leg sweep and simultaneous swipe at Alex's head with the pound-stick. Surprisingly, Alex managed to dive between both attacks and catch the commander with a thump on the back. Trod winced in pain.

"Not bad for a monkey boy, huh?" Alex shouted.

Commander Trod flashed a sinister smile and grabbed his pound-stick with both hands. He swung it from left to right, forcing Alex backwards. The commander then repeated the move several more times, driving his rival out of the combat circle. While dust swirled in the fading twilight, Alex darted back and forth to avoid being clobbered by Trod's staff. Just as he was about to be pushed out of the ring, Alex crouched low and vaulted over the mighty warrior's head. Soaring twelve feet above the ground and swinging hard with his pound-stick, he struck Trod's head with a mighty *clang*. The wooden staff bounced off the commander's four-horned helmet, nearly knocking it from his head.

Apparently frustrated at his inability to land a single strike on his human rival, Commander Trod turned and growled. His orange eyes appeared to glow red in the last rays of the setting sun. After a moment to recover from the blow to his head, he roared and lunged at Alex with every ounce of force his seven hundred pound body could carry.

I can't believe I'm doing this, Alex thought when he saw Trod's charge. Without time to plan his next move, Alex sprinted directly towards the commander. Trod raised his staff and brought it down forcefully while Alex leaped and used both hands to push his own pound-stick upward. The impact split the commander's pole in two. Sharp splinters flew from the broken ends. Before Commander Trod could react, Alex lunged forward and pushed his shoulder into Trod's midsection. Momentum from the attack sent the commander flipping over Alex's hunched body, sending him to the ground with a heavy thump of falling armor and flesh. Prostrate on his back, Commander Trod grunted from the shock and pain of his defeat. Chanting from the sidelines stopped. It was the first time the gathered warriors had *ever* seen their leader fall in combat.

Wiping dust and splinters from his sweaty arms, Alex stood over the commander and asked, "Ever hear the story of David and Goliath?"

With a look of humiliation on his face, Commander Trod pursed his scaly lips and shook his head.

In the crowd, Jean stood and shouted, "You just got schooled by a monkey boy!"

The Survivors were the first to laugh, followed by the children and a few of the Wounding Teeth. Even Commander Trod managed a toothy smile when Alex helped him back to his feet.

"We will not underestimate you again, Alex Hidalgo," the commander grunted, thumping his chest in salute and conceding his victory.

A chant began among the crowd. Even the Diapsids were saying, "Hidalgo ... Hidalgo ... Hidalgo." Katherine ran over to her brother and gave him a big hug.

Later that evening, the five humans gathered around a campfire with Tupi, Bity, Ketoo, and Talitha. Yin, Rahona, and the two other members of the "Zeus Crew" were sleeping on a bed of grass close by. While the friends chatted about their lives, Commander Trod and his three most trusted lieutenants sat down on a cluster of large stones flickering in the fire's glow. "Congratulations again," Trod said in Alex's direction. In the orange light of the campfire, his face looked more sinister than ever.

Lieutenant Tarik's gaze fixed on Jean. "Are you injured?" he asked.

"Nah, man, I'm cool."

"You know you could've killed him," Marie scolded.

Teeth flashing in the firelight, Tarik pointed to the sharp horns on his helmet and snarled, "If I wanted to kill him, I would have used *these*."

After a quick glance to make sure Euplos and Stygi—his adopted dinosaur hatchlings—were sleeping safely, Ketoo cleared his throat and announced, "I think I've found a way to overhaul the engines on your invasion discs, commander."

"Will they get us back to Jupiter?"

"I think so."

"And what about the weapons systems?"

Ketoo leaned forward and said, "Remember your goal is to get back onto your mothership, *not* to destroy the Swift Runners."

Commander Trod shook his head. "We can't get back on that destroyer without a fight."

"If you're planning to kill Swift Runners, I won't help you."

All that followed was tense silence.

In an apparent attempt to make friends with Lieutenant Tarik, Jean turned to him and asked, "What you doin' with an Arabic name? I thought y'all was from another planet."

The lieutenant straightened himself and answered, "I took my name from a human conqueror."

"You talkin' about General Tariq ibn-Ziyad from North Africa?"

"That's the one."

"Who's that?" Marie interrupted.

With pride in his voice, Jean answered, "General Tariq led a force of African soldiers across the Strait of Gibraltar in the year 711 and conquered most of Spain."

Lieutenant Tarik explained, "We thought taking names from your greatest conquerors would command respect among humans."

Jean pointed to Lieutenant Genghis next. "I'll bet you took your name from Genghis Khan!"

The muscular Wounding Tooth lieutenant nodded his head once in reply.

"How'd you know that?" Marie gasped.

"Genghis Khan was one of the greatest conquerors of all time!" Turning to Lieutenant Cyrus, Jean asked, "Where'd you get your name from?"

"It comes from Cyrus the Great," the Diapsid boasted. "He was a Persian emperor who lived 2,500 years ago."

"Why did you pick a guy from *that* long ago?" Ghet chuckled.

"My duty was going to be overseeing the Middle East," Lieutenant Cyrus sighed. "There weren't many other conquerors who both the Israelis *and* Iranians would like."

"Where'd y'all learn this history?" Jean asked.

Commander Trod replied, "Legion Destroyer 3176 picked up a satellite feed from *The History Channel* shortly after we arrived in your solar system."

"Y'all watched TV up there?"

"That's how we learned your languages. We were going to have to talk to humans sooner or later, even if we hadn't gotten captured."

Voice trembling and seemingly fearful to speak up in the presence of such monsters, Katherine nevertheless asked, "What were you gonna do with us if you didn't get captured?"

Commander Trod scanned the gathered beings with his orange eyes before grumbling, "It would be better not to discuss such matters."

"You were gonna *kill* people, weren't you?"

Trod didn't reply.

"Well, what are you gonna do now?" Alex asked, hoping the Wounding Teeth had changed their minds about destroying human civilization.

"We don't know, Alexander the Great," Trod replied with a slight smile. "Humans aren't as worthless as we once thought."

"Hey!" Ghet exclaimed, "Alexander was a conqueror, too!"

"One of the best."

"Wow," Alex muttered.

"Maybe you'll follow in his footsteps," Trod hissed.

"What did he do?"

"He killed thousands of people and enslaved many more."

"That's why he's a hero?"

"In my culture," Commander Trod explained, "a Diapsid's honor is measured by his kills in battle."

"How many have *you* had?" Katherine gasped.

"In war, I've had two hundred nineteen thousand, eight hundred and twenty one," Trod boasted. "Plus quite a few in the Battle Dome."

Alex was horrified by Commander Trod's comments. He wanted to be a hero, but the thought of killing others made him shudder. *There must be another way.*

Seconds later, a thin smile cracked across Ketoo's scaly lips. "Commander, let's leave this talk of war and death behind us, shall we? Why don't you instead tell everyone how you got names for ranks in the Diapsid Military Forces?"

"That's what I meant to ask you!" Ghet blurted. "My dad was in the Navy for a couple of years, so how come all your titles are Navy ranks?"

Commander Trod scratched the thick scales on his shoulder and shifted a strap on his body armor. "Our Diapsid Clans have been receiving television signals from your planet for many years," he began. "The closest Scipion listening posts to your solar system are positioned forty light years away from Earth."

"That means they're currently receiving television programs from forty years ago," Ketoo explained.

Trod resumed his story. "We were bored by most of your transmissions, but one caught our attention. It was a television program about a group of humans who traveled through the galaxy on a five-year exploration mission."

"Sounds like you were watching *Star Trek*," Ghet chuckled.

"That's right," Trod snarled defensively, baring his teeth and glowering in Ghet's direction.

His face flushing red in response to Trod's anger, Ghet stammered, "Oh . . . I . . . um . . . I-I-I like that show."

"So do we," Commander Trod grunted. "And we changed our military organization to honor that TV program. That's where the terms admiral, captain, commander, and lieutenant came from."

Ghet looked at Ketoo and whispered, "These mighty warriors are a bunch of *trekkies?*"

"*Trekkies* who could crush you in an instant," Commander Trod warned.

CHAPTER 24

Chinatown Mischief

When summertime rolled around, Yin and Rahona had caught up to Katherine in size. They'd also become extremely smart, gaining most of their knowledge from educational software on *atarkya.com*. By July, both had mastered college-level astrophysics, calculus, and spoke several languages. Alex wished he could learn as fast as they, but he hadn't been engineered to reach adult size in six months.

Mom was delighted to have two more children in the house, even if they weren't human. She was so happy, in fact, that she began planning family outings with them once Ketoo felt they were old enough. Though Mom interacted with the leopard gecko on a daily basis at the farm, she still hadn't figured out that Ketoo and Sikandar Tendulkar were one and the same. No one let her in on the big secret, either. It was too fun to keep her guessing.

As soon as Ketoo gave the green light, Mom discussed with Katherine the possibility of taking Rahona to the mall for a "Girls' Day Out." In a similar vein, Alex and *Tío* Ramiro made plans to take Yin to Philadelphia's Chinatown so he could practice the languages he'd been learning. Before long, all six developed a plan to dress each dinosaur in long pants, sweatshirt, gloves, shoes, a hat, scarf, and ski goggles. They'd look strange walking around in the midsummer heat, but the disguises would guarantee that the true forms of their bodies would be protected from even the sharpest eyes.

And so it was one day that *Tío* Ramiro and Alex boarded a train to downtown Philadelphia with a companion who appeared to be a boy nine years of age. Yin held the hand of each of his caretakers while skipping along, his tail hidden under a black cape from Alex's old Halloween costume. Muffled questions about city life poured from Yin's scarf-covered beak, sometimes in such a rapid sequence that Alex and his *tío* couldn't answer them all.

Unloading at Market East Station in central Philadelphia, Yin clutched *Tío* Ramiro's arm while the trio navigated among throngs of people rushing to work. Alex kept his hands firmly on top of Yin's bony head to make sure the dinosaur's hat wouldn't come off while searching for an exit. Endless conversations shouted through cell phones and earpieces added to the confusion.

Air outside was hot and humid when *Tío* Ramiro, Yin, and Alex finally opened a pair of doors at street level. They walked past two noisy bus stations and continued west. After a few blocks, signs in storefronts switched languages.

"What's that sign say?" Alex asked Yin upon spotting a sign written entirely in Chinese.

Peering through his dark goggles, Yin translated the store's name within seconds. "It says 'Happy Fun Pretty Photograph.'"

Tío Ramiro pointed to a restaurant with fish tanks in the front lobby. Crabs, eels, pink fish, and frogs could be seen inside. Another restaurant had more than a dozen roasted ducks hanging by their necks. "You hungry?" he asked the two, patting his stomach. One thing Alex loved about his *tío* was that he always seemed to find the best food wherever he went.

True to character, Yin nodded his head enthusiastically. The little dinosaur *never* passed up a chance to eat.

Alex scanned the colorful signs jutting from soot-stained buildings on both sides of the street. Spotting one that read "All You Can Eat Buffet," he tapped his uncle on the shoulder and shouted over the city's rumble, "That's the one we need!"

All three entered the restaurant and took a table in the back corner. Yin sat with his back to the other customers so they wouldn't see his face while he ate. Twenty heaping plates of food and eleven trips to the bathroom later, the manager rushed over to the table and said they'd have to leave. The "All You Can Eat" motto didn't seem to apply to those with *monstrous* appetites. Fortunately, Alex was able to cover Yin's face before the manager realized the biggest eater among them wasn't human.

Back on the sidewalk—cracked and pocked with old gum—Yin shouted, "That looks like me!" and pointed towards a poster on the other side of the street. It showed a green, dragon-like creature in an advertisement for a new video game. Yin looked up at *Tío* Ramiro and asked with a voice full of confusion, "Is that a dinosaur or a dragon?"

Tío Ramiro shrugged his shoulders. "We can go inside to ask, but you'll have to ask the questions *in Chinese*."

The trio crossed the busy street and entered the store. Once inside, a strong scent of incense burned everyone's nostrils. Yin lurched forward and sneezed, nearly losing his scarf in the process. Alex then bent down to Yin's ear and whispered, "You probably need to learn more about Chinese culture, so ask the man behind the counter if he has any good movies." Truth was, all Alex knew about Yin's homeland was General Tso's chicken and *Kung Fu Theater* on television every Sunday.

Shaking his head vigorously inside of his baseball cap, Yin whispered, "I can't . . . I'm too shy."

Alex kneeled beside his green "brother" and patted him on the shoulder. "Soon you'll have problems way bigger than talking to a nice man in a video store, Yin. What if you're called to an emergency meeting with the President of China someday? And how will you negotiate peace with the Diapsid Military Forces if you're too scared to speak up?"

Yin looked at the ground and gave the carpet a kick. "All right," he sighed. "I'll do it."

Alex smiled and encouraged Yin to step forward. "Go ahead, big guy," he said, pushing the nervous dinosaur towards the counter. Once they had the man's attention, Alex said, "Excuse me, do you speak Chinese?"

The man nodded and answered in accented English, "I speak Cantonese. That one kind of Chinese. And Mandarin, too."

"Great!" Alex responded. "My little brother speaks Mandarin *and* Cantonese. He has a question for you."

The man pulled his head back and looked at the figure dressed in heavy clothing. "Why he all wrapped up?"

Alex fumbled for a moment as he tried to think of a believable answer. "He . . . um . . . was adopted, and . . . uh . . . has a skin disease that . . . um . . . means he can't be in the light."

The man nodded cautiously, then asked Yin a simple question in Cantonese. Yin responded in a soft voice at first, but their conversation quickly became much louder. After five minutes of talking, the owner began walking around the store with Yin following close behind. A pile of DVDs, books, and magazines started to grow next to the cash register. The man returned to his place behind the counter and smiled broadly when *Tío* Ramiro pulled out his wallet to pay for everything.

His arms loaded with plastic bags full of merchandise, Yin bid farewell and bowed respectfully to his new human friend.

Returning the gesture, the store owner exclaimed, "Take care, Moon Dragon!"

Alex felt a flush of fear and nearly dropped the bags he was carrying. *Just what had Yin told that guy?* Before he could find out what Yin had said, however, the man behind the counter chuckled, "That boy has good imagination!"

"Yeah," Alex responded, "He likes to make up stories."

"But I told him the truth," Yin insisted.

Alex looked nervously at the man behind the counter and shook his head with a sigh before guiding Yin through the door and returning to the busy sidewalk.

Once outside, Alex scolded his adopted brother. "Yin, you can't go blabbering about where you came from. It's gotta stay a secret."

"Why?"

"Because people wouldn't understand. It'd blow our cover and ruin the whole operation."

"What whole operation?"

"The one the Survivors and Wounding Teeth are developing."

"The one where we're gonna fight the bad guys in space?"

Alex glanced all around, hoping no one heard Yin's last comment. "That's what I'm talking about," he huffed, "We can't talk about these things in public."

"Keeping it a secret will be better?"

"Exactly."

After an uneventful train trip back to New Nottingham and a short ride to the farm in *Tío* Ramiro's pickup truck, Yin ripped off of his clothes and stripped down to Alex's hand-me-down underwear. He then proceeded to beg for permission to watch the first movie they'd bought in Chinatown. When *Tío* Ramiro finally nodded his approval, Yin sprinted across the backyard to get Rahona. She was in the barn, changing into clothes Mom and Katherine had bought at the mall.

Alex bit his lip when he saw Rahona charge out of the red and white building and run towards the house. The purple-feathered dinosaur was wearing gaudy clip-on earrings, a glittering pink bathing suit top, and a yellow skirt. *That's the weirdest thing I've ever seen!* Still, Alex tried to keep a straight face until she darted past him. Flapping her arms, Rahona leaped high onto the deck and charged into the house.

Before they knew it, speakers on the living room entertainment center were blasting the movie's opening music. "Turn that racket down, Yin!" Alex's mother shouted from the wooden deck behind the house. The volume went down a few decibels, but it still rattled the walls. "Kids these days . . . or dinosaurs . . . whatever," she grumbled, shaking her head.

Alex, Mom, *Tío* Ramiro, and Katherine all took seats on the wooden deck and recounted the day's activities. They talked for nearly an hour and a half before the sound of a terrible crash interrupted their conversation. Everyone half-stood in their chairs, trying to figure out what happened and what to do next. *It sounded like a wrecking ball went through the side of the house!* Alex was nervous someone might have fired a shot at his home. *Were Swift Runners attacking?*

Rahona's shrieks could be heard once the sounds of breaking glass stopped. Concluding that their dinosaur siblings might be in danger, Alex grabbed Katherine and ran to the side of the house. Grass there was littered with glass shards, sheets of drywall, and wooden splinters. Rahona lay on the lawn, appearing to be dead. Yin was watching her and laughing through a five-foot hole in the side of the house.

"What happened?" Katherine screamed.

Yin's eyes opened wide when he seemed to realize he'd done something wrong. Rahona propped herself on her elbows and nervously picked at an earring. Up above, Alex's mother screamed when she saw how the living room had been destroyed. Startled by the outburst, Yin leaped through the hole and landed on the grass next to the house.

"Yin," Alex said in his calmest voice possible, "could you tell me what happened?"

The green dinosaur looked at the ground, adjusted his underwear, and mumbled, "It's better to keep it a secret, like the other stuff you don't want me talking about."

"No, Yin, this is different. You've gotta tell me."

Having caught the gift of gab from her adopted sister Katherine, Rahona spoke next. "We were playing . . . just like we saw in the movie."

Alex crossed his arms and looked at Yin. "What's the name of that movie? I thought it was going to teach you Chinese culture."

His gaze still fixed on the grass, Yin replied, "It's called *Kung Fu Masters of the Dragon Fist*."

When *Tío* Ramiro hobbled around the side of the house, Alex turned to him and sighed, "That guy in Chinatown sold us a bunch of kung-fu movies."

"I told him that's what I wanted," Yin admitted.

"But how'd that hole get in the house?" *Tío* Ramiro asked.

Yin rubbed the bony ridges that went around the back of his head while mumbling, "I kicked Rahona through the wall. She was pretending to be the evil warlord and I was the hero. That's why I needed to kill her."

"Why?" Alex snapped.

"Well, heroes should kill the bad guys, right?"

Unsure of what to say, Alex looked to *Tío* Ramiro for advice. The old man shrugged his shoulders and said, "I guess he's got a point."

Alex's eyes opened wide in disbelief. "Are you *serious*?"

"I guess so . . . why?"

Alex gazed skyward for a moment, searching for inspiration. He recalled Commander Trod's boasts of more than 200,000 kills in battle and the uncomfortable feelings that came when Trod suggested he could do the same. "I don't think Yin and Rahona should think that way," he finally said.

"Think what way?" Rahona blurted.

"I just don't like the idea of killing all the bad guys, and I'm pretty sure Ketoo and the other Survivors don't like it either . . ."

"But don't the Survivors want us to fight?" Yin asked.

Running a hand over his closely-cropped hair, Alex said, "I don't know what to tell you, Yin. All I can say is that we shouldn't see things the way Commander Trod does."

"Why not?"

"Well, Commander Trod's probably about as bad as they come, and the Survivors didn't kill him . . . Maybe there's another way to be a hero."

The look on Yin's face was one of confusion. "What way?"

Is Yin catching up to me already? Alex asked himself. It was the same question he'd been pondering recently. *Time's going too fast—pretty soon Yin's gonna be a grownup.* Realizing this might be the last time Yin would look up to him, Alex said, "Maybe a hero can start by saying he's sorry when he does something wrong . . ."

"Sorry, *Ale*," Yin replied. In the moments that had passed, his voice had become deeper and more mature.

"It's not *me* you need to apologize to," Alex scolded. "Mom has a mess up there and you kicked your sister through a wall."

"I'm okay, though," Rahona piped in.

Glancing down at the grass, Yin mumbled "I'm sorry" to Rahona and then shouted his apology to Mom through the gaping hole in the wall. Microbots inside Rahona's body had healed her injuries in little more than five minutes, so she flapped her wings and returned indoors to help clean the living room. Alex was curious to see if his own microbots would protect him as well as they did Rahona, but he didn't want to get kicked through a wall to find out. While helping clean the mess, Alex wondered how he could teach Yin and Rahona to be a different sort of hero . . . if such a thing actually existed.

CHAPTER 25

Swim Lesson

A few days later, Ghet O'Malley stood on an empty parking lot in a threadbare tee shirt and shorts. The July heat was brutal, but he didn't mind. Commander Trod and his three most trusted lieutenants were determined to learn a new skill that very evening, and Ghet volunteered to help. Wrapped inside of his towel were the keys his father used to enter the community pool. He'd stolen them in order to teach the Diapsids how to swim.

In the skies above, stars were hard to see and humid air wrapped the night within a suffocating blanket. Since Ketoo had recently covered each Diapsid spacecraft with the same camouflaging skin as the Drifters, the arrival of Trod's invasion disc was signaled by nothing more than a rumble over the parking lot and scraping noises on the asphalt.

The main access ramp opened after the disc touched down and four muscular warriors trudged to where Ghet was standing. Sword-axes and body armor clanked while the Diapsids proceeded to follow him across the parking lot and up the steps to the pool entrance. Once Ghet jiggled the key into the lock, he turned to Commander Trod and said, "Um . . . you'd better remove that armor before you get into the water."

"Why?" Trod responded in a stern voice.

"You're gonna sink with all that metal on."

The Diapsids exchanged glances and grunted their disapproval, then became even more uneasy when Ghet added, "You guys should also leave those sword-axes outside."

"We must keep our weapons close," Commander Trod insisted.

Unsure of what Commander Trod would do if he didn't get his way, Ghet decided to compromise. "All right, you can bring them in," he sighed. "But you'll have to keep them in the corner."

Entering the darkened building and creeping cautiously onto the pool deck, the Wounding Teeth scanned the area for danger. Moonlight poured through windows overlooking the glassy water and the scent of chlorine was heavy in the air.

"It smells like the second planet of the Anzac system," Trod snorted. His lieutenants nodded in agreement.

Ghet just shook his head and whipped off his tee shirt. He had no idea what the commander was talking about, but he was curious to know more. *These guys must have hundreds of stories from all over the universe!* What interested Ghet even more at the moment, however, was why the Diapsids seemed so uneasy . . . *is something bothering them?*

Removing their armor piece by piece, the Diapsids undressed in the far corner of the pool deck. Pointing to Ghet's red and black bathing suit, Commander Trod snarled, "Do I need *that* in order to swim?"

Ghet chuckled, "I don't think that we have swimsuits to fit your kind, commander. You guys will be skinny dipping!"

The head of Lieutenant Genghis snapped up in surprise. With confusion in his deep voice, he asked, "What is skinny . . . dripping?"

"Skinny *dipping* means swimming without any clothes," Ghet explained. "You guys'll be swimming naked tonight!"

After a few remaining bits of armor clanged to the ground, the four unclothed Wounding Teeth clutched their sword axes and followed Ghet towards the shallow end of the pool.

"Remember, guys," Ghet reminded them, "you're supposed to leave your sword-axes in the corner."

Without warning, Lieutenant Genghis bellowed and fell backwards with a loud slap. The other warriors reacted immediately, crouching into defensive postures while they surveyed their surroundings. A metal pole holding a string of triangular blue and gold flags fell into the water. It had been sliced in two by the lieutenant's blade.

Checking the deck and noticing water spilled about, Ghet scolded, "You've gotta be careful, guys. That floor is *very* slippery." When he spotted the flag pole in the water, he pointed and whined, "Now what am I gonna do about *that*?"

"Leave it to me," Commander Trod assured. "I can fix it."

Lieutenant Genghis carefully returned to his feet and grumbled, "I hate water."

"Is that the problem?" Ghet dared to ask.

"What do you mean?" Trod grunted, his tone defensive.

"I noticed you guys are on edge. It's got something to do with the water, doesn't it?"

Commander Trod looked at his fellow Wounding Teeth in the dim light and admitted, "It makes us uneasy . . ."

"Water? You drink it, don't you?"

"We don't mind small amounts of water," Trod hissed. "But when the water's deep we get . . . scared."

This is crazy, Ghet thought. *A warrior who's fought battles across the universe is afraid of a swimming pool?* Choosing his words with great care, Ghet shrugged, "Well . . . it's not bad once you get used to it."

Neither Trod nor his lieutenants responded, instead keeping their eyes fixed straight ahead—as if they were about to enter a war zone.

By the time they'd reached the shallow end of the pool, all four Wounding Teeth were visibly uncomfortable. Lieutenant Tarik even began picking at his teeth with a curved thumb claw. Commander Trod pointed towards a pile of floating tubes and water noodles and asked, "Can those things keep us from sinking?"

"Yes, but only if you leave your sword-axes in the corner," Ghet responded firmly.

Once they'd placed their weapons on the pool deck, the mighty warriors trotted over to the pile of flotation equipment like little children.

"No running!" Ghet scolded. He had to catch himself before he added, "boys and girls."

It wasn't long before the four Diapsids began scuffling over floaties and inner tubes. "That's mine! Give it back!" one yelled. Commander Trod even asserted his authority as leader to yank a pink life preserver from Lieutenant Cyrus. Soon the reptilian conquerors had flower-print tubes around their bulging biceps and clutched clusters of swimming noodles their hands. Lieutenant Genghis struggled to strap a Styrofoam water bubble onto his back, but his chest was far too broad.

When everyone was ready to go, Ghet smirked to himself, *they look like the kids in my little sister's swim class!* He then asked everyone to step towards the edge of the pool.

The Diapsids shuffled timidly to the pool's edge. Ghet almost suggested they hold hands, but decided that might be going too far. "Why don't you all sit on the side and dip your feet in the water?" he proposed, trying his best to remember how swim instructors taught terrified children.

The four crouched down at the poolside with great care.

"I-I-Is it c-c-cold?" Lieutenant Tarik stuttered.

Ghet made a quick dive through the smooth surface and swam over to his nervous students. Standing chest-deep in the water, he reassured, "It's fine, guys."

Each Wounding Tooth touched the water with one claw, then two, and finally eased a foot into the water. Gripping onto the pool's edge with strength unmatched by humans, the warriors each lowered the other foot as well. No one was willing to descend further, however, no matter how hard Ghet tried.

Frustrated by their unwillingness to enter the pool, Ghet suggested, "How about we kick our feet a little?"

Though hesitant at first, the four warriors began swishing their feet through the dark water. Moments later, they were kicking so hard that water droplets reached the ceiling. Ghet was pretty sure Commander Trod flashed a smile once or twice, and Lieutenant Genghis even let out what seemed to be a chuckle. Everyone's demeanor changed, however, when Ghet asked, "Now, who's going to get in with me?"

As the highest-ranking Wounding Tooth, Commander Trod pulled back from the poolside and ordered Lieutenant Cyrus into the water. The battle-hardened Diapsid pulled his pink inner tubes high, slumped his shoulders, and shyly reached out to Ghet with his massive, three-clawed hands.

When his rump slipped from the tile, Lieutenant Cyrus pushed forward and clasped his bulging biceps over Ghet's face. After shrieking to release his grip and nearly losing his head in the process, Ghet managed to maneuver Cyrus into a floating position. "Try to blow some bubbles for me," he suggested.

Once Lieutenants Cyrus, Tarik, and Genghis had progressed through basic water skills, the time came for Commander Trod's lesson. Ghet tried to ease the cowering warrior into the water, but Trod bellowed, "Save me! I'm drowning!" as soon as his hands left the poolside.

Ghet struggled to stabilize his seven hundred pound student. "Hold still and put your feet down!" he shouted.

"I can't! I'll sink!"

Ducking his head underwater, Ghet shoved Trod forward with all of his strength. A second later, the commander's feet tilted downwards and touched the bottom. The pool was shallow enough for Trod to walk—his head cleared the surface by more than three feet.

Ghet's face broke through the surface and he took a deep breath. "How is it that you guys have never been in the water before?"

"We're land conquerors," Trod explained, his orange eyes peering downwards while stepping carefully along the bottom. "And our sagas say even our primitive ancestors avoided deep water."

"Sagas?"

"They're the legends of our beginnings, stretching to the time when our ancestors lived on Earth."

"Dinosaurs weren't into swimming, huh?"

"Certainly not."

After thirty minutes of watching the lieutenants whip each other with water noodles and try their best to dunk Commander Trod, Ghet called the warriors out of the pool and handed a pile of towels to each of them. Once he was no longer dripping, Trod wrapped an oversized towel around his waist and trotted across the parking lot to fetch his laser welder. The flag pole Lieutenant Genghis had slashed was repaired a few moments later.

As moonlight flooded through the windows and sparkled along the empty pool's surface, something caught Ghet's eye. Its shape looked familiar, so he walked along the deck for a closer look. Once he was a few feet away from the floating mass, his worst suspicions were confirmed.

"All right, guys," he griped, "who pooped in the pool?"

Trod, Tarik, and Cyrus immediately pointed at Genghis. Apparently ashamed, the lieutenant lowered his head.

With a sigh, Ghet walked over to the equipment corner and grabbed a small net attached to a long pole. He then walked over to the guilty Wounding Tooth and handed him the pool skimmer.

"Lieutenant Genghis," Ghet shouted in military fashion with his back perfectly straight. "Welcome to the wonderful world of pool cleanup!"

CHAPTER 26

The Big Test

In September, the new school year started much like any other—except that Ghet was in sixth grade, Marie in fourth, and Jean had moved on to high school. Billy DeGrace also slithered into ninth grade by earning D's on his report card, but he didn't stay in school for long. Events quickly forced him to flee school in a panic, never to return again.

One day in the middle of the month, Ghet was riding the school bus with two of his younger sisters. Zig-zag was in third grade and the third-youngest O'Malley, a redhead named Roller, was just starting kindergarten. On this particular occasion, Roller was sitting on an aisle seat with a spotted white horse in one hand and a dark-skinned doll in the other. Ghet and Zig-zag did their best to ignore the noise she was making.

Marie and Jean boarded the bus a few stops later. They took a seat directly behind Ghet and began an excited conversation among themselves—careful to speak in coded language to ensure Zig-zag and Roller couldn't understand.

"So," Jean whispered, patting Ghet on the shoulder, "The birds are gonna fly soon, right?"

Ghet nodded. "The spotted guy says the discs will be ready within a week. Trod's prepared. The guy with a Y and the girl with an R are fully grown, too."

"Really?" Marie squealed. "I can't wait to see them!"

"*Dag,*" Jean responded. "Seems like they hatched only yesterday."

Zig-zag looked at her brother with a wrinkled nose and stuck out her tongue. "I *hate* when you talk like that," she grumbled.

Brakes squeaked and everyone lurched forward when the bus pulled to its next stop. Billy and his friends thumped up the stairs and shoved towards their usual seats in the back. As the rowdy hooligans heaved along the aisle, Roller O'Malley dropped her favorite plastic horse on the ground.

"Oh no!" she screamed, reaching down to get it.

Roller lost her balance and fell at the same time Billy pushed his friends from behind. The kindergartener shrieked when a ninth-grader tripped over her and the others jostled around. One sound, however, rose above the other commotion—a *crunch* of splitting plastic. Billy had stepped on Roller's toy horse.

"What's that stupid thing doing there?" he shouted, kicking the pieces towards the back of the bus where his friends proceeded to crush them.

Roller's cries became unbearable as Zig-zag tried to help her little sister up from the floor. Full of rage and no longer able to restrain himself, Ghet forced his way out of his seat and shouted, "Hey, man! What's your problem?"

Jean also rose to his feet.

Billy turned towards Ghet with a face twisted in hatred. "You're talking to *me*?"

"Yeah, I'm talking to you! Why'd you break my sister's toy?"

"You wanna be the next thing that gets broken around here?" Billy snickered, cracking his knuckles.

Blinded by anger and ignoring the fact that his bleeding problems would cause terrible injuries if he got into a fight, Ghet stepped forward and said, "You don't do crap like that to people in *my* family!"

Right before the two came within swinging distance of each other, the bus driver stood up, pointed at Ghet and Jean, and shouted, "You two! Off the bus!"

"What?" Jean snapped. "We didn't do nothin'!"

"Off or I call the police!" was the reply.

"Better get going before I hurt you *worse* than your lizard lover friend," Billy scoffed.

Bodies trembling from the adrenaline rush, Ghet and Jean slinked from the bus with their sisters and started walking. Billy made threatening gestures through a cloud of diesel exhaust as they continued on their way.

"What am I gonna do *now*?" Ghet whined as the reality of what he'd done started to set in. "Billy's gonna get me . . . just like he got Alex."

"Don't worry, I got your back," Jean assured.

"But you can't protect me all the time!"

Marie smiled. "I'm going to call Katherine and see what Alex, Yin, and Rahona are doing this afternoon. They might be able to help . . ."

Jean coughed in the cloud of exhaust, pulled his saggy pants and inch higher, and mumbled, "Whatever, yo."

* * *

Seven hours later, a whistle of rushing air could be heard over Sweetbriar Park. It was soon joined by sounds from a second invisible spacecraft, and the two touched down on a barely-used playground in the woods where kids dared not venture. Billy and his fellow troublemakers had succeeded in driving most people from the park months ago. Right before the cargo bay doors opened to betray their presence, Alex went over the rules of engagement with his passengers.

"Remember, Yin," he explained, "our goal is to keep Ghet safe—*not* to take revenge on Billy."

"I understand," the deep-voiced warrior replied. Now fully grown, Yin was three hundred pounds of muscle and stood seven feet tall. Still a fan of kung-fu movies, he often wore custom-made silk outfits in the style of Bruce Lee and Jackie Chan.

Turning to the other passenger, Alex asked, "Did you follow what I said, Euplos?"

Euplos was a member of the "Zeus Crew" who'd been raised by the Survivors. He was tall and thick-bodied, standing over eight feet tall and weighing nearly a thousand pounds. Descended from a genetically-engineered *Ankylosaurus*, he had bony armor plating on his back, head, and eyelids. His principal weapons were a clubbed tail and two steel hammers Commander Trod had fashioned for him. With a face suggesting that his undersized brain was struggling with the instructions, Euplos grunted, "No hurt people?"

"As little as possible."

Inside the Princess Drifter, Katherine was going over the same plan with Rahona and Stygi. The purple-feathered dinosaur had reached adult size, as had the grey-scaled warrior who sat by her side.

"We need to make sure Big Billy never bothers anyone again," Katherine insisted. "But Alex doesn't want anyone getting hurt."

Rahona stretched out a long arm and glanced at her newly-painted claws. "You don't have to worry about us girls," she squawked with confidence. "We can handle it."

"We'll try our best," Stygi affirmed. Derived from a dinosaur known as a "bone head," she had slender limbs and a delicate build. Appearances could be deceiving, however, since Stygi was lightning fast and unbelievably strong. Since Ketoo had given her special attention, she was also incredibly smart.

Katherine cut her lecture short when she spotted Marie walking along the perimeter of the playground. The Princess Drifter's cargo bay doors opened and Katherine shouted, "Over here!"

The Free Bird's rear door opened seconds later. "So much for a quiet entrance," Alex mumbled while the two girls squealed and hugged each other. Turning to see four pairs of reptilian eyes waiting for his next order, Alex motioned for Yin, Euplos, Rahona, and Stygi to disembark from the Drifters and move to their hiding places. In a matter of seconds, they were gone.

Alex walked over to the girls and handed each of them a small package. "These are the latest video cameras from *atarkya.com*," he said with a smile.

Both girls unzipped the black cases and gasped when they saw the tiny cameras inside.

"How cute!" Marie exclaimed.

"Just point and press the button, right?" Katherine asked.

Alex nodded. "And remember there's only one chance to get everything on tape."

The trio jogged to Billy's stomping grounds and hid behind a large mound of dirt. It was the exact same spot that they'd found themselves ten months earlier—before their lives were forever changed by the Survivors. Things didn't look much different from that fateful November day when Alex saved Bluey, though it was a little warmer and leaves were still on the trees.

Even before climbing over the ridge to peer at the bike trail, Alex could feel Billy's presence. It made him feel worried and excited at the same time. Butterflies in his stomach competed with his determination to stop Billy's reign of terror and help a friend. *I just hope this plan works!*

When he crept higher, Alex saw five boys on their bikes arguing over candy, gum, and soda which they'd probably shoplifted from a nearby store. Billy was yelling all sorts of horrible insults at the others (and snatching the best loot for himself in the process).

Peering upwards, the biggest of the hooligans elbowed Billy and asked, "Isn't that the kid we clobbered last spring?"

"Holy crap ... it *is*," Bully said, taking his friend's soda in hand.

Alex strutted down the hill with a phony smile on his face. Katherine and Marie followed, video cameras in hand.

"I thought you already learned your lesson, wheat bread!" Billy sneered.

"You remember me?" Alex replied.

"Friggin' illegal alien."

Energy surging through his chest, Alex began to feel a confidence he'd never felt before. Billy seemed smaller, weaker ... less of a threat. *What was I so afraid of?* Then memories flashed of the day when Billy and his gang attacked. *Oh yeah ... that's why.* Struggling to keep his jitters under control, Alex stammered, "It-It's about time you learned a f-few things, Billy."

Billy threw his bike down and ran a hand through his hair. "*You* should've learned something when we beat the crap out of you."

Remember your lines and stay under control, Alex repeated in his mind, trying to recall the words he'd been rehearsing since the morning. "You go around making people scared," he began, "but no one really likes you. Once people stop being afraid, you'll be nothing. You hear me? Nothing!"

Billy took off his jacket and threw it on the ground. Cracking his knuckles while strutting towards Alex, he growled, "I guess I gotta show you why everyone's afraid of me all over again ..."

Alex pulled his video camera from a jacket pocket, pressed the record button, and pointed it at Billy and his friends. Katherine and Marie also started recording with their own cameras.

"Oh, I see," Billy snarled through clenched teeth. "You and your little *girl*friends are gonna get me on video and take it to the police." He then glanced at his friends and yelled, "Get those cameras and bust 'em up! I'll get this little punk!"

Though he was within striking distance of Billy's fists, Alex no longer saw any need to worry. "You're about to do something you'll *really* regret, so I'll say I'm sorry before it happens," he chuckled.

"Before what happens?"

"Hit me," Alex dared.

Billy pulled his fist back for the first punch while his friends closed around the two girls. Alex, Katherine, and Marie remained perfectly calm and continued filming. Billy's weight shifted to let his fist fly, but a powerful hand clamped on his arm before he could release. Billy looked to see what stopped him and his eyes opened wide with shock. Fingers on the hand were muscular, scaly . . . and *green*.

With a smile on his face, Alex stepped aside and shouted, "Remember, guys. Be gentle!"

Billy let out the highest shriek ever made by a ninth grader when he turned to face the monster who'd grabbed him. Tugging his arm in a vain attempt to free himself, Billy began to whimper. The muscular beast roared and snapped its sharp beak inches from his face. Aiming to punch the creature's stomach with his free arm, Billy cried out when Yin's other hand clamped on his fist and squeezed. Yin then swept a leg at Billy's feet and knocked him to the ground.

The remaining teenagers turned upon hearing their leader's girlish scream. Two who'd planned to grab Marie immediately darted off in the other direction. They didn't get far before a clubbed tail swatted their legs and sent them tumbling to the ground. As they looked up, a thick-bodied monster raised a pair of steel hammers and grunted, "Break good!" Both boys instinctively began hugging each other in horror.

Katherine's would-be attackers also tried to run. One went to recover his bike, but two slender, grey arms clutched his midsection and lifted him high in the air. The other hoodlum tried dashing over the dirt pile, but an immense bird swooped down from the trees and shrieked. Eyes rolling back into his head, the teen fainted and tumbled back down the hill.

Yin maintained his unbreakable grip on Billy's fists and snarled in his face. Billy tried to kick Yin between the legs, but it had no effect (a dinosaur's private parts are better protected than those of people). In response to his hopeless situation, Billy quickly transformed into a sobbing, pleading mess. Hunching over, something warm and wet began trickling through his pants.

Katherine, Marie, and Alex had been filming different parts of the action until Billy peed himself. That was the point when they all focused on Billy's sobs of, "Please, please don't eat me!" His voice was more than an octave higher than usual.

"You hurt my brother," Yin growled in his deep voice, flexing his muscles and snapping his sharp jaws. "That makes me mad!"

"Brother?" Billy gasped.

"He's talking about me!" Alex exclaimed.

Billy closed his eyes tightly and began to mumble, "Oh no . . . oh no . . . oh . . . no."

"Would you like to say something?" Alex asked, zooming his camera on Billy's crumpled form.

Hands still frozen in Yin's powerful grip, Billy screamed, "I'm sorry for all the bad things I did!"

Alex steadied his camera and asked, "Are you, Billy DeGrace, making an apology for all of the bad things you've ever done?"

"Yes!" Billy shrieked, "I'm sorry!"

"Are you also sorry for what you did to Roller O'Malley's toy horse this morning?"

"I'm sorry for everything!" Billy cried. "I'm sorry! I'm sorry!"

Zooming out and panning across the scene, Alex asked, "How about your friends? Are *they* sorry?"

A chorus of "We're sorry!" and "We'll never be bad again!" erupted among the three teenagers who remained conscious. Rahona was checking on the boy who'd fainted.

After one last shot of every goon sobbing like a baby, Alex switched off his camera and said, "I'm glad we've come to this understanding." Turning to his green-skinned "brother" dressed in silk, Alex sighed, "You can let him go, Yin."

The hulking warrior released Billy's fists and took a step backwards. Stygi and Euplos did the same. Billy and the others seemed too frightened to move, so the dinosaurs helped them to their feet and dusted them off.

"You need change pants!" Euplos grunted with a smile, pointing at Billy while he mounted his bike.

Rahona determined the unconscious boy was fine, so she carefully carried him to a bed of dry leaves and pulled a packet of smelling salts from a satchel around her neck. He awoke moments later and walked his bike home.

When the three children checked their video cameras and verified that everything had been recorded, the group moved towards a nearby boulder. Many months earlier, Billy had spraypainted an eye on the rock to show he was always looking over Sweetbriar Park. His reign of terror, however, was now finished.

Alex nodded his head towards an eager Euplos. The mighty ankylosaur lifted his gigantic steel hammers and drove them into the thick block of stone. Shattering into dozens of pieces, the eye crumbled. Sweetbriar Park had been liberated from its dark past.

Everyone returned to New Nottingham thirty minutes later and unloaded next to the Hidalgo's barn. Alex, Katherine, and Marie rushed through an open doorway and climbed the creaky stairs, raising a cloud of dust in the process. Once they reached the top, the three found Bluey chatting with Ghet and Jean about the social complexity of human middle schools.

"Sounds worse than how the Diapsids live," the blue-tongue skink grumbled before turning to the new arrivals and greeting them with his typical, "G'day!"

"Did you get anything?" Ghet asked.

"Oh yeah!" Katherine shouted.

Bluey smiled politely and scratched the back of his neck while explaining, "Ketoo isn't sure if he supports this little project of yours, but he'll be in Princeton until late."

"Why's he spendin' so much time over in New Jersey?" Jean huffed. "I mean . . . c'mon . . . *Jersey?*"

"Princeton's different than the rest of the state," Bluey replied. "Ketoo's sneaking into scientific meetings where he's learning a lot from you people."

"What do you mean, *you* people?"

"You know what I mean," Bluey joked, "Humans all look the same to me."

Jean shook his head and turned to his little sister. "You didn't hurt nobody, did you?"

"We didn't hurt *anybody*," Marie corrected her brother.

Glancing back at Bluey, Jean said, "Ketoo's gotta keep that in mind. Nobody got hurt, and y'all know that we *had* to do something to help our friend Ghetto. With all those hemophilia troubles, Billy might've *killed* him if we stayed quiet."

Once Jean, Ghet, and Marie had departed for Philadelphia under the brilliant reds and oranges of an autumn sunset, Alex and Katherine began editing video footage. When Ketoo returned, they convinced him to upload their final production onto *atarkya.com*. Billy's nightmare was to become the featured video of the day.

* * *

The next morning, Billy arrived at the bus stop early. Still shaken from his encounter with the monsters in Sweetbriar Park, he was nevertheless determined to keep it all a secret. In order to maintain his reputation, no one could *ever* know that he'd been scared, that he'd cried, or—above everything else—that he'd peed his pants.

Only two of Billy's friends showed up at the corner before the yellow bus squealed to a halt in front of them. When the door opened, the three put on their most intimidating expressions and swaggered up the steps.

Boarding the bus, Billy immediately sensed something was wrong. The bus driver had a hand over her mouth, as if she were trying to hold back laughter. Children in their seats peeked from behind cell phones and wireless Internet devices to point and giggle, "That's him!" When a little girl leaned into the aisle and glanced at Billy's pants, a wave of horror shot through his body. *What's happening?*

After a walk down the aisle that seemed five times longer than usual, Billy found another friend in the back of the bus. Head in his hands, he was hunched down as low as possible. Billy gave him a hard elbow to the side and grunted, "Yo, man, what's going on?"

His friend didn't look up. Mumbling through his hands, he whimpered, "You don't know what happened?"

Oblivious to the crisis, but extremely uncomfortable over nonstop glances in his direction, Billy lowered his face and snapped, "Why's everybody looking at their phones and stuff?"

The other teen dug into his sweatshirt pocket and retrieved a cell phone. When he looked upwards, bloodshot eyes indicated he'd been crying. Punching up the buttons to access *atarkya.com*, he showed Billy the tiny screen. In the "Check out this video" section, there was a big headline with bold letters that proclaimed, "Philly's Biggest Bully Pees His Pants!"

Besides several shots of Billy and his friends crying, screaming, and apologizing for every bad thing they'd ever done, one cut jumped to Billy's bladder accident and zoomed out to show him crumpled on the ground. Careful editing had removed every last trace of the monsters who'd attacked them. The final scene showed a banner which read, "Sweetbriar Park is open to everyone again!"

Mouth open in shock, Billy watched the video repeat a second time. Tension gripped his insides. Tossing the cell phone out the window as if it were on fire, Billy quickly joined his friends in the same hunched-over position.

When the youngest children stepped off the bus in front of William Henry Harrison Elementary School, Roller O'Malley waved her tiny hand towards the back of the bus and shouted, "Bye-bye, Mister Wee-wee!" Her sister Zig-zag then giggled and yanked the red-haired kindergartener's hand towards the door.

The bus stopped in front of William H. Taft High School a few minutes later. Right after the four thugs stepped from the bus, the driver shouted, "Try not to piss yourself today!" and slammed the doors with a cackle of laughter.

Shuffling into the building and sliding into his seat in Mr. Dover's homeroom, Billy pulled a jacket over his head and hoped no one in his class had been looking at *atarkya.com*.

Just as he did every morning, Mr. Dover turned on the television for the high school's morning broadcast. Unlike most days, however, the calendar of events didn't appear. Instead, every television within the building was showing the Sweetbriar Park video. Mr. Dover smiled and leaned back in the swivel chair behind his desk with a look of intense satisfaction. Peals of laughter began sounding throughout the halls.

Hopping from his chair and darting out the classroom, Billy's eyes began to fill with tears. *He was ruined.* Even if he tried to fight and threaten his way back up the pecking order, his reputation would never be the same.

Out in the hallway, Billy saw one of his friends and shouted, "Wait up!"

The other teen didn't respond. He just covered his face and ran.

Big Billy DeGrace learned a valuable lesson that day. *When people lose their fear, no one likes a bully.*

CHAPTER 27

Freedom?

The Zeus Crew had passed their first test with flying colors—not a single member of Billy's gang was hurt (not physically, at least). That weekend, Alex traveled with his human friends to the Sikandar Tendulkar Nature Preserve in Brazil for a celebration. Commander Trod had some sort of ceremony planned, and the humans were invited to join them.

Peering down from his Drifter, Alex could see a herd of *Triceratops* trudging across the dry grasslands. Flocks of purple and yellow *Gallimimus* galloped across the open plains as well. Along the margins, small groups of *Tyrannosaurus rex* were guarding territories among the trees. The sight of living dinosaurs never failed to fill Alex with amazement, so he took a few extra minutes cruising overhead to drink in the scenery before selecting a place to land.

Alex's time for quiet thoughts ceased as soon as Katherine pointed towards the ground and shrieked, "What happened down there?"

Near the Wounding Tooth camp was the carcass of a freshly killed *Alamosaurus*. More than fifty warriors were using sword-axes to hack chunks of meat from the long-necked beast while lines of Wounding Teeth carried the dripping flesh to tables for a feast.

Alex shrugged, "I guess they have to eat."

When the Drifter landed and the children stepped outside, Katherine averted her eyes from the carnage. The smell of death hung heavy in the humid air and swarms of flies buzzed in every direction. Nearby Wounding Teeth—all spattered with dried blood—stared at the humans while they crossed the field before returning to the task of distributing dinosaur steak among their ranks.

"Was *that* Commander Trod's ceremony?" Katherine snapped.

"I guess so," Alex replied. "You want something to eat?"

"I'll bet it tastes like chicken," Ghet laughed.

With an expression showing she wasn't in the mood for jokes, Katherine huffed, "Can't those monsters just learn to eat tofu or something?"

"I don't think you'll convince *those* guys to be vegetarians any time soon," Alex replied.

Commander Trod wasn't with the butchers, but was instead sitting with three lieutenants and a dozen other warriors around a fire on the edge of the field. Bluey and Tupi were with them. Wounding Teeth banged on crude drums and chanted ancient Diapsid sagas while Tupi played on his mandolin and Bluey added to the unusual symphony with a *didgeridoo*—a traditional Australian instrument which hummed hauntingly across the plain.

Without breaking the cadence of his chanting, Commander Trod motioned for Alex and his friends to join the group. Another minute of deeply spoken verses passed before the instruments stopped. The gathered warriors then hummed for several seconds at a pitch so deep Alex felt it rumble through his body.

"It's amazing, commander," Bluey said, lifting his mouth from the end of the tube-like *didgeridoo*. "Your language isn't much different from our way of speaking sixty-five million years ago."

"Is that a surprise?" Trod replied, "After all, we must have learned to talk from your kind."

"That's true, but you'd think that after thousands of generations under alien overlords, your culture would've changed more than it actually has."

The commander smoothed a hand over the metal armor on his chest and boasted, "Ketoo told us we're probably the most perfect warriors the Scipions ever saw. That's why they allowed us to maintain our culture and traditions for so long."

"You *were* the most perfect warriors, commander," Tupi clarified, "since it seems the Elektyls will soon take your place."

"Not if we can stop them," Trod growled. With orange eyes scanning his fellow Wounding Teeth, he then commanded, "Get something to eat . . . you'll need your strength for tomorrow."

"What's tomorrow?" Alex blurted while mighty warriors rose from their stones and moved towards the dead *Alamosaurus*.

Commander Trod glared at Alex, his face devoid of all that could be considered kind and peaceful. "Tomorrow we launch our attack against Legion Destroyer 3176."

"You're gonna fly out to Jupiter?"

The commander nodded. "We're going to crush the Swift Runners."

Surprised to hear about the plan on such short notice, Alex looked at Bluey and asked, "How long have you known about this?"

"We made this decision right after the Zeus Crew proved they could fight carefully, without using too much violence."

"You mean after they took on Billy DeGrace?"

"Yes," Bluey sighed.

Anger surging inside of him, Alex yelled, "Why didn't you tell me?"

Tupi flicked his pink tongue and explained, "Yin and Rahona didn't want you worrying about them."

"They're going, too?"

"I'm afraid so."

Alex didn't know what to say. Waves of different emotions surged through his body. Yin and Rahona were going to war, and his heart cried against it. Though both dinosaurs were bigger and stronger than he, Alex still felt responsibility for their safety. *I've gotta try to stop this plan*, he decided. "W-w-well haven't you thought about what'll happen if the Wounding Teeth win?"

"What do you mean?" Commander Trod snarled.

"You're not ready to go back yet. There's lots more we can show you down here."

"Such as?"

"Well . . ." Alex fumbled, "How about democracy?" Since he was supposed to be studying for a test on the U.S. Constitution, it was the first thing that came to mind.

Trod's thin lips pulled back into a sneer, exposing his full complement of two-inch teeth. "What can I learn from *that*?" he spat with contempt.

"Maybe you should change your society."

"How?"

"People in the United States broke away from a bad king and started a country where people could live in freedom. If you stick around, we could teach you guys how to do the same thing."

Jean pulled a headphone from his ear and griped, "Not *everybody* lived in freedom, Alex. My people was oppressed in America back then, and many still is today."

"*Your* people?" Marie shrieked. "Jean, we were born in Senegal! Our ancestors weren't slaves in the United States!"

"Those was the brothers and sisters of *our* ancestors who was sold into slavery!" Jean shot back.

"Those *were* the brothers and sisters who *were* sold into slavery," Marie corrected her brother.

Jean shouted, "Lots of slaves was taken from Senegal! The House of Slaves and the Door of No Return was both in Dakar, *our* hometown!"

Glaring at Alex, Commander Trod snorted, "Sounds like your civilization has plenty of problems."

"Well," Alex answered, "how does your society work?"

"It's simple," Trod explained. "The Scipions select three leaders—the Keepers of the Golden Skull—who create laws for everyone else."

"And if someone doesn't follow the laws?"

"Then they are executed."

"But you're going to rebel against those leaders. Won't you be killed?"

"Not if we win."

"You're only a couple of hundred warriors," Alex scoffed, astonished that he actually had the courage to argue with Commander Trod. "How are you gonna win?"

"Once we take Legion Destroyer 3176, we'll return to our homelands and kill our leaders with a Zokana Device. Whatever remains of the Diapsid Military Forces will then be forced to accept me as their Supreme Commander."

Alex realized he wouldn't get anywhere with that line of argument, so he decided to change tactics. "Why don't you organize an election when you go back to your home planet? If you stay a little longer, we could show you—"

"Nonsense!" Trod interrupted. "Citizens cannot be trusted to think for themselves."

"That's not true!" Alex exclaimed. "You have freedom right now! Why not share it with everyone?"

"Freedom . . ." Commander Trod grunted in disgust.

The word "freedom" had been tossed about for as long as Alex could remember, but he wasn't quite sure how to explain its benefits—especially not to a warrior who didn't seem to care. "Maybe you can borrow one of my history books and learn more before you launch your attack," he offered weakly.

"No time," Trod grunted.

Tupi shuffled over to Alex and put a hand on his knee. "We overheard a communication from the Swift Runners that said reinforcements will be arriving within a week. Time is running out, *amigo*. If we don't move now, there's no way we'll stop them."

Rising from the stone where he sat, Commander Trod snarled in Alex's direction, "Your civilization has existed for little more than two hundred years. Ours has survived for *three hundred thousand* times longer. Tell me, monkey boy, which society works better?" Not waiting for an answer, the commander stormed off towards the feast.

Eyes full of disbelief, Alex looked first at Bluey, then at Tupi. "Didn't Ketoo say he wouldn't help if they planned to kill Swift Runners?"

"That's what he said," Tupi replied, "but he had to face reality."

"What reality?"

"We'll have to support the Wounding Teeth no matter what."

"But they should change first!"

"There's no time!" Tupi exclaimed. "Wounding Teeth might turn the tide of this coming invasion. If we don't help them, we're finished."

In a flash of insight, Alex saw Tupi's point. If the Survivors pushed Wounding Teeth to change, Commander Trod might grow angry and rejoin efforts to conquer Earth. If, however, they helped Wounding Teeth return to their homeworlds and Commander Trod rose to power, he might decide to spare Earth from invasion. Options were few. Regardless of their high ideals, Alex and the Survivors would have to support this Wounding Tooth mission.

Before the conversation continued any further, the air shook with the arrival of ten invisible spacecraft. Dark silhouettes of the vehicles became visible in the fading sunlight when they landed. Everyone cheered when Yin, Rahona, Stygi, and Euplos stepped from the open hatches of their brand-new Interplanetary Fighters. Maintaining the "flying egg" appearance of the Drifters, Interplanetary Fighters sported a shark-like fin on top, a larger engine in the rear, and high-powered laser blasters on the wings.

Yin strode over to Alex and hugged his human "brother" with muscular arms. He then reached over to Katherine and pulled her into a group hug.

After the embrace, Alex stepped back and looked at Yin. It was hard to believe only six months had passed since the little runt hatched on *Tío* Ramiro's porch. Words couldn't describe the pride Alex felt at watching the tiny green hatchling develop into a powerful defender of the Earth. Nowadays, even the most aggressive of the Wounding Teeth treated Yin with extreme respect.

"What about me?" Rahona whined as Alex and Katherine continued staring at their green-skinned brother.

In response, the two quickly ran to hug their six-foot tall "sister" with purple feathers.

"Where were you guys?" Katherine asked.

"Training," Yin responded. Taking a CD from inside his silk outfit, he then handed the disc to Ghet and said, "I enjoyed the music. It helped focus my fighting ability."

"I thought it would," Ghet replied with a smile.

"Hold on now, Ghetto," Jean interrupted, removing his earphones. "What'd you give 'em?"

"Nothing you'd like, my man. I burned this CD from my dad's heavy metal collection."

"Oh no!" Jean exclaimed, "You gotta get him some hip-hop before tomorrow!"

Alex's heart sank. "You're going with the Wounding Teeth tomorrow, aren't you?" he asked Yin with a trembling voice.

Yin looked at the ground and ran a muscular hand along the ridge on the back of his head. "You weren't supposed to know anything until it was over," he mumbled.

"Why not?"

"Because you'd worry about me."

The words reminded Alex of the time his mother had told him, *"You won't understand my pain until you have a child of your own."* Though Yin wasn't Alex's child, he now understood what she meant. "Can't I go with you?" he cried.

"No!" a familiar voice commanded. It was Ketoo, dressed in some sort of metallic spacesuit and hovering on a pair of foot-long wings. "It's too dangerous. There could be terrible casualties, and I don't know how many of us will be coming back."

"I could take my own Drifter and stay camouflaged," Alex suggested.

"Who will help you if you get into trouble?"

Alex glanced at Katherine and noticed she had tears in her eyes. Even Jean, who always maintained his "tough guy" demeanor, was dabbing at his eyes with a shirt sleeve.

Ketoo removed the helmet from his spacesuit and peered into Alex's eyes. "You and your friends are our hope for the future," he sighed. "That's why we need you to stay safe."

Before another word was spoken, the deep howl of a mother *Tyrannosaurus* sounded over an evening chorus of insects.

"Female tyrannosaurs have been nesting recently," Tupi explained. "I'm not sure if we can handle even *more* dinosaurs around here."

"They will return with us to the Diapsid Homelands once we win tomorrow," Commander Trod growled, returning from the feast with bloodstained teeth.

"And may Unim protect you in the struggle," Ketoo proclaimed.

Bluey motioned for Alex to come close. "Don't let the Wounding Teeth know their god Unim isn't real," he whispered.

Careful to keep his voice low so Trod wouldn't hear, Alex asked, "Why?"

"Those beliefs made them the most powerful warriors the universe has ever seen, and we don't want to mess anything up before tomorrow."

The whole experience was completely overwhelming for Alex. All he wanted to do was get some sleep.

Alex, Katherine, Marie, Jean, and Ghet slept that night with the Zeus Crew by their side. Their slumber was disturbed by crackles and rumbles from Wounding Teeth who were testing their invasion discs. In times of war, Diapsid warriors rarely sleep.

Morning broke with roars from four hundred invasion discs taking to the skies. Diapsid ships were camouflaged, but the noise was still deafening. While the humans scratched bites from blood-sucking insects which had bitten them in their sleep, they watched the Zeus Crew and the Survivors prepare their own ships for action. Commander Trod remained on the ground as well, reviewing the final plans with his three lieutenants. When all was ready, the commander strutted over to the humans one last time.

"Pray to your gods for us," he implored.

"*Gods* or *God*?" Jean replied.

"Whatever it is humans believe," Trod grunted.

Marie shrugged her shoulders and said, "People believe lots of different things."

"No one *forces* you to accept such beliefs?"

All five children just shook their heads.

"Freedom . . ." Commander Trod grumbled dismissively, turning to board his invasion disc. Taking to the sky, the fearsome spacecraft quickly turned invisible and raced to join the rest of the fleet.

Once everything was ready, Alex and Katherine ran out to embrace Yin and Rahona one last time.

"You guys take care up there," Alex whimpered.

Katherine was so overwhelmed she couldn't even speak.

Yin sighed, "I'd better go." Placing a comforting hand on Alex's shoulder, he added, "But I'll be back."

Tears rolling down his face, Alex nodded and hugged his huge green brother one last time. He did the same with Rahona. Both dinosaurs then boarded their Interplanetary Fighters, turned on the camouflaging skin, and disappeared. Those who remained on the ground watched the sky until the rumble of their engines could no longer be heard.

CHAPTER 28

Space Combat

An alarm sounded in the Throne Room, waking Vice Admiral Hati from his slumber. He opened his good eye and looked down from the silver chair where Admiral Dromeus once sat. Captain Ripu was standing at the base of the steps, staring at a video screen with a look of concern on his face. In the time since Dromeus had been killed, the two had worked out a power-sharing agreement in which both Hati and Ripu oversaw affairs on Legion Destroyer 3176.

"What is it, captain?" the vice admiral asked.

Ripu pivoted to face his commanding officer. "We have visual contact with invasion discs leaving Earth orbit."

Hati struggled out of his seat and ambled down the marble steps. Captain Ripu flipped a switch to project three-dimensional views of Earth for them both to see. Sure enough, hundreds of slender invasion discs were heading into deep space.

"Are they ours?" Hati hissed.

"They must be," Ripu replied. "Wounding Teeth are returning."

"But I thought you drained their power cells."

"I did."

"Then how are they flying?"

Captain Ripu shrugged. "Maybe it has something to do with five-fingers, like we suspected when Commander Trod was defeated in southern Africa."

The very mention of five-fingers seemed to put Hati on edge. "What can be done, captain?"

Ripu stomped his foot and snarled, "I will take a force of Nychus Fighters out to stop them! No Wounding Tooth can defeat our Swift Runner pilots—not even Trod!"

Studying the projected images, Vice Admiral Hati said, "It appears other ships are on their way, too." He pointed to an egg-shaped spacecraft with a large fin on the back and asked, "Who's flying in *that*?"

"I doubt it's human . . ."

Sword-axe in his only hand, Hati said, "You lead the attack from space. Commander Nicci will be in charge of the particle beam cannon and our shipboard defenses."

"Keep the Zokana Device on standby," Captain Ripu growled while walking towards the door. "It might be wise to use it before our invasion begins."

"Time will tell," Hati snarled in reply.

* * *

The battle began when a thick beam of yellowish light sliced through space to the left of Commander Trod's invasion disc. It came from the main weapon on Legion Destroyer 3176—a massive particle beam cannon. Flying higher and watching its path of destruction, Trod saw several spacecraft explode upon contact with the death-ray, including the one belonging to Lieutenant Genghis.

"May you feast with Unim," the commander offered in remembrance of his trusted companion.

Behind the main phalanx of invasion discs, Yin answered a call from Ketoo.

"Yin," Ketoo's voice rattled. "Don't forget your mission. Stop the Swift Runners, but don't kill them."

"Understood," the young warrior replied, "but where should I strike the Nychus Fighters to avoid injuring the pilots?"

"You'll have to figure it out on your own, but please try your best. Commander Trod says he won't attack disabled Swift Runner vehicles."

"I'll do what I can."

"And don't forget your headpiece!"

Yin sighed in annoyance and strapped a metallic structure over the bony ridges on his skull. It looked something like a helmet, but Ketoo insisted its purpose was to connect his thoughts to the shipboard computer on his Interplanetary Fighter. "This plan better work," Yin muttered to himself.

* * *

Two hundred sleek boomerangs left the Legion Destroyer's main hangar and approached the invasion disc flotilla. They stayed close and flew fast, but most hadn't been serviced in several months. Engine trouble on one of the Nychus Fighters caused it to explode, damaging three other spacecraft nearby.

Watching four blips disappear from his command screen, Captain Ripu pounded his seat and cursed their lack of preparation. He then accelerated his spacecraft towards the front lines of invasion discs. A second blast from the

Legion Destroyer's main cannon obliterated another score of enemy ships before the two sides engaged in battle.

* * *

Yin located the particle beam cannon on the Legion Destroyer's face and increased his velocity. Rahona, Euplos, and five invasion discs covered his flanks. They flew in a wide spiral to avoid fire from a squadron of Nychus Fighters in hot pursuit.

"Rahona!" Yin shouted through his communicator. "Get those Fighters on the starboard side!"

Looking to her right, the purple-feathered dinosaur broke from the trio and hurtled down to face the Nychus Fighters. Two invasion discs joined her. Using her headset to focus on targeting the lead fighters, she placed claws on the triggers of her laser blasters and let loose a volley of greenish light. Surfaces of the first three Nychus Fighters lit up and disintegrated in blinding explosions. Rahona continued to dive downwards, flying from side to side to avoid yellowish particle beams fired by the remaining Swift Runner vehicles.

Slowing her descent and letting loose another rapid sequence of laser blasts, two more Nychus Fighters soon flashed and fell apart. Unfortunately, one of the invasion discs flying with Rahona was hit by a particle beam immediately afterwards, sending a cloud of metal scraps into her Interplanetary Fighter. Though the wing and laser cannon on her right side were damaged, Rahona continued a steady stream of laser fire from her left blaster and pulled a wide arc over the remaining enemy spacecraft.

When the Nychus Fighters passed below and trained their weapons on Yin and Euplos, Rahona's spacecraft swung around in pursuit. Three of the enemy spacecraft were destroyed and four others disabled with another succession of green laser strikes. Despite the fact her spacecraft was rumbling and shaking when she pushed the engine to high speeds, Rahona repositioned herself behind Yin's right flank.

"Rahona!" Yin shouted over the speakers, "Remember the mission! We're not supposed to destroy Swift Runner vehicles!"

Checking the control panel and realizing her ship was losing power fast, Rahona replied, "I'm not gonna last much longer, Yin."

Yin responded, "None of us will last against that particle beam cannon. We've got to hit it immediately."

"I'll keep you covered . . . and I'll be more careful."

Legion Destroyer 3176 grew in Yin's navigation screen, filling the front view in a matter of seconds. Using his sharp vision to determine when the cannon's long tube was taking aim on a target, Yin decided he should take a shot right before the weapon discharged. *That's when I'll have the greatest chance of destroying it.* Nearing the gigantic mothership, he pushed his fighter into a steep dive when the particle beam cannon moved into firing position. Euplos followed.

Rahona tried to keep close, but her Interplanetary Fighter wouldn't obey. The blast that pounded from the particle beam cannon grazed her left side, rendering the spacecraft useless. Should the Swift Runner operating the cannon decide to take aim on her, there was nothing she could do to save herself.

Yin focused on targeting the tube of the particle beam cannon a second time. Once the weapon selected its target—Rahona—Yin took aim down the tube and fired. His shot was perfect. The entire cannon exploded in a bright flash of orange. Rahona was safe, at least for the moment.

* * *

Invasion discs and Nychus Fighters streaked through Jupiter's skies like warring dragonflies over a pond of tumultuous brown water. Dozens of damaged spacecraft disappeared beneath the great planet's clouds, never to be seen again. Sleek Nychus Fighters operated by Swift Runners were bringing down two Wounding Tooth discs for every one of their ships that was lost.

Contrary to one's expectations, battles in space are quiet. Without any air to carry sound waves, even the most spectacular explosions are deathly silent. Lacking oxygen to fuel a fire, objects will flash for an instant and then quickly cool in the frigid temperatures of deep space. Such oddities were occurring all around Commander Trod when he pushed his invasion disc into a breakaway squadron of Nychus Fighters. Catching his victims by surprise, he destroyed nine enemy spacecraft before any of them managed to fire a shot. Three undamaged ships in the rear of the formation, however, discharged their weapons before Trod could escape. Two blasts from particle beam blasters shook the rear of the commander's disc, breaching the hull and penetrating the ship's interior. Air began to rush violently from the commander's cockpit as it depressurized in the vacuum of space.

Trod watched the Nychus Fighters close in for the kill. Never one to show weakness, he snarled and bellowed defiantly. To his surprise, the enemy spacecraft burst apart with bright flashes. *Did I do that?* the commander asked himself.

Before he could determine what had happened, an invisible force began tugging on Trod's ship, dragging it from danger. The breach in the disc's exterior was repaired with a metal panel that was placed over the hole and bolted shut. *Are five-fingers saving me?* Trod never expected to be pulled from the brink of death by his ancestors' mortal enemies.

* * *

Traveling at a speed unimaginable to humans, Yin streaked across the Jovian sky and looped behind a formation of Nychus Fighters that was closing in on Rahona's damaged spacecraft. Though it would have been easy to destroy the five enemy craft, Yin remembered Ketoo's order to *damage* as many fighters as possible. The young warrior lowered power on his lasers and took aim on the closest Nychus Fighter. One shot into the propulsion system of the boomerang-shaped craft caused the engine to sputter and burn out. Yin fired on the four remaining ships in the same fashion. All five began drifting aimlessly in the coldness of deep space. Rahona had been saved a second time . . .

* * *

"*Ketu seeta ratasa*," Captain Ripu cursed when the engine of his Nychus Fighter went dead. One of the fast-moving enemy spacecraft had caught him completely off guard. Pounding his control panel in frustration, Ripu didn't know what to do. He was now what the humans called a "sitting duck."

Ripu turned his external viewer and peered at the egg-shaped Interplanetary Fighter behind him. It was close—so close he could see the pilot had green skin, a sharp beak, and a strange looking helmet. As Captain Ripu wondered where such a creature had come from, he waited for the enemy craft to attack. To his surprise, however, nothing happened. The mysterious spaceship dipped down and banked to the left. Captain Ripu's breathed a sigh of relief that his life had been spared, but he didn't understand why.

* * *

Commander Trod was being towed to a heavy transport ship when a voice chattered over his communicator.

"Commander," the voice said, "Your ship won't fit inside the cargo hold. You must eject from your invasion disc."

Recognizing Ketoo's voice, Trod pressed his radio switch to reply, "These ships aren't meant to be unloaded in space. How will I get out?"

"The only way is through the access ramp on the bottom. My retrieval robot can position your ship so you'll be in the open for the shortest interval possible."

Trod knew of war stories in which Diapsids escaped from one damaged ship or another and survived for brief periods in the frigid vacuum of space. Unfortunately, there were also many tales of those who didn't. If the commander were exposed to the extremes of deep space for more than a few seconds, lack of air pressure would bring his body fluids to a boil inside his body and start damaging his internal organs. Any longer than a minute in the open and even the most powerful warrior was dead, frozen, and drifting through the cosmos. Still, Trod knew his only chance of survival was to get off the invasion disc.

"What should I do?" he snarled into his radio box.

"Open your access ramp and let the air carry you out. Keep your eyes and mouth closed. I'll use my robot to take you through the cargo doors of the transport vessel. Tell me when you're ready to move."

"Understood," Commander Trod replied. Unstrapping himself from the chair, he floated towards the access ramp and banged his head on the ramp controls. Trod mumbled a string of Diapsid curses before bellowing through his communicator, "I'm in position, Ketoo!"

"Then move!" was the reply.

Muscular hands gripping the ramp controls with all his strength, Trod remembered his swim lesson. *A leap through space is nothing compared to a swim in the water.* Air began rushing violently from the disc as soon as he pulled downward. The access ramp was torn from its moorings and slammed it into the side of the transport vessel. Commander Trod closed his eyes, exhaled, and leapt into the abyss. Frigid metal claws grabbed his body seconds later and thrust him through a jet of air. Before he knew it, Trod was inside the cargo bay of the heavy transport vessel with Ketoo's retrieval robot standing nearby.

"I survived?" Trod gasped with surprise. Besides a few spots where the robot's cold metal had frozen his skin, the commander had endured his ordeal without a scratch.

Ketoo leaped from the top of his robot and landed in front of the commander's face. Air in the cargo bay blew refreshingly warm when the leopard gecko removed his helmet and took a deep breath. Sorrow in his voice, he said, "Commander, I have a favor to ask of you."

Trod propped himself on his elbows and replied, "You saved my life, Ketoo. Tell me what you wish."

"I was the one who destroyed the Nychus Fighters who'd been closing in on you. I didn't want to kill those pilots, but it all happened so fast . . ."

"You acted honorably," Trod grunted.

"No, my friend," Ketoo replied, shaking his head. "There's no honor in killing others. I ended the lives of three Swift Runners today, and I want you to apologize to their clan for my actions."

"Apologize to the *enemy?*"

"You owe that to me, commander!" Ketoo shouted. "I saved your life!"

Reluctantly, Commander Trod nodded his agreement to Ketoo's demands. Without another word, the leopard gecko replaced his helmet, climbed back into his robot and gave a signal for the bay doors to open. In response, Trod sprang to his feet and wrapped his arms around a well-anchored pole so the vacuum wouldn't draw him back into space. After a brief blast of wind, Ketoo was gone.

Slumping to a sitting position in the ship's artificial gravity, Trod wondered why *he*, and not Ketoo, would have to give an apology to the Swift Runners.

* * *

In the skies above Jupiter's banded clouds, only thirty of the original two hundred Nychus Fighters remained. One hundred had been completely destroyed; seventy ships and pilots had been captured. Of the four hundred invasion discs flown by Wounding Teeth, one hundred and twenty still cruised through the cosmos.

While lingering Swift Runners attempted to regroup for a last-ditch effort against the Wounding Teeth, a brilliant light burst from the top of Legion Destroyer 3176. Upper reaches glowed when a shiny metal cylinder, pointed in front, left the battleship. It was huge—taller than a dozen skyscrapers stacked on top of each other. Strangely, it didn't attempt to engage the enemy. Soaring around the action, the mysterious object headed towards the Sun.

Once Yin discharged his lasers into the engines of three Nychus Fighters that were headed back to the Legion Destroyer, he noticed that domes on the gigantic battleship were closing.

"Yin," Bluey's voice crackled through the communicator, "hit those energy generators on the inside! Swift Runners are going to retreat! We need to stop them!"

Upon hearing the blue-tongue skink's orders, Yin accelerated ahead of the disabled spacecraft and pushed his Interplanetary Fighter towards a gap between the closing domes. If he managed to hit the negative energy generators, the ship's propulsion system would be dismantled and the Swift Runners would be forced to surrender. Just as he was about to race into the breach and select his target, however, Yin's thoughts turned towards the massive cylinder he'd seen moments before. *Was that the Zokana Device?* A terrible feeling of desperation shuddered through his body. Without a second thought, Yin pulled hard to the right and searched for the fleeing object with his keen eyes.

"What are you doing?" Bluey hollered through Yin's speaker.

"Bluey," Yin responded, "what just left the destroyer?"

"We don't know! It might be an escape vessel for Swift Runners, but that's not important right now!"

"If it's an escape pod, why's it headed towards the Sun?"

"We'll discuss it later, Yin!" Bluey shrieked, "Just hit those energy generators before it's too late!"

Voice full of worry, Yin asked, "What if it's the Zokana Device?"

The speaker was silent for several seconds. "Uhhh..." Bluey finally moaned. "That's a possibility..."

Without another word, Yin darted after the object. *I must save Alex and Katherine*, he resolved; right foot pressing on his fighter's accelerator.

In a matter of seconds, Yin's spacecraft began surging to unsafe speeds, but the Zokana Device went faster. It wasn't until emergency alarms began to ping and buzz that Yin felt he was gaining on the weapon. A fearsome rumbling began to shake the rear of the craft. *I'm breaking up*, Yin realized. Not willing to give up, he accelerated even more.

Yin finally passed the deadly projectile after crossing the orbit of Mars, then placed himself in the Zokana Device's path and focused his thoughts to a single point. Setting the signal of his communicator to beam towards Earth, Yin wanted to send one last message to his human family.

CHAPTER 29

Hero

Alex returned to the farm in New Nottingham shortly after the last ships bound for Jupiter had departed from Brazil. Jean, Marie, Ghet, and Katherine joined him sitting around a machine in the barn which enhanced radio signals, allowing them to follow communications between the Survivors, Zeus Crew, and Wounding Teeth in deep space. At about noon, *Tío* Ramiro joined them. He'd originally planned to spend the day in church, but the suspense was apparently too much to bear. Pulling up a folding chair into the circle where the five sat in silence, the old man tried his best to follow events taking place five hundred million miles away.

Talitha the chameleon radioed a special message every fifteen minutes to update Alex and the others on what was happening. Her communications were always one-way, however, because back-and-forth dialog would take more than an hour to complete over such tremendous distances.

And so a ragtag jumble of humans kept abreast of the first space battle to rage between Survivors and the Scipion Legions in sixty-five million years. They cheered when Rahona was saved from certain death and cried upon learning that hundreds of Wounding Teeth had been killed. The emotional roller coaster led Alex to wonder what would have happened if he'd never saved Bluey on that fateful day in Sweetbriar Park. *What a difference one little act of bravery can make.* When Tupi's voice came crackling over the speakers, however, Alex ceased his daydreaming and stared fixedly at the radio signal enhancer.

"*Carajo*," the black-and-white tegu exclaimed, "What is that thing?"

Salvator's voice patched in next, "It's probably some sort of escape pod for their leaders."

"I hope you're right."

Conversation returned to typical wartime communication after the mysterious object was sighted, but Alex had a sinking feeling something was wrong. Yin's radio question about the Zokana Device confirmed his suspicion. Twenty painful minutes then passed before they heard anything else about the object. Everyone clutched each other's hands in fear. *The end of life on Earth could be imminent.*

Alex was at the point of fainting from anxiety when Yin's voice again rattled through the speaker. His words were free from the static of most communications that day, indicating he was much closer to Earth than the other spacecraft.

"Alex, Katherine, and *Tío* Ramiro," he said deeply, "I only have a few moments to act. The Zokana Device is hurtling towards Earth with nothing to stop it but me. My laser guns aren't powerful enough to destroy it, but an explosion from my engine might be sufficient." Pausing for a moment, Yin's voice cracked with sadness as he continued, "Alex, I know you've tried to teach me what it means to be a hero, so I'll tell you what I've learned. True greatness isn't measured by how much evil you destroy. It lies in how much good you can save. Remember this and remember me . . . I love you all."

In a vain attempt to reach his brother, Alex leaped up and pressed the communicator switch. "No, Yin!" he screamed, "Don't do it!"

Alex's words came too late. Yin had actually encountered the Zokana Device fifteen minutes earlier, and it was only now that his words were reaching Earth. A squeal and hiss of intense static came over the radio signal enhancer, then the twilight outside became intensely bright. Alex and the others rushed down the stairway and pushed their way through the rickety wooden doorway. Tripping when he charged out into the open, Alex fell flat. Cries from the others alerted him that something horrible had happened. He craned his neck upwards and saw remnants of a massive explosion streaking across the heavens.

Katherine ran over to her brother in tears and collapsed next to him. Heavy sobs echoed through the autumn air. Nothing else on Earth seemed to move.

Tío Ramiro hobbled out of the doorway and moaned after spotting the inferno's fading glow. "He's gone!" the old man bawled, collapsing to his knees. "Yin is gone!"

Earth and her inhabitants were safe, but it wasn't violence that saved them. *Love* ensured humanity would survive.

CHAPTER 30

Aftermath

Everyone who knew about Yin's death slept in the barn that night, too sad to move. As a result, Mom didn't know about the tragedy when she left for Philadelphia the next morning. After hearing nonstop news reports in her car about a mysterious flash in the sky which had been seen across half the world the previous evening, Mom arrived at work to hear a surprise message from Sikandar Tendulkar.

The voice recording said, "Ms. Hidalgo, I fear I won't be able to guide the activities of *atarkya.com* anymore. I'm passing leadership of the company into the very capable hands of Ashoka Mehta and yourself. Consider yourselves partners from this day forward. When you have a chance, speak to your son about the way forward. He's gained knowledge about certain secrets I've guarded for many years. Thank you."

In faraway Mumbai, India, *atarkya.com*'s CEO Ashoka Mehta awoke to hear a similar message on his cell phone. Ketoo had spoken the words several days earlier and programmed the recording to be sent if he didn't return from Jupiter. When the battle ended, only nine Survivors made it back to Earth. The leopard gecko wasn't one of them.

Wounding Teeth had suffered a mighty blow above the clouds of Earth's giant neighbor. Of the four hundred and ninety-nine who departed, only one hundred and twenty-eight came back. Commander Trod was among them, as were Lieutenants Cyrus and Tarik. According to their traditions, the Diapsids held remembrance rituals for their fallen comrades and moved on quickly. Years of constant warfare had given them little capacity to reflect on the past.

When Legion Destroyer 3176 made its escape from the attacking invasion discs and Interplanetary Fighters, more than eighty Swift Runners were left behind—including Captain Ripu. With nowhere else to go, the lizards took them to the Diapsid camp in Brazil. True to Ketoo's wishes, Commander Trod apologized to the Swift Runners for deaths inflicted during the conflict. Such humility enabled former adversaries to put aside their mistrust and work in friendship for the first time in sixty-five million years. While the arrangement wasn't perfect, hostilities were usually resolved through *capoeira* matches and non-lethal duels with the pound-stick.

Sadness among the humans was handled differently. Since the Mexican holiday known as *El Día de los Muertos*—or The Day of the Dead—was fast approaching, *Tío* Ramiro showed Alex and Katherine how to construct a shrine-like altar to honor Yin and Ketoo. Marie and Jean helped with the preparations. Artist that he was, Ghet contributed by drawing pictures of the fallen heroes. They sat among flowers and food offered in their memory, accompanied by a photograph of Alex's *Tía* Elena.

Once pain from the battle began to fade, the lizards gathered over the town of Princeton, New Jersey with Alex, his friends, and three Wounding Teeth. It was their way of remembering Ketoo, since Princeton was the place where the leopard gecko seemed most happy. All sat silently inside a camouflaged heavy transport vehicle while it hovered over the playground of a local elementary school. Children below were frolicking on the slides, swings, and monkey bars. Sounds of youthful joy radiated up to the invisible spacecraft. The day was cool, but many of the children refused to protect themselves from the chilly air of late fall.

Commander Trod seemed to be mystified by the sight of youngsters skipping and running in tee shirts and shorts. "Those hatchlings down there don't feel cold?" he asked.

"Nah," Ghet replied, "Kids don't get cold like grownups do. They're not hatchlings, though. Humans don't come out of eggs."

"You are strange creatures," Trod snorted. His trusted Lieutenants Tarik and Cyrus nodded in agreement.

Jean looked at the Diapsids and snapped, "I thought y'all watched television up on that battleship . . . Why wouldn't you know a thing like *that*?"

"We only watched shows that interested us," Trod grunted in reply.

"Like what?"

"*Star Trek, The History Channel*, and *The Three Stooges*."

"You're kiddin' me, right?"

"We liked Curly the best . . . but Shemp and Joe had some entertaining moments, too."

Jean shook his head with a smile, then looked down and elbowed his sister. "Is that what things are like at *your* school?" he asked. "Look at how they're all playin' together. White kids are runnin' around with black kids. It's like they don't see any differences between each other."

"That's how most children are," Marie replied.

"*Dag*, I guess we *all* could learn a thing or two from little kids."

"Little kids?" Katherine snapped angrily.

"You know what I mean."

"We could all learn to coexist better," Commander Trod boomed. "Even Wounding Teeth and Swift Runners will need to manage our affairs in peace. That's what Ketoo would have wanted."

Soft chirps could be heard at the commander's feet. In the first compassionate act of his life, Commander Trod had rescued a baby *Tyrannosaurus rex* when its mother was torn to pieces by a pack of rival tyrannosaurs. The little creature, not much larger than a rooster, was covered in soft, white feathers. Trod named the hatchling "Kusa" in remembrance of a *Tyrannosaurus* who'd fallen on the battlefield in Zimbabwe. Lifting the baby dinosaur and cradling it in his arms, Trod patted it on the head and stroked the downy feathers on its back.

Tupi, Bluey, Talitha, and Bity were in a heated discussion over the future of *atarkya.com*. No more Ketoo meant no more Sikandar Tendulkar. Notwithstanding the leopard gecko's foresight in dividing the company between Ashoka Mehta and Alex's mother, Tupi and Bluey were convinced they should pull the plug on the whole operation. To make matters worse, Chelonius had been describing the presence of some mysterious entity within *atarkya.com*'s computer system. "I feel that I am not alone anymore," was his best estimation of the problem.

As his brown eyes scanned the scene through the transparent floor of the heavy transport vehicle, Alex wished he could return to the days when he'd been ignorant of the sorrows of war and death. *Those days are long gone.* With a sigh, he thought about looking for a place to be alone with his thoughts when a heavy hand and three curved claws clamped down on his bony shoulder.

"Alexander the Great," Commander Trod hissed, cuddling the infant tyrannosaur in his other arm, "Tell me more about this idea of 'freedom.' Maybe it's worth considering."

Sketches from the Notebook of Ghet O'Malley

Bluey
the blue-tongue
skink

Tupi
the Argentine black
and white tegu

Ketoo the leopard gecko

Salvator the water monitor vs a Sleeran!

Talitha
the veiled chameleon

Togo
the fire skink

Bity
the beaded lizard

Suzikha the crested gecko

Aira the
Eastern water dragon
(on a Humboldt Penguin)

Mama
Taonga
the
tuatara

Commander Trod on his Tyrannosaurus rex

Vice Admiral
Hati

Captain Ripu
(they say Admiral Dromeus looked pretty much the same!)

Lieutenant Tarik with a pound-stick

Trod struggling
to keep his dinosaurs
under control
on Earth

Yin's growth in five months!

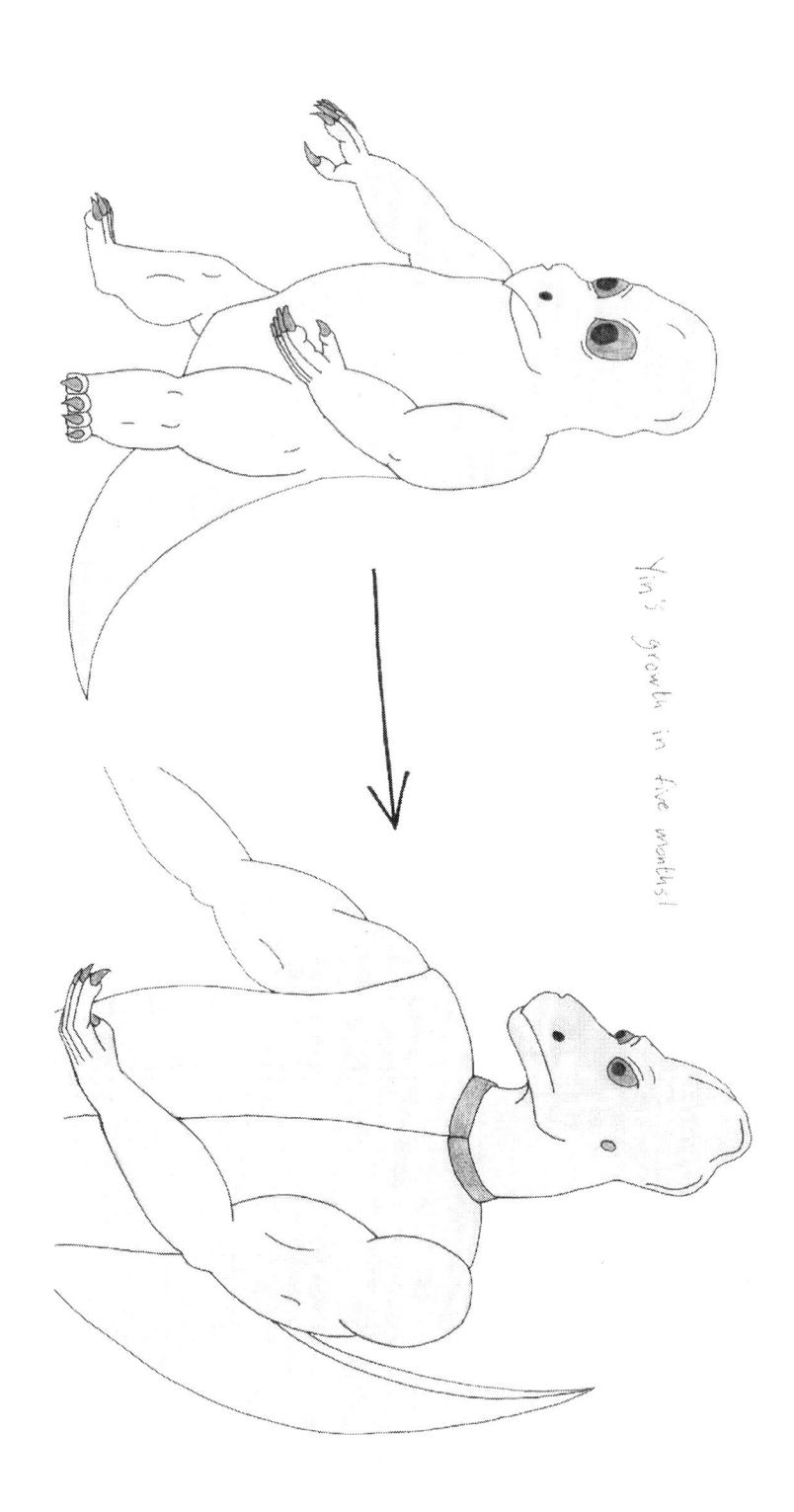

Rahnas growth

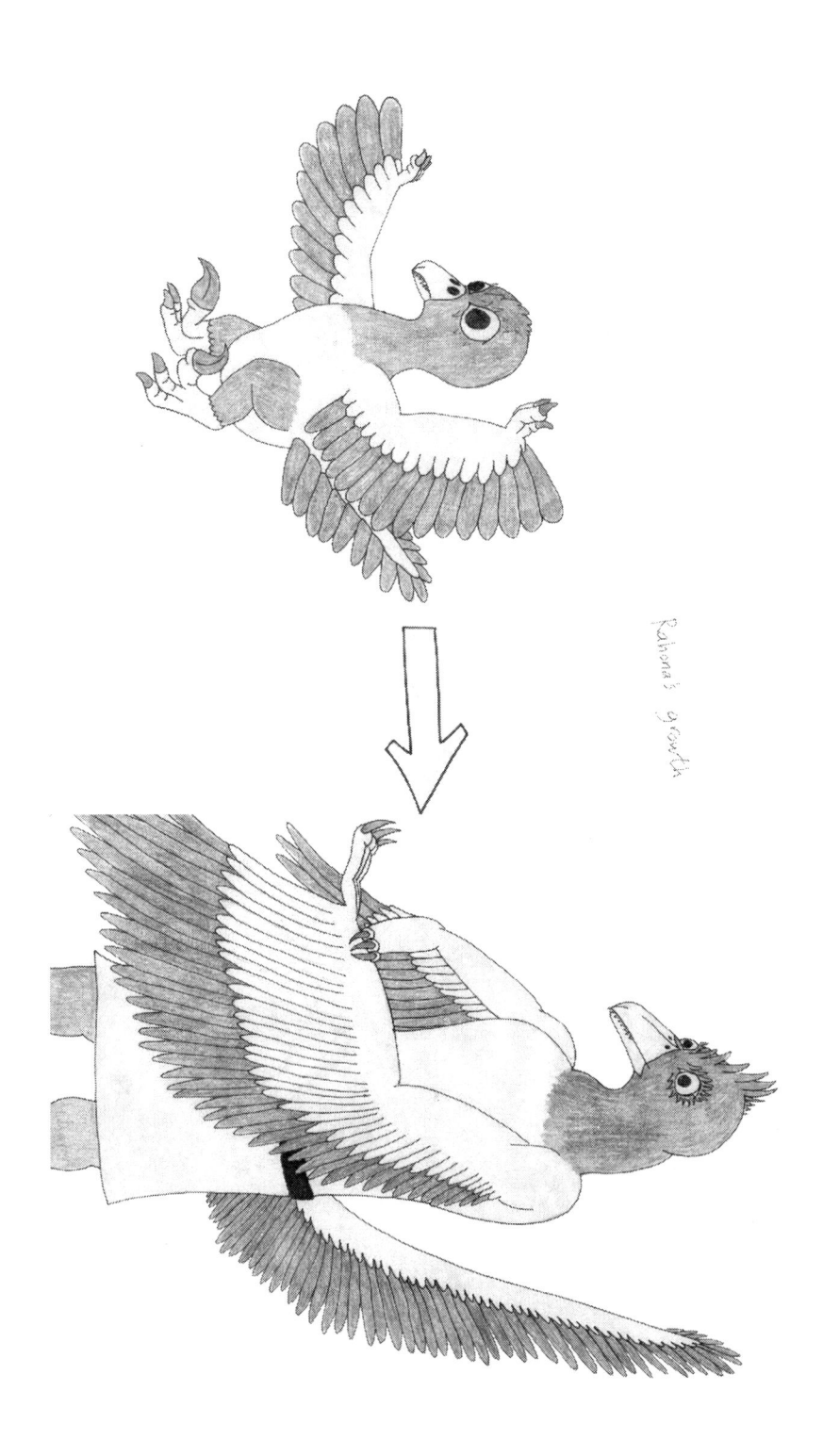

Stygi's growth

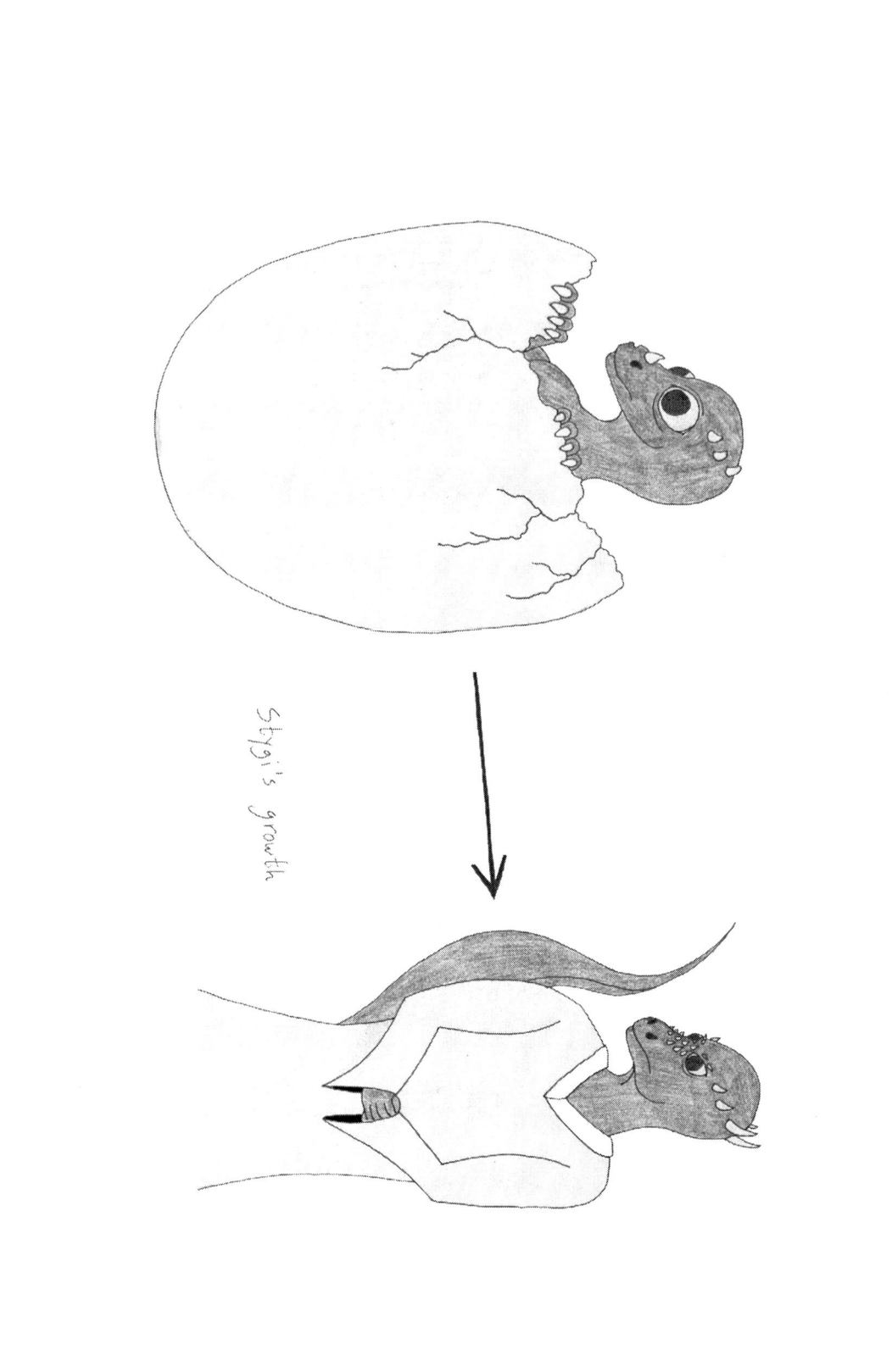

The maturation of Euplos (my how he grew!)

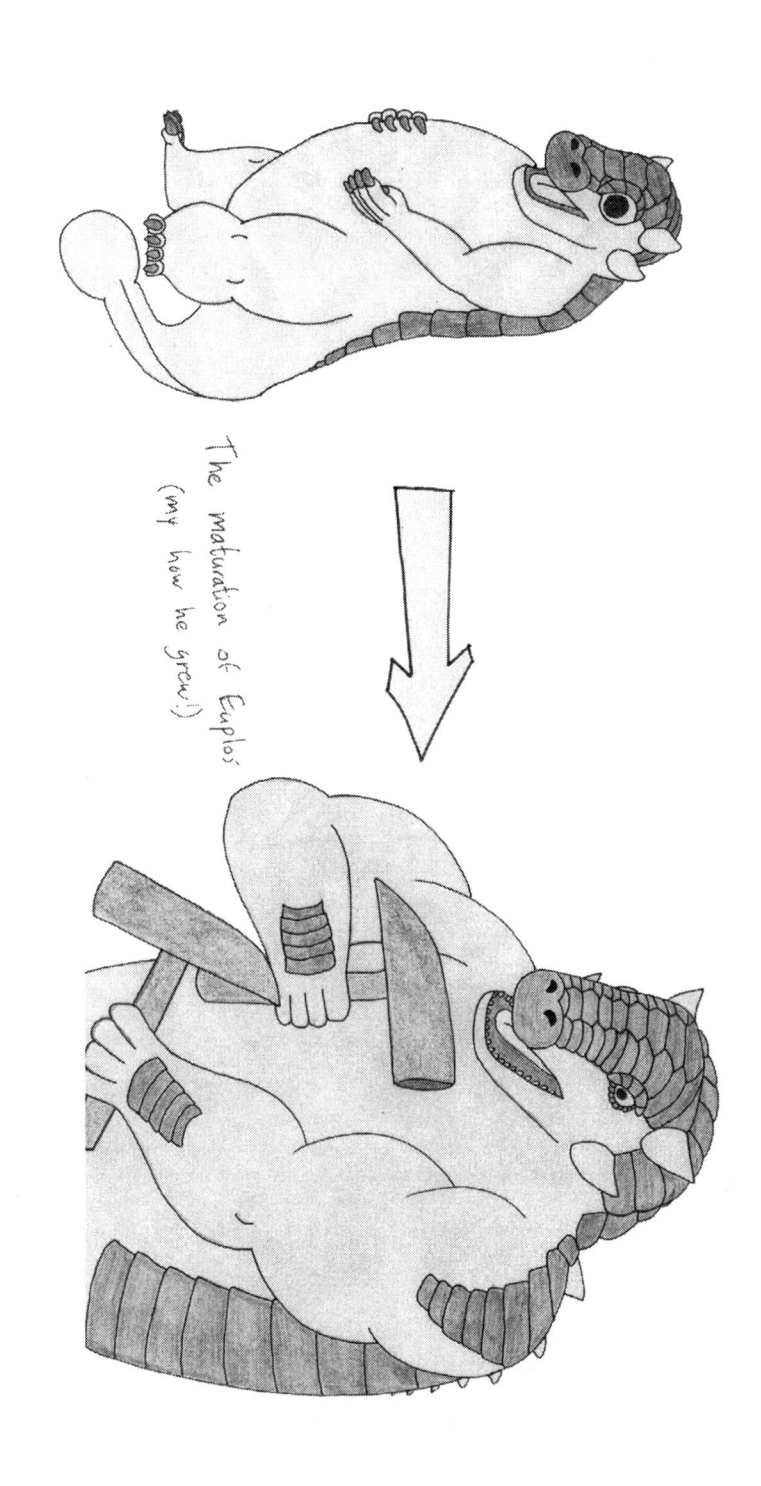